Christmas
at
Red Robin
Cottage

BOOKS BY SUE ROBERTS

My Big Greek Summer

My Very Italian Holiday

You, Me and Italy

A Very French Affair

As Greek as It Gets

Some Like It Greek

Going Greek

Greece Actually

What Happens in Greece

Take a Chance on Greece

SUE ROBERTS

Christmas at Red Robin Cottage

bookouture

Published by Bookouture in 2022

An imprint of Storyfire Ltd.
Carmelite House
50 Victoria Embankment
London EC4Y 0DZ

www.bookouture.com

ISBN: 978-1-80314-538-9
eBook ISBN: 978-1-80314-537-2

For all those who still appreciate the magic of Christmas.

ONE

'Why on earth would you go to all that fuss?'

I unwrap a chocolate from a box of Quality Street as I listen to the presenter on the television, as they show viewers how to upgrade cheap Christmas crackers. I'm enjoying my day off from the local cinema where I work, and have spent an enjoyable morning watching the endless festive craft shows, listening to Christmas tunes on the radio, and adorning the house with pretty decorations.

As I glance around the cosy room, I feel rather proud of my efforts. I've chosen a traditional colour scheme of red, gold and green. The garland on the banister is my favourite thing of all, threaded with holly berries, little robins and gold baubles – it makes me smile every time I step onto the flagstone floor in the hall. Ellie helped with the decorating, even though she had tried to persuade me to try the current trend of grey and pink that we'd spotted when out shopping in town the previous week. I declined. I quite like keeping up with current trends, but I wasn't about to completely desert tradition. Santa will always be red in our house.

As I lounge around in my soft, grey velour tracksuit, my

shoulder-length blonde hair scraped back into a ponytail, enjoying my day off, I'm captivated by the shimmering baubles, placed artistically on branches. The white angel, hand-knitted by my friend Cassie, smiles down at me with her little red woollen mouth, sitting proudly at the top of the real fir tree bought from a farm down the road. One thing about living in a small village is that the local farm sells fir trees at Christmas and pumpkins at Halloween, the illuminated pumpkins being quite a sight when the locals display them outside their houses throughout the month of October.

I really ought to be using the time to go through the tall larder cupboard in the kitchen and throw out the jars of cranberry and chutneys, some of which are probably still there from last Christmas. I was planning on going for a walk with my friend Helen, from the Penny Farthing pub, this afternoon but she texted me earlier to say she'd sprained her ankle, so there's really no excuse for me not to be sorting out those cupboards. I've been putting off them doing for weeks.

'Who are you talking to, Mum?' My daughter Ellie is smiling as she enters the room, having just arrived home from school.

Ellie, who people say is a miniature version of me, with the same large, green eyes and natural blonde hair, drops her school bag onto a chair, before flopping down next to me on the couch. She smells of cold, crisp air and school corridors.

'This woman on the telly,' I tell her. 'She's showing people how to make fancy crackers by tying velvet ribbon around cheap ones and inserting better quality toys into the centre.'

'Why wouldn't you just buy a box of posh crackers in the first place?' says Ellie, rolling her eyes.

'My thoughts exactly! So how was your day at school?' I ask.

'Fine.' Ellie shrugs as she helps herself to the chocolate with the purple wrapper from the tin.

I hadn't expected anything other than 'fine', to be honest.

Ellie never tells me much these days. I know she is keeping up with her studies though, courtesy of the online school system that I log into occasionally, just to make sure. She's leaving school this summer after her GCSEs and attending sixth form, although in truth I'm surprised she's on track to make the required grades. I rarely witness her doing any actual studying.

'What do you fancy for tea?' I ask, popping the lid onto the tin of chocolates. Glancing at the pile of discarded cellophane sweet wrappers, I might need to rein myself in, otherwise I'll need to get a larger size of the dress I'm going to buy for the cinema Christmas party. 'Unless you fancy a wander into town later?' I add. 'There's a Christmas market stall that sells the most amazing pulled pork rolls. Maybe we could have a Baileys hot chocolate too, as it's Christmas?'

'Umm... no, thanks, Mum. I don't really like Baileys.' Ellie pulls a face.

'You could have a hot chocolate with marshmallows,' I venture, although it is obvious Ellie has already made up her mind.

'I'll pass. I'm going out later anyway,' she informs me.

'Oh, right, okay. Anywhere nice?'

'A few of us are just going to hang out near the ice rink in town.' Ellie shrugs.

'Right, okay. Be careful, though. Give me a ring when you want a lift home,' I offer.

It's a twenty-minute bus ride into the city centre, and, as most of her friends live in or close to the centre, I worry about her getting home to our small village as the last bus stops around nine o'clock in the evening. And it's pitch-black at five.

'Mum, I'll be with my friends. Stop being such a worrier. Anyway, I'll be going to Izzy's afterwards; her mum will probably give me a lift. If not, I'll call you.'

Ellie grabbed a packet of crisps from the cupboard and bounded upstairs and left me with a sudden, and, perhaps, selfish feeling of disappointment. I couldn't shake the feeling that my sixteen-year-old daughter was slipping away from me, hurtling into an adult world that didn't include her mother. I'd naively imagined us going on shopping trips together and having a wander around the cosy Christmas market this year, looking at the wooden toys and hand-crafted gifts, maybe having a bite to eat. Then again, what teenager behaved like that? It would maybe take a good few years for Ellie to mature and appreciate mother-and-daughter time, as, on reflection, I would never have gone out with my mother in the evening when I was my daughter's age. Not when there were groups of friends to hang out with, that usually included good-looking boys.

I decide to crack on with the cupboard clearing, as I've had a nice, relaxed day, wrapping presents, watching TV and tidying a messy part of the fairly large garden. The lawn is long and narrow, the fence panels painted a sage green, the same colour as the front door. At the end of the garden is a huge ash tree that stretches out and overlooks some farmland beyond. I filled the bird feeder full of seeds, but they seem to be emptying more quickly than usual, as squirrels are helping themselves too. As always, I glanced around for the red robin that sometimes appears in the garden, but today there was no sign of it.

The redundant BBQ near the patio area is covered over for the winter and it made me think how quickly the seasons change. It barely seems five minutes since I was sitting with family and friends soaking up the summer sun, which the south-facing garden is blessed with throughout the daylight hours. Even early this morning, the winter sun streamed through the lounge windows, despite the frost on the grass.

After rinsing some out-of-date tins and jars, I place them in the recycling bin, and breathe in the frosty air outside, before quickly heading inside in search of a cardigan. Despite the cold weather, I feel a little restless having been indoors all afternoon, so I'm still considering wrapping up well and heading into town.

I'm sitting pondering my next move, when my phone rings, and the caller display shows that it's my friend Cassie. I had been debating calling a couple of my friends in the village for a get-together here, which we do from time to time, but thought it was maybe too short notice. Maybe I'll have some company after all – the good thing about living in a village is that there is usually always someone to chat to, and neighbours very quickly become friends.

'Hi, Sarah, how are you doing?' says Cassie. She's always bright and cheerful, and hearing her voice brings a smile to my face. 'Fancy having a potter around town? There's mulled wine at the Christmas market to warm us up!'

'I absolutely would!' I tell her. 'I asked Ellie but she turned me down. I thought you were out with James tonight, or I would have called you.'

'He's had to work an extra shift. A couple of the staff have gone down with a sickness bug. He said he'll make it up to me, which probably means he'll bring a takeaway home after his shift.' She laughs.

Cassie has been married to her husband, James, a paramedic, for twenty years and they're still very much in love.

'Great, shall we say six thirty? Meet you outside the coffee shop on Church Street?'

'Okay. See you in a bit.'

I tap on Ellie's bedroom door, only entering when she invites me in. I think it's fair to respect her privacy, although boys in her room are completely off-limits. Eyeing a pile of clothes on her bed, I watch my daughter hold a black top against her, her slender legs clad in ripped denim jeans. The top is sheer and ever so slightly low cut. And entirely inappropriate for a night at the skating rink.

'You'll freeze to death in that,' I tell her, not mentioning the fact that I think it looks far too sexy as I don't want an argument before I leave.

'I'll be wearing a coat, Mother. I'm not stupid,' Ellie replies, shaking her head at me.

'There's no need for the attitude, my girl, remember who you're talking to.'

If there is one thing my daughter will have in life, it's good manners and respect for her elders.

'Anyway, I only came up to let you know that I'm meeting Cassie in town for one of those pork rolls. Make sure you have something to eat before you go out.'

'I will. Enjoy your time with Cassie,' she says, her voice softening a little.

'Thanks. I'll give you a lift if you're ready in fifteen minutes.' I glance at my watch. 'The last bus will be leaving in half an hour.'

'It's okay, Mum. I'm not ready yet.'

The bus stop is only across the road, so I try not to worry that it's getting dark already.

I tell Ellie that there is a pizza in the fridge she could heat up, and she tells me she will grab something in town with her friends. I resist telling her that she should make sure she gets something warm inside her as it's freezing outside before I grab my coat and scarf from a stand in the hall, and head out.

TWO

Little Newdale has often been described as one of the prettiest villages in the North of England. With its eighteenth-century church, old coaching house pub and several thatched cottages, it's not difficult to see why. The village dates back to 1760, and the houses in the village are all individual, from half-timbered dwellings, to red-brick detached residences. There's a row of five sandstone two-bedroomed houses, and a gorgeous house set back from the road slightly that looks like the cottage in the movie *The Holiday*, which I am lucky enough to call home and I count my blessings every single day.

Red Robin Cottage has been handed down through the generations. My great-grandfather, once the village blacksmith, told stories of how a robin would visit the garden daily in the winter months, so he made a metal plaque in his forge depicting the daily visitor, which is displayed next to the front door to this day. I used to fastidiously clean the plaque that looks a little weather-beaten these days, yet somehow it all adds to its rustic appeal. A red robin still makes an appearance in the garden, but not every single day, which makes it even more special when one does decide to pay a visit.

The property was originally named End Lane Cottage, and I think its change to Red Robin Cottage makes it sound far more inviting. The cottage is surrounded by rolling farmland and on a clear day you can glimpse the water on the Wirral Peninsula, the sun dancing upon it. Living here is like having the best of both worlds as it's also only a half-hour drive to the sands of Formby and Crosby beaches.

Driving along, I pass the pretty houses, most of them with holly wreaths on their glossy red and black front doors. My own cottage really stands out from the rest, with its thatched roof and sage-green wooden front door, the garden surrounded by a white picket fence. I have a huge fir tree in the front garden, currently strung with coloured fairy lights, and all it needs now is to be covered in a light dusting of snow to make it the perfect cover of a Christmas card.

The courtyard in the village – an old stable block that was bought by developers seven years ago – is covered in twinkling lights and looks so festive as I go by. It boasts a café, flower shop and a dog-grooming parlour and has been a real addition to the community. Especially the Hot Pot café, that serves the most incredible hot chocolate. As its name suggests, it also serves up the most delicious hot pot with red cabbage and crusty bread, which is the best comfort food in the cold, winter months and I find it difficult to resist.

I take a right turn out of the village, and pass the red-brick house which is known around these parts as the Christmas House, which never fails to bring a smile to my face. A middle-aged couple started decorating their house ten years ago, slowly adding to the colourful creations over the years, with ever more elaborate decorations. Eventually, when they retired, they set up a little charity box and invited parents to wander around the garden with their children to admire what had become a magical winter wonderland attracting visits from people far and wide. They even serve hot chocolate and mulled wine from a stand at the front of the house, as Christmas songs play in the background.

I remember the first time I took Ellie there, and she wandered around in complete awe, giggling at the singing and dancing snowmen, her little eyes marvelling at the sight of all the moving figures and twinkling lights, barely able to take it all in.

I can't remember the exact year she decided she was too old to visit, I think she was about thirteen, but I remember it saddened me a little. My ex-husband and Ellie's father, Robbie, laughed, saying he thought I enjoyed it more than she did. That might have held a grain of truth. Visiting the Christmas House always got me in the holiday mood, so, the year Ellie had said it was for little kids, I persuaded Robbie to come with me, but ended up feeling a bit daft wandering around watching families with young children, and it tugged at my heartstrings a little. It was one of the times I regretted not having any more children. We had been told by the doctors that there was nothing medically wrong, when we investigated things, but I simply never got pregnant again, so I guess I'm lucky to have been blessed with even one child.

Turning left, the sound of a motorbike roaring around the corner startles me as I'm lost in my own thoughts. Josh Hunter, whose father runs the village pub the Penny Farthing, roars along, heading back towards the village. Josh lives there with his father, Paul, and my friend, his stepmother, Helen. Josh has had several brushes with the law for speeding on his motorbike, and getting himself into scrapes at the pub, that sort of thing. He was never the same after his mother died four years ago, and it's common knowledge that he has never enjoyed an easy relationship with Helen. I imagine how hard it must have been for him, losing his mother at such a difficult age, and in the year following her death, his father sought comfort in a whisky bottle. Helen came along at the right time, and is really good for

Paul. She put a stop to his drinking and I know she's a good stepmum to Josh too, even though it isn't always smooth between them. There's no denying Josh's brooding good looks and it's easy to see why he's considered a bit of a heart-throb in the village, especially to the young girls, who all seem to love a bad boy.

I park up in the city, feeling the chill of the crisp night air as I step out of the car and pull my grey woollen coat tightly around me, lifting my black-and-white checked scarf up over my chin. A few minutes later, I approach the coffee shop, and see Cassie walking towards me from the opposite direction.

'Hi, Cassie, that's good timing. I'm glad neither of us had to stand around waiting,' I say as I rub my hands together to warm them up.

'I know, me too.' She hugs me and I smell her perfume that she's worn since I've known her, and it's like a comfort blanket, wrapping itself around me.

'Right, where to first?' asks Cassie, who's wearing a quilted silver jacket and a multicoloured beanie hat that she knitted herself. Her brown curly hair is hanging down below.

'I don't mind. I do have to head to Boots for a few bits for Ellie, she's into her Soap and Glory bath stuff, then maybe John Lewis. I might as well have a look for a dress for the cinema's Christmas party while I'm here.'

'Great, I need John Lewis to grab a voucher for the in-laws.'

Cassie told me she had given up buying gifts for her mother-in-law, as every gift she purchased was met with cool indifference, sometimes asking Cassie if she had kept the receipt. Her father-in-law's reaction was always completely in contrast, expressing sincere gratitude when he received a gift, whatever it might be.

My own parents passed away three years ago, within a few months of each other, so my gift to them will be a pretty, hand-made wreath that I've ordered from the flower shop in the village courtyard from my friend Frances. Strangely enough, the sun always shines on the day I visit their grave and I like to look up at the clouds and imagine them smiling down on me.

We walk along chatting, before stopping and listening to a brass band play on Church Street, which really puts me in the Christmas mood. I especially love when they play 'God Rest Ye Merry Gentlemen' and I find myself singing along. I've always loved to sing, even though I never fulfilled my dream of singing on a stage in front of an audience.

'So, how's things at the cinema?' Cassie asks as we walk through the streets, where the crowds seem to be out in force this evening, taking advantage of late-night shopping and soaking up the festive atmosphere.

'To be honest, things have been really quiet lately. In fact,' I tell her, hardly bringing myself to say the words, 'we've basically been told unless we get some more bums on seats there's a chance the cinema may be faced with closure. I guess most people go into town for the cinema, rather than use the local one.' The smell of food from a nearby food hut hits my nostrils.

'I can imagine how hard it must be competing with the huge chains,' says Cassie. 'Not to mention Netflix and Prime streaming films almost right away these days.'

'You're right, that's the biggest issue. The big chains don't have the romance of an old-fashioned cinema, though, do they? At least, I don't think so.'

'But they do have reclining leather seats, which is what most people want these days,' she reminds me.

'I suppose you're right. Maybe I'm just an old romantic.'

'Maybe you are. There's nothing wrong with that, though.' She links her arm through mine as we walk on.

The Roxy is such a wonderful cinema and I love working in a place that gives a glimpse of days gone by. The chairs are still pink velvet with polished wooden arms, and red velvet curtains hang proudly at the front of the cinema screen. The frontage is wonderful too – art deco in design and something new visitors to the cinema often comment on. Okay, the chairs can't compete with the luxurious leather recliners, and are a little cramped, but the cinema gives an old-fashioned theatre experience, unlike like the modern, homogenised buildings of today.

I love the smell as soon as I enter the building, feeling like I'm stepping into the past. I often think of the couples who must have walked through the doors on date nights in years gone by. I imagine them snuggling in the back seats, the ladies dressed in smart dresses and pillbox hats, the men in dapper suits, the scent of the women's perfume mixing with the men's tobacco. I think of all those people who met the love of their life at the Roxy. I reckon love was a whole lot simpler back then. Or perhaps that's just my romanticised perception of it.

'Pensioners' afternoon is still popular, though,' I tell Cassie. 'But I think we need some ideas to get more people inside. Persuade them that local is just as good as heading into the city.'

'Try screening *Magic Mike*. I bet the pensioner ladies would love that.' Cassie giggles.

'You could be right there,' I say, thinking of the spirited ladies who love their cinema afternoons, laughing uproariously when we screen a particularly amusing comedy. Occasionally, men will pop in for the matinee, but generally only when we have a special screening of a war film. *Dunkirk* was very popular, despite some of the older guys grumbling that it was factually inaccurate.

I can't bear to even think about the possibility of the cinema being under threat, so I decide to put it out of my mind, for the time being at least, and enjoy my evening with my friend. I've always loved Christmas and feel happy as I walk along, taking in the bright lights of the city.

· · ·

We step inside John Lewis, glad to be inside away from the biting air, and where gorgeous displays greet us at every turn. It would so easy to overspend with so many tempting things on offer, so I try and focus on what I came in here for. My eye is drawn to a large copper pan in the kitchenware section, that I think would look good on display in my country cottage kitchen. I momentarily consider making home-made jam, although wonder if I would ever actually get around to doing it. In the end, I walk on as the last thing I really need in my kitchen is another pan. There's already a rack full of them, hanging from a Victorian airer, half of which I barely use. I waver over a waffle maker – Ellie loves waffles – but glancing at the price tag, I'm sure I could purchase something cheaper online.

Walking through the cosmetics area, Cassie stops and sprays some perfume on her wrist from a sample. An over-eager assistant from a make-up counter approaches us asking if we would like a makeover, which we politely decline.

'I might do when I go on the Christmas night out, though,' I tell Cassie as we continue to explore the store. 'I've never had my make-up done professionally before.'

'Ooh good idea, I bet you would look amazing,' says Cassie as we ascend the escalator to the first floor. 'I maybe wouldn't go for the sparkly eyeshadow, though. Someone at work had it done once and the falling sparkles ruined her black dress.' She laughs.

My eyes are large and a light-green shade and people often comment on them. Robbie told me it was the first thing he noticed about me when we first met in the Empire Theatre, where I was working at the time. It's a pity they couldn't captivate him forever.

There are racks of gorgeous dresses on display, some in shimmering gold or covered in sequins, ideal for the party season, side by side with more classic styles. Rifling the racks, my eyes soon fall on a pretty wrap-over in shades of black and mustard.

'I think I might go and try this on,' I tell Cassie as she looks at handbags that are heavily discounted in a pre-Christmas sale.

'Okay, I'll be over in a minute to have a look,' she says, turning over a brown leather designer bag.

Five minutes later, having regretted wearing two layers of clothes, I finally get the dress on. Opening the curtain of the changing room, and seeing Cassie waiting outside, I give her a twirl.

'Ta da!'

'Oh, Sarah, that's gorgeous. It's really flattering. You should definitely buy it,' Cassie enthuses.

'You don't think it's too low, do you?' I ask doubtfully, although I have to admit it does look good and I feel great wearing it, as it really shows off what you might call my hour-glass figure.

'No, it's perfect for a party and not that low-cut at all. It really shows off your waist. You have to buy it,' she says firmly.

'I think I will,' I say excitedly, relieved to have found a dress. I also manage to find a pair of black suede boots to go with the outfit.

Cassie treats herself to the bag and buys the in-laws their annual gift voucher, along with some fancy chocolates, so we head off back into the cold streets.

THREE

An hour later, having done some more shopping, we take a little break, finding a bench close to one of the food huts outside St George's Hall. The building in front of us looks resplendent bathed in a soft purple light, its huge columns with stone lions peering out from a platform at the top, proudly glancing out across the market square. St George's Hall is a wonderful Grade I listed neoclassical building, often described as one of the finest buildings in the world. It was once the old law courts. Nowadays, you can visit the holding cells below ground, where they display memorabilia and photos of prisoners in days gone by, many of whom were deported to Australia. The building also holds classical music concerts, recitals and readings. In years gone by, Charles Dickens was a frequent visitor to the hall to give readings of his novels and poetry recitals. They even have a room especially for wedding venues, and I can't think of a nicer place to tie the knot.

We purchase a pork roll each from a nearby food stall in the market and watch the world go by. It's not the largest of Christmas markets, but has the usual food, drink and wooden toys stalls. Stallholders, wearing thick coats and caps, are stamping their feet behind their stalls in an effort to keep warm. They welcome us with smiles as we pass, hoping we might purchase something.

'I've been looking forward to this,' I say, before sinking my teeth into the tasty hot pork with cranberry stuffing, encased in the soft white roll. We're sitting beneath a tree threaded with white lights, and from here, we can hear the strains of music from the brass band.

'And I've been looking forward to this.' Cassie takes long glug of her warming mulled wine. 'Ah that's really hit the spot.' She smiles.

So, how's everyone? Are the kids enjoying the Christmas break from college?' I ask. Cassie has eighteen-year-old twins, Zak and Jessie.

'They are, thanks. Jessie has got a few things booked with her mates over the holidays, including a trip to the theatre to watch *Hairspray*. Zak will try and spend most of his time gaming in his room, but I'm determined he'll go out a few times too.'

'Have they started applying for university?' I ask, smiling at a couple of rosy-cheeked revellers who have just strolled by, dressed as elves and looking slightly the worse for wear.

'They have. Jessie wants to spread her wings and go somewhere down south. Maybe it's selfish of me, but I was kind of hoping she would apply for John Moores and stay here in Liverpool,' she reveals. 'Zak, on the other hand, keeps banging on about how you don't need a degree to be successful and how people have made a living from YouTube, blah blah. Honestly, I could shake him sometimes. They're both going to stick at their education, though. James and I will make sure of that,' she says firmly. 'How's Ellie doing?'

'Yep, she's fine.' I take a sip of my mulled wine, enjoying the soothing cinnamon taste. 'Although she doesn't tell me much these days, if I'm honest. But she's a good girl. In fact, she's in town tonight at the skating rink near the Albert Dock. I'll walk down later and see if she wants a lift home.'

'She probably won't thank you for cramping her style.' She laughs. 'Although I guess she is only sixteen.'

'Exactly. She's growing up so quickly.' A bit too quickly, I think to myself, recalling the outfit she was wearing this evening. I take a bite of my roll, wiping my chin with a napkin as a bit of cranberry stuffing escapes it. Why do they taste so much nicer purchased from these food stalls? I could never make a pork roll taste so good back home.

'I know. I can't believe the twins are eighteen. Will Ellie be spending time with Robbie over Christmas?' Cassie asks.

'Yeah, probably. I'm pleased her and Robbie are so close, but I do miss her when she stays out,' I find myself admitting. 'Pathetic really.'

'Maybe you ought to go on Tinder,' suggests Cassie with a wink.

'I have actually thought about it, but I'm not sure I can be bothered with a bloke at the moment. And if I was, I'd kind of like to meet someone organically. Maybe I really am an old romantic.'

I imagine someone walking into the cinema through a cloud of smoke, wearing a suit and looking a bit like Clark Gable. I really must stop watching those old black-and-white movies.

'Is Robbie still with the current girlfriend?' asks Cassie.

'As far as I know, yes. Current being the operative word.'

Robbie doesn't tend to stick around once the initial passion has waned. This is his third partner in the two years since we split. At least Ellie is the one thing that seems to be a constant in his life, and for that I'm grateful.

The divorce was difficult at the time. I realise now that Robbie and I should never have married so young, but he totally swept me off my feet. I'd finished college, where I'd been studying musical theatre and drama, and was getting a couple of small parts in the theatre. Unfortunately, the rejections outweighed the jobs, so I ended up working at the box office instead. At least it meant that I was part of theatreland, and I loved working there and I did still get offered the occasional leading role in the local amateur dramatics group. Robbie asked me out one evening at the theatre where he had treated his mum to the musical *Anything Goes* for her birthday – earning immediate brownie points from me for treating his mum well. We met the following evening, and that was it. I'm not sure Robbie will ever settle down with one woman, being one of those guys who thinks he's forever twenty-one. A Peter Pan who will only realise his life has passed him by when he's cashing in his pension. Even then, with his undeniable good looks and charm, he'll probably bag a rich widow and live out his days in comfort somewhere nice. Robbie Dunn could literally fall into a dung heap and come up smelling of roses.

A brass band strikes up a rendition of 'We Wish You A Merry Christmas' and all thoughts of Robbie disappear, as my Christmas spirit soars listening to my all-time favourite Christmas song. The surrounding crowd start singing along to the music and by the time they reach the line, 'So bring us some figgy pudding', the whole of the little market seems to have joined in, finishing up with a round of applause and whoops and cheers.

'Ooh, I feel all Christmassy now. Shall we head down the road and have a look at the window display in the art shop?' asks Cassie and I eagerly agree as we throw our paper cups and napkins into a nearby bin.

We link arms as we walk, heading for one of my favourite little places in the whole of the city. Queen Street is a tiny alley sandwiched between a large hotel, and it's one of the city's best kept secrets, the sort of place you only know about if you've lived here. It's a far cry from the generic chain stores, a row of buildings with Dickensian windows and specialist shops.

There's literally a handful of outlets that include a wine merchant, an art shop and a tiny café with an outdoor seating area in the summer. One of the empty units has a sold sign on the window and I look forward to seeing what might be opening up here next.

Ten minutes later, we step onto the narrow street and I'm drawn to a display in the window of the art gallery. There's a huge oil on canvas painting of a train that looks just like the one in *The Polar Express*, the old-fashioned steam train driving through a snow-covered landscape, with lights glowing from distant buildings. A little train track has been set up in the window, surrounded by snow fashioned from cotton wool, and is chugging along through little tunnels. The window has gold stars hanging down and little figures of skating children are placed around the snowscape – it all looks completely magical. The striking painting of the train shows a price tag of eight hundred pounds, the painting created by a well-respected local artist.

'Ah, do you remember taking the kids on the Christmas train when they were little?' says Cassie as she stares at the painting, with a look of nostalgia on her face.

'I most certainly do.'

I smile as Cassie reminds me of the times we used take the children to Haworth in Yorkshire. We would go for the weekend, staying at an inn with a roaring log fire and four-poster beds. A black-and-red steam train, the carriages adorned with Christmas decorations, would whisk us along a track to a junction box that had been transformed into Santa's grotto. I don't think I'll ever forget the look on the children's faces the very first time they saw Father Christmas sitting in a green velvet chair to greet them. Afterwards, we would take a walk around the Victorian Christmas market on Main Street, where all the market traders would be decked out in Victorian regalia, the women in long, red velvet dresses and muffs, the men wearing heavy capes over shirts and waistcoats. As we walked, we would smell chestnuts roasting over a fire and sample mulled cider from a stall. Robbie and James were friends back then, mainly as Cassie and I were, but their friendship never independently survived the divorce.

'Why do they have to grow up?' I sigh. 'All the magic disappears then, doesn't it? These days, it's all about money or iPhones.' Remembering those times always fills me with a mixture of joy and sadness. I'd hoped me and Robbie would grow old as a couple, maybe one day even welcome grandchildren together, rather than apart. I knew deep down that Robbie wasn't ready to marry, but maybe I foolishly thought I could persuade him to settle down. When his first affair came to light, after five years together, I forgave him for the sake of Ellie. Nine years later, and after finding out about several more affairs, I'd finally had enough and we parted ways two years ago. I often wondered why Robbie wanted to stay married. I think it gave him a feeling of security, despite his casual affairs.

'Maybe one day we will be lucky enough to have grandchildren and all the magic will come back again,' says Cassie, who was clearly thinking along similar lines, about the twins, as she watched the little train chug around the track, with its flashing lights and whistling sounds.

'Or you could have another,' I say and Cassie looks aghast.

'What? No chance.' She gives a little shudder. 'I haven't worked all these years to get where I am, to then start all over again.' She laughs.

Cassie has a fabulous job as a librarian in the wonderful Central Library next to the World Museum. The library is definitely worth visiting in the city, as it has a spectacular glass-enclosed staircase leading to an upper floor that has a viewing terrace, where you can enjoy fantastic views across the city.

'Well, you're still young enough, is all I'm saying.' She doesn't bother telling me that I am too, as she knows how no more children came along after Ellie. The doctors told me to relax, saying the more I worried, the less chance I had of conceiving. Maybe it turned out to be a blessing in a way having no more children with Robbie, considering his behaviour. I guess everything happens for a reason.

Occasionally over the years, usually when I'd been having troubles with Robbie, previous relationships would pop into my mind, especially my first crush. I imagined what things might have been like if we had got together, but I guess it does no good to think of 'what ifs' and 'if onlys'. Life isn't like that, and we have to deal with the life the cards deal us. Besides, it was so long ago, and we were so young.

Luke Watson was the older brother of my best friend Kay when I was sixteen years old, and I worshipped him. I can still see his smiling, handsome face, soft-brown eyes that crinkled at the corners when he laughed and that mop of gorgeous dark-brown hair. He was nineteen and he wasn't even aware of my teenage crush for a while, even though we chatted all the time when I was at their fabulous house near the sea. We went to the cinema a couple of times, as we were both film buffs, but with the age difference it never got serious. He was often out with his friends in town, where I couldn't join them. I longed to be old enough to go to the pubs and clubs they frequented with my own friends. I imagined bumping into him in a bar somewhere, where he would see me suddenly in a different light, grown up and as a more viable girlfriend. We'd fall madly in love, become engaged and marry in one of the cathedrals in the city – we could take our pick as the city has two. But, at eighteen years old, I was heartbroken when this future was snatched away as the family moved to America. I never saw him again.

The crisp night air closes in and I wish I'd worn a warm woolly hat like Cassie, as I feel an icy nip on my ears as we stroll. The car park is close to the skating rink, so we head back along Church Street and stop for a warming hot chocolate on the way. Cassie buys two mince pies from a stall, knowing I can't resist them.

'You're a bad influence,' I tell her, but I take a huge bite of the warm, delicious mince pie all the same. I make short work of it, before cupping my hot drink in my hands. Soon enough, I spot the skaters dressed in woolly hats and long scarves gliding around the large, man-made ice rink. Scanning the crowd, I spot a few faces I recognise and head towards them, although I can't seem to spot Ellie.

'Hi, Maisie,' I say to one of Ellie's school friends, who turns around in surprise.

'Oh, hi, Mrs Dunn.'

It makes me feel old when her friends address me by my surname, although maybe they feel disrespectful calling me Sarah. These teenagers must see me as an older woman, even though I'm not even forty yet.

'Have you seen Ellie this evening?' I ask, slightly concerned, as I still don't seem to be able to see her on the skating rink.

'Erm, no. She said she was coming, but she never showed up.' She shrugs.

'Oh right. Maybe she's with Izzy,' I say.

'Yes, I think she said something about that actually.' She nods, as if recalling a conversation between them.

'Okay, right, thanks. Enjoy the rest of your evening.'

'Sure,' she says, before resuming her conversation with her friends, who glance after me and Cassie as we leave.

'I'm sure she's fine,' says Cassie, clearly noting the look of concern on my face as we head towards the car park. 'You know what teenagers are like.'

'I'm sure you're right, but I think I'll give her a call anyway.' I'm surprised I don't have a head full of grey hair. It seems parenting doesn't get any easier as your kids grow older. If anything, it seems to be ten times worse.

I dial her number, but the call goes to voicemail, so I leave a message asking her to call me if she needs a lift home.

I load my shopping into the boot, and hug Cassie goodbye before we climb into our respective cars. Driving home, I can't help worrying about Ellie. Maybe she's right, I am a worrier. One of those over-anxious parents that fret over everything. On the other hand, she is only sixteen and I've had to be mother and father to her these past few years since Robbie and I parted. I say a silent prayer that she will be there when I arrive home.

FOUR

'Hi, Mum, how was town?'

I breathe a sigh of relief when I see Ellie sitting at the kitchen table, nursing a hot chocolate and eating some cheese on toast.

'It was great, thanks, really Christmassy. When did you get home?' I throw my bag onto a chair as relief floods through me.

'Literally ten minutes ago.' She's dressed in cosy red-and-white reindeer pyjamas and fluffy white slippers.

'Do you want a hot chocolate?' she offers.

'No, thanks, love, I've just had one in town. I might have another mulled wine, though.'

I grab a tall glass from a cream wooden kitchen cupboard, that contrasts beautifully with the solid oak worktops. The flagstone floor in the hall flows through to the kitchen, that has a large Victorian Aga against one wall. The larder-style cupboard is strung with cream-and-red bunting across the top, that spells out the word Christmas. On the windowsill are pots of herbs and Christmas plants, including a fake robin nestled in the pots.

'Talking of town. I had a wander down to the ice-skating

rink; I never saw you there,' I say, taking a sip of my mulled wine.

'Checking up on me, were you?' she says, a half-smile on her face, but meaning every word.

'Not exactly. I just went to see if you needed a lift home, that's all. I saw some of your friends there.'

'I decided not to go in the end.' She shrugs. 'I went to Izzy's and we ended up ordering pizza and watching a film. It was freezing outside anyway.'

'I can vouch for that. Still hungry after that pizza, then?' I ask as she finishes her cheese on toast.

'What? Oh, yeah, well, I only picked at it, I suppose. Did you buy anything nice?' she asks, changing the subject. Even though I'm not sure she's telling the truth, I pull out the dress I bought for the party.

'Ooh, that's pretty, Mum. It will really suit you.'

'Thanks, Ellie, I think so too. You don't think it's a bit young for me, do you?' I ask, knowing I will get the complete truth from a teenager.

'Mum, you are young! Well, okay, nearly forty isn't *that* young.' She smiles.

'Oi, cheeky.'

'But you've always looked and acted way younger than your age anyway. And what is it they say? Age is just a number.'

'That's true, I suppose.'

'Honestly, that dress is really lovely,' she says definitely.

'Thanks, I'm glad you approve.' I smile. 'It's ages since I've bought a new dress.'

I feel cheered by her comment, but I'm still dreading my fortieth birthday on New Year's Eve. I quite like having a birthday on the same day as another event, but I'm hoping the next ten years don't go as quickly as the last ten, or I'll be drawing my pension before I know it.

We chat for a while about town and Christmas, and when Ellie has finished her hot chocolate, she yawns.

'Right, I'm going to go to bed now, Mum. Night.'

'Night, love.'

Glancing at the clock, it's just after ten. I'm a little tired myself this evening. Maybe it's down to the mulled wine and all that walking around town.

Wandering into the lounge, I take in the unmistakeable scent of my Christmas fireside Yankee Candle. It has burned down quite a bit, the pool of wax swimming around at the top. This makes me question whether Ellie has been out at all this evening. But why would she lie to me?

Wondering what is going on with her, I turn off the lights and head back into the kitchen. I take a tall tumbler from a cupboard and, before filling it with water, I notice some vodka has gone from a bottle on the shelf. Ellie didn't seem as though she had been drinking, though. Maybe she has had company here this evening. Suddenly something doesn't quite sit right with me and I can't help wondering what on earth she has been up to.

There were eight pensioners in for the afternoon matinee of *The Last Bus*, starring Timothy Spall. Most of them had bought cups of tea, bags of Revels and mince pies that we currently have on offer. The pensioners hardly ever buy popcorn, complaining that it gets stuck in their teeth. Quite often I give the younger people a large bucket for the same price as a small one, otherwise we would have to bin loads.

'What did you think, then, ladies?' I asked a couple of our regulars as they left the cinema. The general consensus was that the film was very good, although one lady said she found it a bit depressing. We had six people in for the matinee yesterday, so at least the numbers aren't going down. We have to be thankful for small mercies, I guess, and there's usually at least twenty people in for the later showing. Still not enough, though.

'Honestly, I can't think of what else we can do to attract numbers. It seems the younger crowd just aren't interested in coming here; they all head into town,' I say to eighteen-year-old Shelley, one of my co-workers, who's opened a bag of M&M's and is munching on them thoughtfully. Shelley is tall and attractive, with dark hair in a pixie cut and striking blue eyes that she accentuates with kohl liner. She's studying art at college, and this is only a part-time job for her.

'I hope you've paid for them. We definitely can't afford to be eating the profits,' I tell her, only half-joking.

'I know. Just a little perk, isn't it? I don't do it very often. And the pay is so crap.'

She's right about the pay being rubbish, so I don't push it. Shelley likes it here, as the hours fit around her college course, and she is good to have around. I like her dry wit, and she works hard, on the odd occasion when the cinema is busy – which seems to be whenever a new Marvel film is being screened.

'Maybe munch on some of that popcorn.' I point to the mound behind the glass counter.

'Might do, but I'm not that keen on popcorn. Apart from that toffee one in the red packet.'

'I can't resist that either. Good job we don't sell it here.'

She proffers her bag of M&M's, but I resist.

'What? Don't you want to be complicit to the crime, when the police turn up and arrest us?' She grins.

'Exactly that,' I reply, smiling. 'Or more that I'm watching the pounds. I've bought a new dress for the Christmas party, and it clings to everything.'

Shaking her head, Shelley takes one last handful and puts the bag away on a shelf under the counter, where I also spy a half-eaten Twix that she swiftly covers with a cinema programme.

'I bet the young people would come if there was a Nando's next door. You should email head office to see if they'll open one here,' says Shelley.

'If only it were that simple. Fast-food restaurants tend to open in retail parks or city centres, not on the edge of a village.'

'Motorways.' She sucks an M&M thoughtfully.

'What about them?'

'They have fast-food restaurants at motorway services too. The McDonald's just off the M57 near the airport is my favourite. They give you loads of chips.'

'I'll be sure to remember that.' I smile at Shelley.

It's just after three o'clock and once Shelley has cleaned the auditorium – even though the pensioners never leave a mess, placing all waste into a bin on their exit – there's little else to do until the next movie is screened at five thirty. It's a Christmas family movie, so there's a chance it will be popular over the next few weeks running up to Christmas. Fingers crossed anyway. I suppose we are lucky to be paid for the hour or two between showings. Last time the area manager was here, he hinted at maybe not being able to pay us for that time and even suggested we work a split shift. We argued it would be impossible to go home and back again, and replenish stock for the next viewings, so our wages are safe. For now, at least. It seems the director of the cinema group, Greg Starr, said he wouldn't hear of us not being paid for the time between films, regardless of the economic situation.

After checking the toilets and making sure all the sweets are in place, Shelley spruces up the reception area with some tinsel and a little Christmas tree, and a box of baubles and lights she found in a cupboard that both of us had completely forgotten about. It looks really festive and inviting now for the customers when they enter. After that, we watch *The Last Bus*. Getting to watch movies is a big perk to the job and, to my surprise, Shelley says she really liked the film. I did too. It was a little melancholy but with a real heart, and I really liked the ending. Endings can often be a huge let-down in a film for me.

Thankfully, there is quite a turn-out for the Christmas film. When I say quite a turnout, there are forty people, mainly families with young children. Not bad for a Tuesday evening, though. We watch the film, that includes goodies, baddies, Santa and a golden Labrador that saves the day. The children all have smiles on their faces as they leave, which makes me smile too. *The Dog Who Saved Christmas* seems to be a sure-fire winner.

'Right, see you tomorrow afternoon, then,' says Shelley as we lock up. Another part-time worker, Ed, is here tomorrow for the morning, then Shelley and me. I'm the only full-time member of staff; the rest are made up of part-timers, mainly students, with Ed and Shelley having the most hours. At one time, the cinema was open until ten thirty in the evening, but as hardly anyone came through the doors, the last film is screened at six, and we lock up and leave usually before nine p.m.

'See you tomorrow. Enjoy the rest of your evening.'

It's freezing outside, and I zip my chunky padded jacket up, even for the short walk to the car park. Shelley has headed off in the opposite direction, towards town to meet some of her friends in a bar so has declined the lift I offered her.

FIVE

Driving into the village, it's almost eight thirty when I push open the door of the Hot Pot café.

'Oh, thank goodness you're still open.' I take in the warm smell of home cooking. Jo, the café owner and close friend, turns the sign to closed.

'You made it by the skin of your teeth,' she says as she sashays towards the counter.

'Please say you have some hot pot left.' I rub my hands together in an attempt to warm them up.

'Literally just one or two portions,' Jo tells me.

'I'm not surprised as it's so popular. It's blinking freezing out there.'

'I know.' Jo smiles. 'It's really good for business. So, how has your day been? Have you had many in at the cinema today?' Jo knows all about my concerns over numbers.

'Pretty good, actually, yeah. It usually is when we show a family movie,' I tell her, feeling the warmth in the café.

Jo Hollins – known in the village as Joan Collins, due to her penchant for red lip gloss and wearing her black hair piled up – is the glamorous owner of the Hot Pot café. Today, she's wearing a white blouse with a huge bow and a dogtooth-patterned pencil skirt. Her attire makes her look more suited to working in a high-class department store. I wouldn't say work is something she usually does, though, as she mostly swans around chatting to the customers and occasionally serving a slice of cake. Her daughter Claire is the one who is up first thing in the morning to make a huge vat of the hot pot – or scouse as it's known around these parts. It was her great-grandmother's recipe, apparently. Claire is spraying tables and wiping them down with a cloth.

'Hi, Sarah.' She looks up from under her heavy blonde fringe, her hair chopped into a shaggy bob. Claire is twenty years old and very pretty. I know for a fact a few of the local lads in the village have their eye on her, but she doesn't seem to take them on.

'Hi, Claire, how are you?'

'Okay, thanks. About to head home. After I've served our last customer of the day, of course.' She winks, heading towards the counter.

'You're a good 'un,' I tell her. I'm ravenous and dying to get stuck into some hot food. I hope they have some crusty bread left to go with it.

'I won't be switching the coffee machine on again, though, I'm afraid, as I've cleaned and unplugged it for the evening. But as you're such a loyal customer, I can do you an instant coffee if you like?' She brandishes a kettle.

'You really are an angel, Christmas or otherwise. Thanks, Claire.'

'Not a problem.'

There's a rapping on the glass door, and Jo tuts and says, 'Can't people read the sign?' She'd turned it to closed as soon as I entered the café.

'Maybe it's because they can see another customer inside,' I say a little guiltily as I wait for my food.

Jo walks to the door and a few seconds later a handsome bloke with dark hair streaked with grey has been ushered inside.

'We're actually closed, but... well, maybe there is still something I can tempt you with,' says Jo, with her seductive smile.

'Sounds good.' The bloke, who looks in his fifties, smiles. 'And sorry, I saw the lights on, so I thought you were still open,' he explains.

'I thought as much. Maybe we should switch them off and light some candles.' She raises an eyebrow and he follows her to the counter like he's been hypnotised and I can't help laughing to myself.

'Oh, my goodness, I'm sure that gets better every time I eat it,' I tell Claire as she clears my plate away.

'It's always better at the end of the day,' she says and I agree. The stew was thick and tasty, served with a crusty roll and butter and a little pot of red cabbage. I decided not to bother cooking this evening, as Ellie was heading to a friend's house to revise, and was having dinner there. It's a little extravagant to be eating out midweek on my income, but I justify it to myself as the price is so reasonable. Jo waves at me as I stand to leave, before she returns her attention to the handsome diner.

Jo's age is indeterminate; I'm not sure even Claire knows how old she really is. She moved here six years ago from the city centre having run a successful café near the Royal Albert Dock, but Jo sold up after her husband suffered a fatal heart attack. I was surprised to find out that she had always hankered after somewhere in a village. She said she found the city a little overwhelming at times, but her husband was a townie through and through. She told me that she feels right at home running the café in the courtyard and is much more suited to village life – I'd never have had her down as a country bumpkin. It shows you really can't judge a book by its cover.

I drop a couple of pound coins into the glass jar with a handwritten sign saying *Tips*, wrapped with red tinsel.

'Bye, Jo, bye, Claire, and thanks,' I say before heading out in the cold, fortified by my warming meal.

Passing the village pub, with a large Christmas tree outside, I realise I probably ought to dine there occasionally too and support them, especially as my friend Helen works behind the bar. I know from working at the cinema how valuable local support is. If I'm honest, though, I think the Hot Pot café serves the best food around here. Besides, I remind myself once more that my budget doesn't really allow me to eat out too much. You can't beat the beer in the pub, though, and they always have a good selection of cask ales and decent wines.

Inside, it's cosy and inviting, with several nooks and crannies that have velour chairs in various colours and fashionable, Victorian-style flock wallpaper. A dark-wooden bookcase along one wall matches the oak beams on the ceilings. There's no doubt that Helen has given the place a touch of modern opulence, whilst retaining the original old eighteenth-century atmosphere. She's tried a few drinks promotions recently too, as well as happy hour that unfortunately attracted the wrong kind of customer, so was quickly shelved.

Glancing through a window, I see a roaring fire in the grate and I make a pledge to pop in a little more often, even if it's only for a drink. I know how uncertain things can be, working at the cinema, and how developers can come in the blink of an eye offering to buy up pubs and build houses. It would be awful to lose the village pub. Or the cinema, but I push that thought firmly to the back of my mind.

Back home, I shrug off my thick coat and hang my woolly scarf up in the hall on the black metal wall hangers. An hour later, Ellie arrives home and heads almost straight to her room, yawning, stopping just long enough for me to ask how her study went. She has mock exams in February, so I'm glad to hear that it went well, and that she and her friends had made revision notes in their phones and on little Post-it notes. I don't often get that much from her about studies and schoolwork, so it is encouraging to hear.

I head up not long after her, after watching an old Christmas episode of *Only Fools and Horses* that still makes me laugh. I used to watch it with Dad; it was his absolute favourite and always brings back such happy memories. It's been a long day, so once I'm upstairs and in bed, I'm out like a light.

SIX

Ellie was up and out early this morning. All I heard was a 'Bye, Mum' as I emerged from the shower, so I still haven't had a chance to chat to her about the candle and vodka from the other night, although it weighed a little on my mind in work yesterday. I know we bicker at times about the usual stuff, which I kind of expect – she's a teenager after all – but, to my knowledge, she's never lied to me before.

I don't start work at the cinema until twelve, so I head into the city centre to look for some different shoes to match my dress for the party. I've decided to return the suede boots as, on reflection, I don't think they are dressy enough for a party. It's being held at the Hilton in the city centre, and as it's for the whole of the Starlight Cinema Group; I'd rather be overdressed than under. The annual bash is funded by Greg Starr, MD of the cinema group, and I feel grateful for the invite every year, even though I am constantly worrying that it may be the last one if the cinema closes. I don't often have the chance to wear a pretty dress, favouring nice tops and jeans when I head out for a meal somewhere with Cassie, or my friends in the village. I'm looking forward to going full-on glam, with big hair and high heels. If I can find a pair.

I'm just grabbing a coffee, when I hear a familiar voice.

'Hiya, Sarah, I thought that was you.' I turn to find myself staring into the annoyingly dazzling blue eyes of my ex-husband, Robbie. He grabs the seat opposite me, without being invited to, and plonks himself down.

'So, how's tricks?' he asks, his smile as bright as ever.

Robbie always asks me 'How's tricks?' And my response is always 'Fine, thanks', although I often feel like saying 'Unlike you, I'm not up to any tricks', but manage to bite my tongue. Whilst he heads to the counter to grab himself a coffee, I look in the mirror and check my make-up, even teasing my hair a little. Not that I want to make a good impression, you understand, but I don't want him to think I've let myself go either, since we split.

'What are you doing for Christmas, then?' he asks when he returns with his Americano.

'I'm hosting Christmas lunch. Me, Ellie, Auntie Jean and Uncle Bernie. Oh, and this year, my cousin Heather is joining us. She's on her own this year, having only recently divorced. She's staying at her parents' place for a bit.'

'Have I met her?' he asks.

'Hmm. I think you might have not long after we got married. She was married to Joe,' I remind him.

'Oh, I remember her now. No wonder she's divorced. He was a right misery arse.' Robbie laughs.

'That's a little unkind,' I say, although in truth, yes, Joe could be described as a bit of a misery arse, only coming to life with alcohol, when he usually made a fool of himself slurring his words and being touchy-feely with every woman in sight. She was probably well rid of him.

'How about you?' I ask.

'Umm, not sure. We were hoping to go to the Canaries, but that's kind of been stalled. I think Hannah is heading up to her folks in Scotland, as her dad hasn't been too well,' he says, not giving much away, and I can't help wondering if there's trouble in paradise.

'Anyway, talking of Christmas, are Pandora bracelets still popular? Do you think Ellie would like one?' he asks me as he stirs his coffee.

It's nice that Robbie is still a good father to Ellie, no matter what is going on in his private life.

'I'm not sure really. I think she's into Thomas Sabo jewellery at the moment and I do know she has admired something on their website.'

I flick through my phone and show him a picture of a pretty bracelet.

'Great, send me the link, would you? I'll get her that. Unless you were planning on buying it?' he asks.

'No, it's fine. She's asked me for a pair of boots she's had her eye on.'

'Okay, great.'

Robbie suddenly studies a message that has just come through on his phone.

'Right, gotta go.' He takes a long slurp of his coffee. 'Or Hannah will be wearing my balls for earrings.'

'Great, thanks for leaving me with that image.' I glance down at my untouched Christmas pudding cake, which has suddenly lost its appeal.

'See you later,' he says and the whirlwind that is Robbie departs.

I finish my coffee and head out onto the busy street once more. I sigh when I think of Robbie and how he hurt me. Thankfully, we're in a slightly better place nowadays, although I still wouldn't trust him as far as I could throw him. Despite his commitment issues, I have to admit that he has always been a good father to Ellie – available whenever she needs a chat, which is worth far more than any expensive gift he buys. Even when he does splash out on her, he checks to see if it's something Ellie will like. I'm really happy that they are close, and sad that we didn't make it as a trio, but I guess some things just aren't meant to be.

Walking along, I could kick myself, wishing I'd asked him if Ellie had mentioned having a boyfriend. Then again, I don't suppose teenage girls mention boyfriends to their fathers, do they? I remember being out at a restaurant celebrating Ellie's thirteenth birthday and someone cheekily asked if she had a boyfriend and the talk turned to boys. Robbie told Ellie teenage boys couldn't be trusted and were only after one thing, advising her to stay away from them until she was at least thirty, and everyone laughed. I told him not to judge other people by his own standards – out of earshot of Ellie – and he protested, before flicking his eyes over a particularly attractive passing waitress. He'll never change. At forty-three years old, he is wearing it remarkably well. Possibly with a little enhancement from the local cosmetic dentist and Botox clinic, that is. Always a bit vain, that man.

I head to Liverpool One, where a busker, wearing a Santa hat, is braving the cold and belting out a medley of Christmas tunes, with shoppers in the Christmas spirit generously throwing coins into a hat as they stand around listening to him. An adorable old silver-haired couple do a little jive when the busker plays a particularly catchy tune, which earns a round of applause from the crowd. They give a little bow at the end, looking so happy together, and I feel a little pang as I think of my own parents. I miss them so much, especially around this time of year. Christmas lunch just doesn't feel the same without them. I'm so grateful that they got to meet Ellie, though, and that she has some wonderful memories with her grandparents, recorded in some precious photos in an album.

I fish in my coat pocket, where I always have some change, and toss a two-pound coin into the busker's hat, and he winks at me. He really is a very good singer and I really hope he gets his big break one day.

I stroll on, marvelling at the creative window displays in the shop fronts, some with sophisticated lighting and elegantly decorated silver trees, others covered with tinsel and string lights. I resist buying donuts, even though they look mouthwatering, covered in white icing and dusted with cinnamon or chocolate flakes. Others have red and green icing, adorned with little snowmen and candy canes. I have a really sweet tooth and have to rein myself in at times, otherwise I'll start looking like those snowmen.

I stop at a shoe shop, and my eyes fall on the most gorgeous pair of black stilettos. Not skyscraper high, but tall enough to look glamorous and still be able to walk in. They have a little trio of paste diamonds at the toe and at the top of the heel. Pretty without being over the top. I head inside, and when I try them on, I feel like Cinderella. They are an absolutely perfect fit, which, believe me, doesn't happen very often. I wince a little at the price tag, but they're real leather and will probably last me for years as they will only come out for Christmas parties and special occasions. Happy with my purchase, I'm feeling a little peckish as I abandoned the Christmas pudding cake, so I head away from the main shopping area and head along to Castle Street. My favourite cafeteria beckons as I turn the corner, glancing up at a rapidly darkening sky I wonder whether we might get snow, but decide it's far too cold.

I push open the door of the Castle Street Townhouse and I'm immediately enveloped in a warm hug and the smell of something delicious. The café is housed in an old Grade II listed building, with high ceilings, chandeliers and a long, marble-topped bar. Its opulence belies the friendly, laid-back service and atmosphere of the restaurant, which serves fabulous food from breakfast right through to dinner on stylish dark-wood tables. I take a seat near a window, and order a breakfast brunch. The waiter offers me the bottomless Prosecco option but I decline, as I think getting wasted whilst out shopping is definitely a bad idea. Especially as I'm out alone. Not to mention the fact that I'm in work in an hour or so.

I finish my delicious breakfast of warm waffles, berries and maple syrup and head to the train station, pleased with my shoe purchase. I really don't enjoy shoe shopping, so I'm happy it's something I no longer have to think about. As I walk, the grey sky above is now streaked with orange, and there's a stillness in the air despite the activity on the streets, and it feels a little warmer.

After descending the escalator to Central Station, which is heaving, I shove my way towards the platform, jostling with shoppers carrying multiple bags of Christmas shopping and mums with pushchairs. As I stand waiting for my train, the train on the opposite platform is about to leave.

There's a bloke staring out of the window, and for a second, our eyes meet. As the train pulls out, he smiles at me. He looks so familiar and a memory comes shooting into my mind. It can't be, can it? Luke and his family moved to America many years ago. It was probably just someone who looked similar. Luke must have surely changed a lot in the intervening years. I put it out of my mind as my own train pulls into the station and I'm almost carried along as the crowd surges forward.

On the train, I flop into the nearest seat, thankful not to be left standing. As the train rattles along the track, I find myself thinking of Luke Watson and wondering what he's up to these days.

SEVEN

By the time I step off the train half an hour later, thick snowflakes are swirling to the ground. I quickly head home to change, admiring the cottage, the front lawn already covered in a light brushing of snow. Later on, it will look like a perfect Christmas-card scene, but I hope we don't get snowed in at the cinema later.

I drive the short distance to work, watching the snowflakes fall onto the windscreen, as the wipers busily swoosh them away. Once inside, I struggle to focus on work, as my mind keeps wandering back to the train station.

'Sarah, what are you doing?'

Shelley is looking at me open-mouthed and pointing to the coffee machine that I am about to fill with juice instead of water.

'Oh gosh, what am I like! Sorry.'

'Where are you exactly? You're definitely miles away somewhere,' she teases.

I hand tickets to a quartet of pensioners, who Shelley then serves coffee and snacks. They are here to watch a film starring Pierce Brosnan, who is always a crowd-pleaser.

When the film has started, I tell Shelley all about the bloke on the train.

'It was so strange. He looked exactly like my first crush, the same dark hair and strong jawline. And those brown eyes.' I drift off. 'I can't see how it could have been him, though; the man on the train looked quite young and Luke's a few years older than me. It's definitely stirred up some memories, though.'

I tell Shelley all about my friend Kay and how Luke was her older brother. 'I always blushed bright red when I saw him.' I tell her about their house on Adelaide Terrace.

'Nice,' says Shelley, before she pours a handful of sweets into her mouth.

'Nice isn't the word. It was gorgeous.'

Adelaide Terrace is a row of attractive, pastel-coloured Victorian houses across the road from the sea. One of the houses on the nearby Marine Drive has a blue plaque outside, showing it to have once been the home of the captain of the *Titanic*.

I first met Kay at a local amateur dramatics group, kind of halfway between our respective homes. I'd always loved acting at school, and I once played Frenchie in a school production of *Grease*, to rave reviews. Kay went to a private girls' school across town, whilst I attended the local comprehensive. In a way, we were worlds apart, but we bonded over our love of acting. We enjoyed trips to the Empire Theatre together – sometimes Kay would buy two tickets and present me with one, knowing my family never had that much money to spare. Other times, we watched productions at the Everyman Theatre, which was cheaper and more arthouse, and would sit giggling at some of the more slightly risqué performances: a naked woman performing a monologue covered in blue paint being an example of such. We both dreamt of becoming famous actresses and starring in the West End. Theatre and cinema were always a passion of mine – although working in a struggling cinema was hardly my lifetime ambition.

By the time Kay was twenty-three, she was appearing in *Chicago* on Broadway, whilst I had married Robbie Dunn and was carrying our first child. We wrote to each other for a while after Kay moved to the States. When she sent me the programme of *Chicago* with her name on it, I felt a mixture of immense pride for my friend, along with personal regret. She kindly offered to pay the airfare so I could go and see her, but I was unable to, as I was too heavily pregnant at the time. She was my best friend and was like a sister to me. When she moved away, I missed her greatly and vowed to visit her when my child was born. But somehow, that day never came.

'What would you have done if it was the bloke from your past?' asks Shelley, pulling me back to the present, as she attempts to take another packet of sweets from a stand. I bat her hand away and she rolls her eyes and tuts.

'Well, there wasn't a lot I could have done, as his train was heading off in the opposite direction.'

'Where to?'

'Um, I think it was Southport. I'll probably never see him again. Anyway, I'm pretty sure it wasn't him; as I said, he emigrated to America.'

I should try to forget all about it, even though Luke has been on my mind since I thought I saw him, and I can't stop thinking about those happy memories.

'If you did want to know what he's up to, you could try Facebook?' she suggests and to be truthful I have already looked, but I couldn't see him. Besides, I don't know his situation; he could be married with kids. Although maybe I could have inquired about Kay, to start the conversation.

An icy blast enters the foyer as the door opens and a snow-ball lands squarely in the middle of the red-carpeted foyer, distracting me for now. As the film is well underway, I head to the door and bolt it, spotting a small group of children disappear around a corner, no doubt giggling wildly.

That evening, I pull into the village and Josh Hunter is straddling his motorbike in the courtyard, chatting to Claire from the Hot Pot café, who is giggling at something he said. He lifts a helmet from a bike box and offers it to her. I'm driving slowly over the speed bumps in the village, taking in the scene as she shakes her head. A second later, he revs the engine and does a figure of eight in the courtyard, before roaring past me in the road, the noise of the engine throbbing through the village road. Claire would be wise to give that one a wide berth.

Ellie is sprawled out on the huge red rug in front of the log burner when I get home, browsing through some geography books. Tonight, she's wearing black pyjamas decorated with snowmen.

'Hi, love, doing some revision, I see,' I say as I rub my hands in front of the fire. 'I thought you were going to Izzy's tonight?'

'Change of plan.' She shrugs. 'I thought I might do some more revision by myself, even though I think it's a waste of time.'

'Why do you think that?' I ask as I sit down on the huge, squishy cream sofa, adorned with Christmas cushions.

'Dunno. I'll have forgotten everything by the time I sit the exams. I prefer to do it a couple of days before.'

'I used to think the same when I was at school. But going over things several times embeds it into the brain and helps with memory recall,' I say with certainty, even though I'm not quite sure it worked for me. 'Anyway, have you eaten?' I ask.

'I had some tomato soup after school but I'm a bit peckish now.'

'Do you fancy some pancakes?'

'Home-made?' Ellie abandons her books and follows me into the kitchen, where she sits on a bar stool as I busy myself making some batter mix. She chops some banana and strawberries, before retrieving a jar of Nutella from a cupboard. Fifteen minutes later, there's a pile of fresh pancakes waiting to be devoured.

We chat about our respective days, and it feels good to be sitting here actually having a nice conversation together. Despite me not wanting to ruin things, I do feel the need to talk to her about the other evening.

'I've been meaning to ask you,' I say, placing some fruit on my pancake and resisting the chocolate spread. 'Did you actually go out the other night, when I went to meet Cassie in town?'

She seems to have to think for a moment before she answers. 'Yeah, I told you, I went to Izzy's. Why?'

She's sitting here with me this evening, safe and sound, and I'm almost tempted to backtrack. But I don't like the idea of her being secretive and thinking she's gotten away with it.

'What time did you get home?' I try to act casually.

'What? I dunno, I can't remember. Why are you asking me this?'

'Because' – I try to keep my voice calm and even – 'when I came home, I smelt the Yankee Candle in the lounge. It looked like it had been burning for quite a while.'

Even beneath the subdued pendant lighting, I can see her face colour.

'So. I might have lit it when I got home. I can't remember.' Her voice seems to have risen an octave higher.

'The smell was strong, as if it had been burning for a good while,' I continue. 'If you had stayed home and invited someone around, I wouldn't have minded, you know. Was it a boy?' I ask.

'Oh my God, Mum, I've told you I was out.' She attempts to leave the room, but I stand in the doorway.

'You're not running away, Ellie. I'm only asking you, because I don't want you lying to me. I don't lie to you, do I?

You told me you were going out that evening, so what's going on?'

She looks so young, standing in front of me like a rabbit trapped in headlights. All I really want to do is hug her.

'Sorry, Mum.' She looks as though she is about to burst into tears.

'Ellie, what's wrong? Did something happen?' I ask gently.

'I did have someone round, but it all went wrong,' she tells me, looking down at the floor.

'Was it a boy?'

She lifts her head and nods.

'Anyone I know?'

She shakes her head.

'Was it someone from school?'

She nods. This is starting to feel like a game of twenty questions.

'Yes,' she says in a small voice, and a sudden feeling of dread runs through my body. I hope someone hasn't hurt her.

'Ellie, it's okay. You can tell me. What do you mean everything went wrong?'

'It was probably my fault.' She sighs. 'I got dressed up so maybe he got the wrong idea.'

I remember the tight jeans and the black top she wore that evening.

'He was roaming around the kitchen looking for booze,' she continues. 'And when he found some in a cupboard, he poured us both a vodka. I told him I didn't really want any but he had some anyway. When I put the film on, he laughed and said did I really think he'd come around to watch a film? I felt like such an idiot.'

'Oh my goodness, Ellie. He never did anything to you, did he?' I ask, fear flooding through me.

'No, Mum, chill out. I'm not stupid. We did have a kiss, but when he wanted more I told him to get out.'

'Oh, Ellie.'

'Maybe it's 'cos he's a couple of years older than me,' she says.

'I thought you said it was someone from school?'

'Sixth form,' she quickly adds. 'Anyway, I won't be seeing him again. I really like him, though. Dad did warn me about teenage boys. Maybe he's right.'

Who would have thought Robbie capable of dispensing sensible advice, let alone about relationships?

'Well, I'm proud I've raised such a smart girl. Don't ever think you've enticed someone by wearing the wrong clothes. He's older than you; he should know better. That boy, whoever he is, doesn't deserve you. And, please, don't lie to me in future, Ellie.'

'I promise I won't, Mum.'

An hour later, we're both tucked up in bed, but I lie awake, thinking of how quickly Ellie is growing up. I'm sure this won't be the first boyfriend incident, and one day she will probably get her heart broken before she finds the right one. And even a mother can't do anything to protect her daughter from that.

EIGHT

I wake the next morning and stroll down to the courtyard, where I am greeted by Frances, the owner of Countryside Flowers. Frances is the personification of sunshine, with her halo of curly blonde hair that frames her face and the brightest of smiles. We've become friendly over the years and often head out on a night out together, and she comes round when I host friends at the cottage.

'Hi, Sarah, how are you?' she asks, but she seems to be missing her usual bright smile.

'Good, thanks. You?'

'I'm well, thanks. Although, I'm super tired this morning. I probably stayed up later than my bedtime last night watching a Christmas movie.'

'Oh, I'm forever doing that,' I tell her. 'I don't know why I can't just watch things on catch-up, but once I'm invested in a film, I have to see it through.'

I glance around the stunning floral displays in the shop. Amongst the usual holly and berry decorations are pots of vivid red poinsettia plants, alongside amaryllis and displays of silver-painted twigs in pots with pretty baubles dangling from them. There are pretty ornaments too, including wooden tree decorations bearing children's names. It's a place I could stand in for hours, just staring at the beauty of it all, surrounded by the fresh scents. I notice a pink rose encased in a glass case, and it reminds of the rose from *Beauty and the Beast*.

'That's pretty. Why is it in a case?' I ask, transfixed by its delicate beauty.

'It's poisonous, so I don't want anyone touching it, especially children. But it's so beautiful I think it should be on display,' she tells me. 'It's a bit of a talking point.'

'I bet it is.' It really is lovely. The outer petals are a soft pink, and it has a white centre. It looks completely pure, yet its appearance belies its toxicity.

'It's called the Christmas rose, or to give it its scientific name, the *Helleborus niger*,' Frances tells me. 'Attractive, but deadly. It grows around this time of year.' There's nothing Frances doesn't know about flowers, always able to answer a question about a particular bloom without a moment's hesitation.

'I've got your wreath ready,' she tells me before she disappears into the back of the shop.

I'm here today to collect a wreath for my parents' grave. When she returns and shows it to me, I give a little gasp. She has really excelled herself this year, presenting me with a stunning holly wreath, threaded with cranberries, holly berries and vibrant red amaryllis. She has also added some pretty purple flowers that look like pansies. Frances tells me they are anemones.

'Really? I thought they lived under the sea?'

'Different variety,' she tells me, smiling. 'These ones are plants, the ones under the sea are living creatures.'

'Of course they are, silly me! like sea urchins.'

'Exactly.'

The wreath has been sprayed lightly with fake snow and a shimmering of silver glitter. It's absolutely stunning.

'Fran, I love it, I can't thank you enough.'

'You're welcome. I really enjoyed doing that one. Nothing but the finest for your mum and dad,' she says kindly as she hands it over.

Last night's snowfall has blanketed the ground of the churchyard, leaving no distinction between the looked-after graves, and the older neglected ones. I push open the creaky metal gate of the churchyard and step inside. The graveyard looks so pretty, as people have been to place various floral displays and gifts at this time of year, which makes it look vivid and alive somehow, despite it being a resting place.

I brush the black marble stone and tidy a few stray leaves and grasses and set down the wreath.

'Frances has done a fine job this year,' I say. 'I really like the purple anemones; I hope you do too.

A watery sun has been attempting to penetrate some clouds and I wonder if it's too much to expect it to break through once again this year, but after five minutes of chatting to my parents, the clouds part and the grave is bathed in a shaft of sunlight. I head home with a smile on my face and feeling truly blessed.

'Do you and Ellie fancy going to a concert at St George's Hall? Gerald Dickens is performing again. I missed seeing him last year.'

Cassie is on the phone this morning, making plans. She must have felt the same inspiration from our festive reminiscing the other day. St George's Hall is continuing its programme of classical musical concerts and theatre productions. Gerald Dickens, the great-great-grandson of Charles, is carrying on the tradition of his famous relative and doing readings at the hall.

Cassie tells me he is performing *A Christmas Carol* again, which received rave reviews last year.

'Oh, wow, yes, I'd love that. Are James and the kids going too?' I ask.

'Yes, I thought it would be a nice magical evening listening to the story by candlelight. If the kids aren't bored stiff, that is,' she says with a laugh. 'I hope Ellie will come along too.'

Cassie knows there's a possibility Ellie might roll her eyes and decline, but on the other hand, she gets along well with Cassie's kids. In fact, I'll tell her Cassie has already booked tickets, so she has to come. It was one of her favourite Christmas films as a child anyway.

'She will, I'm sure. Especially if Jess and Zak are going.'

I remember Ellie tucked up in her Christmas pyjamas, the tree all twinkling in the background, the first time we watched the film with a mug of hot chocolate. She was a bit unsure about the ghost at first, but really enjoyed it when she was a little older, when she could understand how it revealed the true meaning of being kind, especially at Christmastime.

'Great. I'll book the tickets then. What date is best for you? They have the twenty-second and the twenty-third available.'

I have a quick glance through my diary, and confirm for the twenty-third of December.

'Okay. Seven o'clock. Ooh, I can't wait! It sounds so Christmassy.'

'I know. Maybe grab some food first if you like, but we'll sort that out later.'

'Thanks, Cassie, I'm really looking forward to that now. I'll transfer you some money for the tickets.'

'Don't do that, we'll sort it out,' she says vaguely, but I will anyway. She's typically generous and often pays for coffees and little treats when we are out, knowing I only have one income, but I don't want to take advantage of her generosity. Besides, I do alright, as Robbie still pays maintenance for Ellie, which will continue until she leaves college. After that, well, I haven't thought too much about it, but I guess I might have to look for another job. It's unlikely I will be able to increase my hours at the cinema.

After making it through the week with no more drama, I wake up on Sunday morning feeling refreshed. I actually have the whole day off, so I decide to take a drive to Crosby and take a walk along the seafront. I ask Ellie if she fancies it, and she considers it for a minute, before deciding that actually she and a friend are thinking about catching the train into Southport.

'No problem. Here.' I peel a twenty-pound note from my purse and hand it to her. 'You and Izzy get some lunch.'

'Are you sure, Mum? I still have some money on my card,' she says.

'Certain. Take it.'

I like Ellie to have a little cash when she's out, in case of an emergency.

'Okay, thanks, Mum, if you're sure.' She takes the note and smiles gratefully.

I pay an allowance onto a debit card for Ellie – from the money Robbie pays me – hoping it will be a lesson in budgeting. So far, she seems to be doing a good job. Well, after an initial blip, when she spent twenty pounds in one week buying lattes after school, but it actually provided the basis for a useful discussion about managing finances.

Driving out of the village, I spot Jo Hollins in a smart red coat that matches her lipstick, stepping into a stylish convertible with a good-looking bloke in his fifties. As I draw closer, driving slowly over the speed bumps, I notice it's the man from the café the other evening, who turned up when it was closed, and I can't help smiling to myself. Jo certainly grabs life with both hands, taking every opportunity that comes her way.

Claire will probably be running the café with one of the part-time staff today. I bet she's glad they don't serve Sunday roasts, or they would be rushed off their feet. In fact, on Sunday they only serve soup, sandwiches and a selection of cakes, usually to day-trippers, either heading home after a day out at the beach in the summer, or shopping trips in the winter. Although, there are still a steady amount of people visiting the beach in winter, walking dogs and flying kites with kids. Lots of business comes from people passing through the village, as it links a main road to the coast and then on into the city centre. I know the village pub and the Hot Pot café are grateful for the passing trade.

Driving along, the sun has made a rare appearance in the sky, and glancing at the bright blue sky from the warmth of my car, it could almost be a summer's day. If it wasn't for the sludge now left on the ground outside from the snow during the week. And the chilly temperature outside. I'm warm and toasty inside the car, and have packed a quilted jacket and woolly hat and scarf for my walk later. I'm already planning this evening's movie in the lounge with the cosy log burner and a glass of something, having enjoyed a bracing walk. I think it is important to go on walks, despite the weather, to keep the winter blues at bay. I'm pretty sure I spotted a Christmas film starring Reese Witherspoon on one of the channels in the TV guide, but there's always *The Holiday* on Netflix if I am mistaken. It's my all-time favourite Christmas movie.

NINE

The wind is more bracing than I thought when I walk along the beach road. I'm grateful I brought my thickest coat and matching woolly hat and scarf, which I had the foresight to buy last summer in an online sale. I cut through a small park across the road from the beach, where I can see the coloured row of houses on Adelaide Terrace lined up like a row of pastel-coloured chalks in a box.

The one with the blue door that my old friend lived in has two silver pots either side of it, with small bushes threaded with lights. It looks almost exactly the same as it did all those years ago – apart from the For Sale sign – and I'm grabbed for a minute by a feeling of nostalgia.

I'll never forget the first time Kay invited me to her house for tea. It was around this time of year, and when I stepped onto the parquet flooring in the huge hall, it was like walking into a different world. It was a far cry from the modest, although pretty, cottage I called home. I remember glancing up at the sweeping, thickly carpeted red staircase, half expecting a princess to descend the stairs from one of the bedrooms.

As it happened, a good-looking, dark-haired boy walked

down the stairs and I felt my cheeks redden. On the far side of the hall stood a tall, real Christmas tree draped with icicle lights and tasteful, blue baubles. I couldn't help comparing it to the tree in our house, covered with silver tinsel and multicoloured lights. I was worried Kay's parents might be a little stuffy, but they were lovely and completely down to earth. Even though we ate at the dining table – chicken casserole as I recall – there was no fancy silver or crystal glasses, which I had been half expecting.

I was a fairly regular visitor after that, each time hoping to get a glimpse of Luke again. Sometimes I was lucky. I remember he always smiled at me, and once or twice he offered me a drink if I was waiting for Kay when she'd gone upstairs to change. His presence always seemed to make me stumble over my words. It all seems like a lifetime ago now, I think to myself as I stroll on, although those memories will stay with me forever.

I find myself wondering what Kay is up to now. Is she married with children? Maybe I ought to look her up on Facebook, but she could have a different name these days. Whatever she is up to now, I'm happy she had the chance of fulfilling her ambition to appear in a show on Broadway. It seems dreams really can come true.

I take a long walk along the beach, watching the crashing waves and inhaling the fresh sea air. A black-and-white dog, off lead, heads towards the water before running away when a wave splashes over its paws. I don't blame it; it's probably freezing.

'Max, come here.' A young woman calls the dog over.

'It's not Mad Max, is it?' I laugh nervously as it bounds towards me.

'No, soft as a brush,' she reassures me.

'Not the day for a swim,' I say, feeling the sting on my cheeks and wondering if I'm crazy coming here on a day like this.

'You're not kidding. It's bright, though, isn't it? I like to get out for a winter walk, blow the cobwebs away,' she says. 'And the dog too, if I'm not careful.' She chuckles, attaching a lead to its collar.

Walking on, I pass several more people walking dogs, a young couple holding hands and a couple with a young boy, who is giggling as the bloke, presumably his father, chases him up and down the sand dunes. At the end of my walk, I head into the Marine Café, grateful to find a table and order a steaming latte and a bowl of thick winter vegetable soup, which really hits the spot. I hope Ellie is enjoying herself in Southport, too, and look forward to spending the evening with her.

It's late afternoon when I arrive back in the village, and decide to call in for a drink at the Penny Farthing. The place has only a handful of customers in today, nursing drinks and chatting. Helen is behind the bar, looking slightly bored, picking at her nails. Her husband, sandy-haired Paul, who's fifty next year and is developing a bit of a middle-aged paunch, is carrying a tray of drinks to a table.

'Alright, Sarah.' He nods.

'Hi, Paul,' I reply, heading to the bar.

'Hi, Helen, a glass of Merlot, please,' I request, sitting myself on a bar stool.

'Large?' She brandishes the bottle.

'Oh, go on then. But just the one, I'm in work tomorrow.'

'It's only four o'clock,' she says, laughing. 'Actually, I think I'll join you.' She retrieves two glasses from a rack above the bar. Today she's wearing jeans and a mulberry-coloured blouse that's the same shade as her cropped, spiky hair.

'How's the ankle?' I ask.

'Quite a bit better. It was only a sprain, I think. Serves me right for lugging boxes of mixers up the step from the yard when

Josh had gone AWOL. Luckily, the swelling had gone down the next morning.'

'That's good,' I reply.

'So, what have you been up to today?' she asks, pouring us each a glass and I tell her about my walk along the beach.

'Are you mad?' She looks startled.

'Probably but I feel really good now,' I say, which is true. 'In fact, I feel great. I should really do it more often. You're welcome to join me any time, once your ankle is fully healed.'

'I'll pass, thanks. At least along a freezing beach.'

Helen and I have enjoyed some lovely country strolls together but, really, she is more of a fairweather walker.

'Bit quiet today?' I say, glancing around at the customers, which is essentially half a dozen blokes, and a couple who look as though they have popped in for a drink after a country walk.

'It's a bit quiet every day.' She sighs. 'We do have a bit of passing trade, walkers and the like, as well as the locals, but I can't remember the last time we were packed out.'

I take a sip of my wine, then tentatively offer a suggestion.

'You'd probably attract more customers if the food menu was a bit more... exciting, if I'm honest.'

It's currently limited to burgers, pies, or fish and chips.

'Have you considered doing Sunday lunches?'

'We did consider it, actually, but Paul said we'd have to hire some new staff, and then it wasn't really discussed further. I suppose we ought to think about serving home-made food, I know people's palates are a lot more discerning these days but Paul doesn't seem that interested,' she tells me. 'I even asked Josh if he would like to help in the kitchen, maybe get a catering qualification, but he just huffed. Probably because I suggested it. He hates me.' She takes a glug of her wine.

'I'm sure he doesn't hate you.' I can't help feeling sorry for her, as I know she does try and make an effort with her stepson.

'Okay, maybe not hate, but he certainly doesn't like me. And for one reason. I'm not his mother.'

'Teenagers can be difficult,' I say gently.

'I know.' She sighs. 'And I've tried to be nice to him, I really have. It must have been awful losing his mum, I realise that, especially as a teenage boy.' She pauses to take another swig of wine before topping up her glass. 'But he's bone idle. He's on the payroll here but complains if he has to lug a crate of mixers up from the cellar, moaning that he's being underpaid, even though he's on minimum wage. His dad can't afford to pay him any more than that. I find I'm constantly biting my tongue with him. He's nineteen now, and really needs to grow up a little.'

We stall our conversation for a minute, when another couple dressed in walking gear, head towards the bar and she serves them drinks in a cosy nook with a burning fire.

'Josh is slacking off somewhere again today,' says Helen, resuming our conversation when she returns to the bar. 'Even though Paul asked him to tidy the yard up a bit.'

'He doesn't know how lucky he is; he should try working out in the real world. Maybe Paul is a bit soft with him,' I suggest.

'Just a bit. He overcompensates for the loss of his mother, I think. Meanwhile I am the bitch stepmother from hell.'

'I'm sure you're exaggerating,' I say, but I suppose you never really know what goes on behind closed doors.

Paul and a couple of other blokes cheer as someone scores a goal in the football match they are watching on the flat-screen television at the far side of the bar.

'Anyway, think about what I said about expanding the food menu. As long as it's not hot pot. You don't want to be in competition with the café.'

'Oh, I wouldn't dare.' She laughs. 'Jo would have my guts for garters. I can make a decent chilli, though. And a curry too, come to think of it.'

'Well, there you go, that's a start. Talk to Paul. In fact, you could have a curry night, Ellie and I love a good curry, I bet a lot of people do.' I realise I'm getting a bit carried away, but I seem to have ignited a spark in Helen.

'You know, that's not a bad idea!' she says enthusiastically. 'Thanks, Sarah, and your drink is on the house.' When I protest, she says it's a thank you for my creative input.

'You can't afford to be giving away freebies.' I slide a five-pound note onto the counter, and head quickly for the door.

Paul collects some pint glasses from the blokes around the table and says goodbye as I leave.

'See you, Sarah.' He smiles.

'Bye, Paul, enjoy your evening.'

Ellie arrives home just after six. The bright sun has long disappeared, and the village is illuminated with street lamps and twinkling tree lights from trees in the windows of people's houses. Ellie texted to say she was on her way home half an hour ago, and it's always reassuring to hear the sound of her key in the lock. Especially in the dark evenings.

'Hi, Mum.' She heads upstairs to change out of her jeans, into her favourite cosy pyjamas.

'Did you have a nice day?' I ask, when she returns downstairs with an art folder.

'Yes, thanks, Mum. Did you?'

'I did, actually. It was freezing down near the sea, but I really enjoyed my walk. You never said you had any homework?' I remark as she flips open her folder.

'It's only a bit of sketching.' She shrugs. As she flicks through her large folder, I notice a beautiful collage of an African sunset.

'That's really good,' I say, impressed with her work. 'The colours are absolutely stunning.'

'Do you think so?' she asks. 'You should see some of the others in my class, they could literally sell their drawings, they're that good.'

'Well, I'd buy this,' I tell her. 'In fact, when school have finished with it, maybe I could buy a frame and display it somewhere.'

'Really?' She cocks her head to one side, and reappraises it.

'Yes, really. Those colours would look really good in the dining room, with their rich mustard and copper shades.' I'm not just humouring her; it's actually the truth.

She continues her work, shading and concentrating hard on a drawing of a kettle. A simple enough sketch using pencils, although it can be tricky to get the shading right, but she's doing a really good job.

Around seven thirty, when she closes her folder, I ask her if she would like to watch a Christmas movie.

'I'm a bit tired, but, yeah, sure. Can we watch *The Holiday*?'

I've probably watched it more than a dozen times but it's still one of my favourites at this time of year. And I love how our cottage looks so similar to the one in the movie.

Her choice of film makes me realise she is at that in-between stage of teenager and young woman. Only last year, she would have preferred something like a Disney movie, not really paying attention to a romantic comedy such as *The Holiday*.

'Do you want some popcorn?' I ask.

'Yes, please. Although I thought you would be sick of the sight of that working in the cinema.' She laughs.

'I'm going to have some ice cream. You can have that too, if you like?'

I enjoy the film as always, cringing slightly at the bedroom scenes, but at least they aren't graphic. I smile, as I do every time, at the scene where Jack Black is in the video store looking at films with Kate Winslet. Before he spots his cheating girl-friend outside the window, that is.

Settled in front of the fire watching a film and eating choco-late chip ice cream, Ellie munching on popcorn with a fleecy tartan throw over her legs, there is nowhere I would rather be. I know these evenings won't last forever and I intend to enjoy every minute.

TEN

Shelley is busy rearranging the sweets in the cinema when I arrive the next day.

'Morning, Shelley, how was your weekend?' I ask, hanging my coat in a small cloakroom behind the counter.

'It was okay. Although, I had to endure the torment of my niece's birthday party.' She pulls a face.

'I thought you would have liked that. Plenty of sweets.' I raise an eyebrow, before I notice a packet of Skittles poking out of the pocket of her jeans.

'Ah. I actually did buy these.' She taps her pocket. 'From the shop near the bus stop. We don't sell these here.'

She pulls the pack from her pocket to prove that we don't stock the tropical variety.

'Where was the party?' I ask, returning to the subject of her niece's celebration.

'The Rumble in the Jungle in town. It was a total nightmare. My sister said it was a right rip-off and the food was crap. Although the kids didn't seem to notice. They were all hyped up on sugar.' She laughs.

'Oh well, as long as the kids enjoyed it, I guess that's the main thing.'

'Yeah, I think I just got roped in as extra childcare, though,' she moans. 'Half of the mums there were chatting, drinking cappuccinos and eating mince pies, and not taking a blind bit of notice of their kids,' she continues. 'I had to break up a fight in the ball pit, and take an overexcited kid to their mother after they'd wet themselves, then carried on down the slide.'

'Oh, Shelley.' I burst out laughing. 'You should have demanded payment. Where were the playcentre staff?'

'One was off sick, and the other so-called employee was so tiny, I think she was actually frightened of the children. She kept wincing every time they charged past her. Complete nightmare. Anyway, my sister bunged me twenty quid at the end, so it wasn't all bad. We should consider having them here, you know,' she says thoughtfully, now chewing on some pink bubble gum that she's pulled from her other pocket.

'No, thanks, incontinent toddlers and fighting five-year-olds?'

'Children's birthday parties.' She blows a huge pink bubble, then pops it. 'Just a thought.'

Children's parties. The thought had never occurred to me before, but suddenly my brain is working overtime.

'When you say the party was a rip-off, how much are we talking exactly?'

'Ten quid per head. That included a play on the climbing frames, pizza and chips, and some cheap squash. It didn't include the cake or the party bags, so my sister said the whole lot probably totalled closer to twenty pounds really.'

I'm already doing the mental calculations in my head. It's six pounds entry here, two pounds for a hot dog, and drinks and bags of sweets are both a pound each. Ten pounds for a cinema party, which sounds better than what Shelley has just described. We could cut the cake at the end of the movie. I could even stick a few balloons and banners around the place. My mind is suddenly full of ideas.

'Well, I know it's almost Christmas, but do let me know if you hear of anyone who needs a last-minute venue for a kids' party.'

'Sure.' She shrugs.

'Although I'd have to move the matinee time,' I muse. 'I hope the pensioners would be alright with that.'

'What, all six of them?'

'There were at least ten at the Pierce Brosnan film,' I remind her.

'I'm sure they would be okay. The coffin dodgers haven't exactly got anything else to do with their day,' she jokes.

'You don't know that.' I try not to laugh at her description of the older customers.

'Yeah, but I can't see them traipsing into town for a cinema. It's more expense, for one thing.'

'True enough.'

I used to go to pool parties at the local swimming baths when I was a kid, but they don't seem to be a thing anymore. Kids love the cinema, though, and I imagine it would be exciting for them to have the cinema all to themselves.

The matinee could be brought forward to one o'clock instead of two, I suppose, which means everyone will have left around three. Or a kids' party could start after school, and be done and dusted before the evening showings at six o'clock. I can't believe I haven't thought of it before. But then I don't have friends with kids that age – they're all teenagers – so I didn't know the cost of an organised birthday party these days. It's definitely an idea that needs some thought, though, especially after Christmas.

ELEVEN

It's another bright morning as I head into work, grateful that the snowfall has disappeared without a trace as the roads were a little icy yesterday. With less than two weeks until Christmas, it might be nice if it stays away until the day itself. I have three days off work then, and wouldn't mind being snowed in, hunkering down with all the books I haven't got around to reading lately that are piling up on a shelf in the lounge.

My shift finishes at three o'clock, when one of the part-time students takes over, so I drive into town to the Central Library to meet Cassie after work. She's finishing work at four thirty, once she's done an after-school book reading in the children's section. I'm calling in to drop off a gold clutch bag she wants to borrow for an evening out with her husband and I want to get to the library a little earlier so that I can have a wander around for a while and soak up the atmosphere.

Stepping inside, I take in the grand staircase that is the first thing you see, swirling and magnificent, with its crisscrossing stairs, encased in glass. At the foot of the stairs is a gigantic Christmas tree covered in red and gold baubles, candy canes and tiny little wooden books. Fitting decorations for a library.

On the ground floor is the large children's area, that I start wandering towards. It's bright and cheerful with chunky furniture in red, yellow and green. The ceiling is strung with simple paper chain decorations made by the children, and a wall display showcases Christmas paintings created by pupils from local primary schools. Young children are settled on bean bags, in anticipation of story time, which is about to be hosted by Cassie, with others sitting at tables with adults who are reading to them.

I used to bring Ellie here when she was a child, to listen to Cassie host story-time morning for pre-schoolers. It's where Cassie and I first met and became firm friends. Ellie used to call out 'Auntie Cassie' and wave at her while Cassie was reading. I would gently shush her, whilst Cassie would smile and continue with the story. She had such a way with young children, she still has it to this day, creating voices of the various characters in the stories, holding the children transfixed as she transports them to another place. She was always hoping to plant the seeds of a lifelong love affair with books. It brings back such joyous memories of being here on Christmas Eve. Cassie would do a reading of *The Night Before Christmas* and have the children completely entranced by the magic of the tale. It's still one of Ellie's favourite Christmas books and it's where she learned the names of all of Santa's reindeer.

The whole library is just so lovely; it would be easy to spend hours here, finding a corner with a comfortable chair and whiling away the hours reading. I remember studying for my A levels here, among groups of other students, being shushed by the rather austere librarians who suggested we go and hang out in the park if we weren't actually intending to do any studying. Thinking about it, it was probably a fair point. I scraped through my A levels, but never actually continued on to uni as – or so I felt at the time – I didn't think I had any more studying in me. The plan was to take a year out, then return to my studies.

In the end, though, I got the job working in the theatre box office, and was quite happy working and earning.

'Are we all ready, children?' asks Cassie, and the little ones nod their heads. Even the children at the tables with their parents slide off their chairs and take a seat on the blue carpet, in anticipation of the tale.

She's chosen *Stick Man* by Julia Donaldson, and the children are completely enamoured by her storytelling. That is, until one child bursts into tears and says she doesn't want the stick family to go on the fire. Cassie soothes the little child by telling her that every story has a happy ending. The child eventually stops crying – although I think that might have been down to the small packet of chocolate buttons the mother has just produced from her pocket – and Cassie continues. By the end of the story, where Stick Man and his family are reunited, the child who had been crying breaks into applause and the other children follow suit.

Once the crowd disperses, Cassie pops over and says she will meet me in the café in fifteen minutes, so I climb the glass staircase for a last bit of wandering. I keep going until I reach the roof of the main building, a glass dome at its summit designed to mirror the reading room below.

At the highest point of the building, I step outside to the viewing area. It's freezing up here and I pull my scarf tightly around my neck. From here, I can see the tall Radio City Tower, and all the magnificent Grade I listed buildings, their rooves covered in a dusting of snow. The architecture of the city is really something to behold, and, at one time, it actually had the most Grade I listed buildings in the whole of the country. I can see the Liver bird at the top of one of the buildings called the Three Graces; the Cunard shipping building, the Liver Building and the Port of Liverpool Building. In the summer months it's a lovely place to sit with a cold drink, contemplating life and taking in the wonderful city views.

Arriving back on the ground floor, I give a final glance at the magnificent staircase I have just walked down.

'It's quite something, isn't it?' says a bloke standing beside me.

'It really is,' I say, still staring up.

'It's hard to believe it was almost destroyed in the Blitz, isn't it? What a transformation.'

I remember the library being closed for two years when it underwent a massive refurbishment, the second one in its time, when the breathtaking staircase was added in 2006.

'I know, thank goodness the building itself survived. I can't imagine it not being here.'

I turn to look at the bloke standing next to me, who's dressed smartly in a navy woollen coat with a grey-striped scarf tucked inside. And this time there is no mistake. I take in the familiar smile, and I can feel a blush rising up my cheeks. As our eyes meet, I find I am staring into the gorgeous brown eyes of Luke Watson.

TWELVE

'Sarah?'

'Oh my goodness, Luke, is that you?' I can't believe I'm standing next to Luke. I realise my heart is beating a little faster than normal. He's still absolutely gorgeous.

'What are you doing here?' I ask, so shocked I can barely speak.

'Shall we grab a coffee and I'll fill you in?' he asks, indicating the nearby ground-floor coffee bar.

'Yes, of course.' I realise I'm smiling like a lunatic. My teenage heart-throb is standing here next to me in the Central Library.

I'm trying to process him being here, as he heads to the counter. I still can't believe it's really him.

Luke places two cappuccinos down on the table, shaking me from my reverie.

'I thought I saw you in Central Station the other day but I told myself it couldn't possibly have been you,' I tell him.

'That was you?' He looks surprised.

'Yes, I was the girl you smiled at through the window of the train. I thought maybe you had recognised me. I kept thinking about you afterwards.'

'Is that right?' He raises an eyebrow as he stirs his coffee.

'I mean, I kept wondering if it was you,' I tell him, feeling the heat rising in my cheeks again.

'I have to be honest, I didn't recognise you at the station. You were wearing a hat and looking kind of cute, though, as I recall, so I guess I smiled.'

He has a slight American accent.

'Oh, I see. Do you often smile at cute strangers, then?' I say and it's my turn to raise an eyebrow.

'I don't make a habit of it.' He grins.

'So, tell me what on earth are you doing here? And how is Kay? I have so many questions!'

Luke takes a long sip of his coffee. 'I've been back here for my uncle's funeral. My dad passed away last year, and Mum is currently recovering from a hip operation. And Kay's good. Married with two children and living in Florida. I live there too.'

'Oh, I'm so sorry to hear about your dad, and your uncle, of course. So, Kay's in Florida? Sounds like a dream place to live. I'm happy for her.'

'I don't know if anyone's life is a dream.' There's a pause. 'Although, yes, she has a really good life there.' He nods.

'Please send her my best wishes next time you speak. I remember your parents so well; they were always so welcoming when I came to you house. Say hi to your mum too.'

'I will. I guess my folks were friendly, weren't they?' His face breaks into a smile. 'We were lucky having such great parents but you take it for granted when you're young. Mum's coming up for eighty soon; Dad was eighty-two when he passed.'

'I can't believe your mum is almost eighty!' Once again, teenage memories come flooding back. I remember his mum and her perfectly painted nails, and stylish clothes. She was an elegant beauty.

'I guess age catches up with us all. Mum actually lives in a bungalow next door to Kay. She looks after her well; they've always been close.' He takes another sip of frothy cappuccino.

'So, where do you live?' asks Luke and I tell him about life in the village.

'Sounds idyllic.'

Luke tells me he is renting a loft apartment and is enjoying exploring the city.

'I'd forgotten what a great place it is. The city has changed so much since I left.'

'I guess it has. The Albert Dock has a lot more shops and restaurants since you were last here. Have you been back since you all left for America?' I ask, which was so long ago now.

'Never. I kept in touch with people, though, and I always intended to, but suddenly the years have rolled by.'

I know exactly what he means. Hadn't I intended to visit Kay, after all? Yet somehow, I never did.

There are so many questions I want to ask. I need to know all about Kay; is she still acting? And how long will Luke be staying here in Liverpool? I also can't help wondering whether he has a partner back home.

'Right, I need to be off,' he says, draining his coffee. 'I have a meeting with a solicitor. I'm sorting my uncle's estate. I've been killing a bit of time.' He glances at his watch. 'Sarah, it's been so great seeing you. Do you fancy doing dinner whilst I'm over here?'

Do I ever!

'Yes, that would be lovely, thanks,' I say, trying to hide the excitement from my voice.

Luke takes my number before he leaves and I'm already looking forward to his call. As he disappears, I glance up to find Cassie approaching me.

'Hi, I enjoyed your reading of *Stick Man*,' I tell her. 'I'd forgotten how good your storytelling skills are.'

'Thanks. But never mind that, who's the good-looking bloke?' she asks, her gaze following Luke out of the main entrance.

'Oh my goodness, you will never guess who that was!' I say, recovering slightly, but still completely open-mouthed.

'Someone who's left quite an impression on you, I'd say.' She smiles as she sits down opposite me.

'It was Luke Watson. Remember me telling you about the older brother of my friend when I was a teenager, that I had quite a thing for?'

'I certainly do.' She grins. 'The one who lived at Adelaide Terrace?'

'The very one.'

We'd sat one evening talking about our first crushes with glasses of wine, and I'd told her about Luke, and the rather disappointing first kiss experience I had at my first school disco, with a boy who must have been practising on his hoover and left me breathless, but not in a good way.

'He's asked me out for dinner,' I say excitedly.

'Oh, Sarah, that's great! I know I only caught a glimpse of him but, wow, he's a very attractive bloke.'

'I know. Oh, it's probably only a catch-up, though. I'm sure he's not interested in me romantically; he's bound to be involved with someone. I'm probably just a friendly face he remembers from the past.'

'Don't you think it's fate, though, that you just happened to be here at the same time?'

'You've been reading too many of those books from the romance section.' I laugh. 'He did say he was just passing some time before an appointment, though. I suppose he could have chosen anywhere to do that.'

'See! If he'd have gone next door to the museum you might

never have reconnected. And there was that moment he drifted away in the train carriage, and your eyes met.'

'You've definitely been at the Mills and Boon. Anyway, we'll see if he calls,' I say, finding myself really hoping that he will.

We walk out together and I hand over the gold evening bag, before she climbs into her car.

'And talking of romance, have a great night with James tonight,' I say. She's heading to the Titanic Hotel for dinner and an overnight stay.

'Oh, I will. It comes to something when you have to book a hotel room with soundproofed walls to have sex.' She laughs. 'Teenagers in the next bedroom are a right passion killer.'

'Good job I don't have any passion to kill.'

'Not yet,' she teases as she climbs into her car and drives off.

THIRTEEN

Driving into the village, I am jolted from thoughts of Luke by a strange sight. I'm not sure if my eyes are deceiving me, but as a woman is crossing the road from Perfect Pooches, I do a double take at the green poodle by her side. I mean, I've seen dogs wearing all manner of Christmas coats, and even a hat with antlers making them look like a hybrid reindeer, but nothing like this.

Later on, I pop into the Penny Farthing for a drink, where Christmas tunes are playing in the background. Despite the pub looking cosy and inviting, it's still half empty. One of the dog groomers, from the same grooming parlour in the courtyard I passed earlier, is sitting alone at a table, nursing a glass of red wine. I nod and smile.

'I think I saw one of your creations today.' I tell her about the green dog.

'Oh my goodness, I know. The customer is always right, though, hey,' she says diplomatically.

'Interesting choice of colour.'

'The owner was hosting a Grinch-themed party, apparently,' she explains.

'Ahh. Well, that makes total sense now,' I say and she laughs.

'Has business been good?' I ask as I order a glass of wine from Paul, who is behind the bar.

'Non-stop at this time of year. Everyone likes their dogs looking pretty for Christmas,' she tells me. 'I've added pretty bows to Pekingese dogs after they've been groomed, and done all manner of beautifying for people's pooches, but I must admit I've never been asked to do a full colour before,' she tells me. 'To be honest, I wasn't even sure whether I ought to or not. But the colour is chemical-free and pet-friendly, and, more importantly, temporary,' she adds, taking a slurp of her wine.

'How's things with you?' she asks.

'I wish business was as brisk at the cinema as your dog grooming is.'

'Haven't there been a few new Christmas films released recently?'

'Yeah, and don't get me wrong, we have had a few families in, so things are ticking over at the moment. The rest of the year has been quiet, though,' I reveal. 'I won't lie, I do worry about the future of the Roxy.'

'I can't imagine that not being around here. It's such a great building and a bit of a local landmark. But everything is about profit these days, isn't it?' she reminds me, which is something I don't really like to acknowledge.

'Right, see you later, gotta go.' She drains her glass and leaves.

As we've been chatting, Helen has emerged from the kitchen and now heads towards my table.

'Ooh, Sarah, just the person. I've made some chilli and wonder if you might tell me what you think,' she says with a beaming smile.

'Great. I'm starved.'

Helen disappears back into the kitchen and returns carrying

a tray with two bowls of chilli and rice, and some slices of garlic
bread.

'Smells fantastic!' I say as she places them onto the table.

I fork the tender chilli beef into my mouth and chew it
slowly, whilst Helen looks on in anticipation.

'That's lovely,' I tell her. 'Just the right amount of chilli, at
least for my taste anyway.'

'Oh, I'm so pleased you like it! I'm going to put it on the
menu tomorrow. I'll offer some dried chilli flakes if it's not hot
enough for some palates,' she says, sounding excited.

'I think it's just the thing for these cold winter evenings. I'm
sure it will be a popular dish,' I tell Helen.

'Thanks, Sarah. Paul said it's nice, but I wanted an honest
opinion, although I have to admit, even Josh said it was "alright"
when he tried it, which is high praise from him.' She laughs.
'I'm doing cottage pie too. Paul can get a really good deal on
meat from a butcher contact. There will be veggie versions as
well, of course,' she says enthusiastically.

'Well, I'm sure it will be a winner with the customers,' I
tell her.

'Thanks. It's a bit close to Christmas now, but in the new
year I might actually think about a curry night, like you suggested,' she says, turning to me.

'Now you're talking. I won't have to order a Friday night
takeaway if there's a good curry on offer here in the village.
Assuming you do it on a Friday, that is,' I add.

'Yes, I've been thinking about that. It does make sense to
host it on a Friday night.' Helen nods.

Ellie is eating pasta when I arrive home half an hour later, after
declining a takeaway sample of Helen's chilli, when I'd texted
her to ask if she'd like some.

'Hi, Ellie, are you okay?'

'Yep, fine.'

Ellie has recently started learning to cook a little and has mastered a really nice tomato sauce with pasta, which she's sprinkled with cheese.

After dinner, Ellie heads upstairs for a shower and I take a cup of tea into the lounge and pick a sudoku book from the shelf, and look around for a pen. Ellie is in the shower, but she almost certainly has one in her school bag. I delve into her bag and grab at what I think is a pen. I pull it from the bag and I gasp in shock. What on earth is she doing with this?

FOURTEEN

I can hear the whirring of the hairdryer upstairs, as my mind simultaneously whirrs down here. A pregnancy test.

How on earth can I explain seeing this? I guess I did stumble on it innocently in my search for a pen.

I think back to the evening Ellie invited a boy over here. She said nothing had happened between them, but was she telling me the truth? I find myself pacing the room, hoping she will come back downstairs, yet I'm dreading having the conversation I'm about to have with her.

After what seems like an eternity, I hear the sound of Ellie's footsteps padding down the stairs.

'What's up?' she says immediately, clearly noticing the look on my face.

'I don't want you to be cross with me, I was simply looking for a pen in your bag when I found that.'

I indicate to the test on the coffee table near the fire, and Ellie's mouth drops open.

'Oh my God, Mum. You've been going through my bag?' The colour has returned to her face that now looks filled with fury.

'I told you, I was after a pen. I'm sorry I rooted in your bag, but can you explain it?' I try to keep my voice even.

'It's not mine.'

'Okay. Then whose is it?'

'Someone from school.'

'Oh, someone from school? Like the boy who came here was just "someone from school". You're being very vague about everything, Ellie.'

She sits down on the sofa. 'I know it must have been a shock finding this, Mum, but I'm telling you the truth,' she says. 'One of the girls in my class is late with her period. We grabbed this on the way home from school. She asked me to stash it for her, so she can do it in the morning.'

'Why would she ask you to do that?' I ask doubtfully.

'Apparently, her mum is always going through her stuff and she shares a room with her younger sister, so didn't want it being found. I said it would be okay here. Seems I was wrong about that,' she huffs.

'Well, I've already said I'm sorry for going through your bag. I only wanted to settle down with my sudoku. Sorry, I should have waited until you were out of the shower and asked you for a pen.'

'Yeah, maybe you should,' she says, her voice a little shaky, and I pray she is telling the truth.

'But you can surely see why I was concerned,' I add as she picks the test up and returns it to her bag, her face like thunder. A part of me wishes I had never gone in the bag. Last night we were sat together, happily watching a movie and eating ice cream. And tonight this.

'I just can't believe you went through my things.'

'I told you I was looking for—'

'A pen, I know,' she snaps. 'It's not as if there aren't any pens in the kitchen drawer.'

'Stop overreacting,' I tell her firmly. 'I'm your mother, I

have a right to ask questions. And actually, there aren't any pens in the drawer that work. I had to throw a couple away yesterday.'

'Whatever,' she mutters under her breath, and it takes all my resolve not to let this continue into a full-scale blazing row.

Ellie grabs her bag and stomps upstairs, and I let out a deep sigh when I hear the sound of her bedroom door slamming shut.

Cassie calls around late the next morning before I go to work, to return the handbag.

'How was your evening?' I ask as we sit in the lounge sipping a caramel latte. I've recently bought some of those syrups to add to coffee.

'It was lovely, thanks. The food was fantastic and the room... wow. Incredible. It had this huge bed too. We had a great sleep.'

'A great sleep?' I raise an eyebrow.

'Yes. We haven't been out for a little while and I got a bit drunk,' she reveals. 'When I returned to bed after going to the bathroom, James was snoring loudly. It was a good job the hotel had those soundproofed walls after all.' She laughs.

'So much for your romantic liaison. I'm glad you enjoyed it, though.'

'Don't get me wrong, we ordered room service for breakfast this morning. After a leisurely lie-in.' She winks.

'Ah, I see.'

'I guess we're lucky that we still fancy each other,' she says dreamily, wrapping her hands around her coffee. 'Our twentieth wedding anniversary is coming up soon.'

'You two were made for each other,' I say, thinking how wonderful it must be to find the love of your life at a young age and go on to live happily ever after. There was a time when I imagined the same for me and Robbie.

I tell Cassie all about finding the pregnancy test in Ellie's bag.

'You don't think it could be hers, do you?' she asks, obviously hearing the doubt in my voice, or maybe seeing the concerned look in my eyes.

'No. I suppose what she told me was quite plausible, but... Oh, I don't know, Cassie. I just feel like she doesn't tell me anything these days.' I sigh.

'That's just her age,' she reassures me. 'The twins were the same. They have matured slightly now, and actually talk to me about what's going on in their lives. A few years ago, I had to squeeze everything out of them, like I was torturing them with questions,' she recalls. 'Give it time.'

'Thanks, Cassie, that makes me feel a little better. Right, sorry to kick you out, but I need to be leaving for work about now,' I say, glancing at my watch.

We walk down the path together and after Cassie closes the gate, she stops and glances back at the cottage.

'You're so lucky to live here.' She sighs. 'It's just so gorgeous. I love seeing the cottage when it snows, it's really magical. See you soon,' she says before climbing into her car.

I glance at the sage door and the pretty holly wreath, handmade by Francis in the flower shop, and I have to agree. Even though I took everything for granted living here as a young woman. Even thinking it inferior to my friends' house in Adelaide Terrace. These days, properties like mine are very desirable and rarely come up on the market. I know I'm lucky. Just then, a little red robin hops onto the front gate, making me smile. I quickly whip out my phone and take a photo. This morning, Red Robin Cottage is living up to its name.

I arrive at the cinema and I'm just hanging my coat up, when my phone rings in my handbag. There's no name on the caller display, and I hesitate for a moment before I take the call. To my great joy and surprise, it's Luke.

'Hi, is this a good time to talk?' he asks, his gorgeous accent drawing me in.

'Hi, Luke. I'm just about to start work, but I have a couple of minutes,' I tell him, feeling excited by the mere sound of his voice.

'Okay, it won't take long. I just wondered if you were free any evening this week?'

'I finish early tomorrow,' I tell him.

'Great. Do you fancy going out for dinner? If you text me your address I could pick you up. Say seven? Unless you would prefer to just meet up in town?'

'I'll meet you in town, if you like,' I say, thinking that Ellie might be home and I don't want to be introducing her to somebody I've only just met. I tell myself I will if things develop between us, before I shake myself and wonder why on earth I'm thinking that way. He'll be heading back to America soon enough.

We arrange to meet at the train station. I feel thrilled by the thought of going to dinner with him, and can't help the smile on my face.

'What's tickled you, then?' asks Shelley, who has just arrived and is shrugging off her coat.

'What do you mean?'

'You're smiling there like you've won the lottery. You haven't, have you?'

'Yeah right, do you really think I would be standing here if I had?'

She shakes her head. 'You disappoint me, Sarah. I thought you were here purely for the love of it.'

'I'm joking. I love my job. Besides, I'd never leave you in the lurch without finding a replacement first. Actually, I'm smiling because I've just been asked out on a date,' I tell her as I head over to switch on the popcorn machine.

'Ooh, nice. Have you been on Tinder?' Shelley takes some Maltesers from a box and replenishes the front counter. Maltesers seem to be the most popular choice with both adults and children.

'No. Would you believe it's my teenage crush. I think I told you about him.'

'The one from the posh house?'

'The very one.'

'So he is really back from America, then?'

'For his uncle's funeral.' I nod. 'After that, who knows? I guess I'll know more when we have dinner tomorrow.'

It's surprisingly busy today for the matinee and evening performance and time flies by. Soon enough we're locking up to go home.

'Oh yeah, I forget to mention,' says Shelley as we're about to go our separate ways. 'Someone's mum at college has been let down with a party venue for their kid sister. The building is flooded, apparently. Could we hold it at the cinema, do you think?'

'Yes, when?'

'Friday.'

'This Friday?'

'Yeah. I know it's short notice, but I said we might be able to help. *The Dog Who Saved Christmas* is still showing until after Christmas, isn't it?'

'Well, I don't see why not. What time?'

'Four o'clock, pretty much after school. Seven-year-olds, I think, so it shouldn't be too bad. There's twenty of them.'

'That's brilliant. I'll make sure we have plenty of hot dogs and buns. A kids' party is not something we've ever done before, but it's something we should definitely be trying to tap into.'

Kids' parties have reached a whole new level these days. Whatever happened to pass the parcel and musical chairs in someone's house, followed by jelly and ice cream? I think I'll nip to a shop and grab some birthday balloons and banners to decorate the place a bit. If the cinema looks welcoming, the woman might spread the word amongst the other mums.

'Night, then, Shelley,' I say, my mind ticking over with thoughts of the children's party.

'See you tomorrow,' she says, before heading off to meet some of her student friends for an open mic night at a nearby pub.

FIFTEEN

I spend hours trying on different outfits, wondering what kind of impression I'm trying to make. Are we old friends having a casual catch-up, which probably means jeans and a top? Then again, I'm not sure we were even that. Should I look like I have made a real effort, and wear something a little glamorous? I guess it would help if I had an idea of where Luke is taking me. In the end, I opt for a classic black wrap-over dress, that I accessorise with a silver necklace with a single ruby stone necklace and matching bracelet.

Things have been a little cool between me and Ellie since the pregnancy test episode. I wonder whether I ought to bring up the subject of safe sex as she's turned sixteen. Especially knowing she had a boy over here the other week. Although, I'd probably stoke up another argument if I did. I'm sure she's not stupid, we've had conversations in the past about relationships and unwanted pregnancy and, of course, she's had sex education at school. No parent wants to discuss these things, but I'm realistic when it comes to teenagers' lives these days, despite my no-boyfriends-in-the-bedroom ban. The least I can do is not encourage casual relationships.

I left it for a day before I asked if her friend at school was okay, and she told me it had been a false alarm. The atmosphere has been a little better this evening when I helped her with her English homework, analysing an act in *Macbeth*. I actually remember that from my own studies. Maths is a different story, though. English hasn't changed, but the way things are worked out these days in maths – or numeracy as it's now called – is a complete puzzle to me. Not to mention pointless if you arrive at the same answer anyway, but I guess some people would disagree.

'You look nice,' says Ellie as I walk into the kitchen.

'Thanks.'

She's standing at the sink filling a glass with water.

'So, is it a date, then?'

I'd told her I had bumped into an old friend from my teenage years earlier.

'I don't know if it's a date as such, or more of a catch-up,' I confess.

'You look like you are dressed up for a date.' She swallows some water.

'Do I? Gosh, that makes me worry that I've made too much of an effort.' I'm now wondering if I look a little *too* dressed up.

'No.' She smiles. 'You look lovely, Mum. A plain black dress is never overdressed. Honestly, you look really nice.'

'Thanks, Ellie. I shouldn't be too late, we're meeting at seven,' I tell her as I pick up my bag.

'Don't worry, I won't wait up,' she says. 'I'll probably watch a film upstairs in my room. I was awake really early this morning, and we had double P.E. so I'm tired.'

'Okay. Right, well, even so, I won't be too late. See you later, then,' I say, feeling happy the bus stop is literally across the road.

I'm just crossing, when a familiar car draws alongside the

bus stop. It's Jo from the Hot Pot café. She winds her window down and asks me where I'm heading.

'Into town,' I tell her.

'Hop in, then. I'm heading there too. You don't want men leering at you on the bus; you look gorgeous,' she says kindly.

'Thanks, Jo, that would be brilliant.' I did consider a taxi, but I don't want to be splashing out on such things, not so close to Christmas. 'I'd have taken the car, but I imagine I'll be having a glass of wine.'

'Meeting someone special?' she asks as we drive out of the village and on to the main roads.

I tell her all about my chance meeting with Luke at the library.

'He sounds divine,' she says.

'Anyway, talking of anyone special, how are things going with your gentleman friend?'

'Rick? He's good enough company, I suppose. Warm and funny, but I'm not looking for anything serious,' she tells me, dismissing the idea of him being anything special. 'You never know who might walk through the door of the café, so I don't want to be tied to someone exclusively.' She smiles a beaming smile. 'Besides, my husband was my one and only,' she says, loyally.

'Can't say I blame you, not wanting to settle down again. You must do what makes you happy. So where are you heading tonight, then?' I ask. Jo is wearing a gorgeous white faux fur coat and her make-up is immaculate.

'The theatre. With an old friend of my husband's. He knows how much I love Michael Ball and he just happens to have two tickets to watch him at the Philharmonic. I'm really looking forward to it.'

'Well, have a great time. And he's a lucky man, having you as a date this evening. You look lovely.'

'Thanks, gorgeous. You have a great night too.'

She drops me outside the train station where I'm meeting Luke, and as I'm ten minutes early, I vaguely browse the station shop, not wanting to appear too eager waiting for my date to arrive. At exactly seven o'clock, I head out to the main entrance just as Luke is walking up the steps.

'Wow, you look beautiful,' he says kindly, his words making me glow inside.

'So do you. Or should I say handsome? Do we call men beautiful?'

'You can if you like,' he teases as we head down the stairs, past a huge Christmas tree. He really does look good, dressed in dark jeans, a green jumper that looks like cashmere, and a stylish brown leather jacket.

'Do you like Italian food?' he asks as we walk.

'It's my absolute favourite,' I tell him.

'Great, I've reserved a table at the Italian Club on Bold Street, if that's okay?'

'Sounds perfect, although I've never actually dined there.'

'You haven't? Well, I think you're in for a treat. I ate there when I first arrived here, and thought the food was lovely.'

We walk along, taking in the Christmas lights suspended across the busy streets with shimmering gold angels, sparkly silver stars and rows of Santas. I take a quick glance at Luke's handsome profile and have to pinch myself that I'm actually here with him this evening, on our way to dinner.

Heading towards the restaurant, we stop at the bombed-out church at the end of the road, where the sound of violins gently fills the air. St Luke's Church, or the bombed-out church, is exactly that – a church that was destroyed in the Blitz, although its outer shell remained. Over the years, various projects have raised money to secure the remains and landscaped the grounds and it's now used as a venue for outdoor theatre and music concerts. This evening there seems to be a rendition of 'The

Four Seasons' playing out from the outdoor theatre that is bathed in soft, amber light.

'It's so wonderful to think a bombed-out building could be used to host such beautiful concerts, isn't it?' I say as we walk.

'It really is. A true example of triumph over tragedy, I'd say,' Luke replies, which I think sums it up perfectly.

Arriving at the Italian Club, a delicious smell envelops us as we enter, and a charming Italian waiter directs us to our table. It's only seven thirty but the restaurant is already busy, the sound of chatter filing the air. Dark tables have red candles at the centre and the cream walls have an assortment of photographs of Italy, including Rome. Luke orders a bottle of Chianti and some water, and pours me a glass as the waiter heads to the kitchen with our food order.

'So, tell me everything that's happened to you since I last saw you,' says Luke, looking at me with those warm brown eyes.

'Have you got a Post-it note? I'll write my life story down.' I take a sip of the delicious wine. 'I'd rather listen to your story; I bet it's far more interesting.'

'But I asked about you, so you go first.' He smiles.

I tell him all about marrying Robbie at a young age, my daughter Ellie and how we divorced two years ago. I also talk about my job at the cinema.

'Is Kay still into acting?' I ask him.

'She is. Bit parts mainly, as well as voice-overs on adverts, that type of thing. She worked on Broadway for a good while when she was younger, eventually playing Sandy in a production of *Grease*. She mentioned you a lot at the time, saying how you'd played Frenchie in a school production.'

'She did?'

'Yeah. I think she always meant to look you up again, but you know how life can get in the way and suddenly you've lost touch. When she had a family, she scaled back on the acting. She has twin boys about to start high school.'

'Oh, that's lovely. I'm pleased she did so well. And you're right about meaning to contact someone, thinking you'll do it sometime in the future.' I realise you should never procrastinate getting in touch with someone if you want them in your life.

Luke tells me how he took over his father's flooring business, expanding it even more. The company have laid floors and carpets in some fashionable, as well as important, buildings and recently supplied new flooring for the Guggenheim in New York. During our conversation, I discover Luke doesn't have a significant other back home anymore, but he doesn't reveal much, other than to say he is happy that chapter of his life is over.

'I guess we got to the point where we knew things weren't right between us,' he admits. 'We were tearing each other apart, so it was the right thing to separate. The relationship had definitely run its course.'

It makes me think how some relationships end in a whole load of angst, others in a whimper, although I think apathy in a relationship is just as destructive as constant drama.

'Did you ever wonder about us?' he says suddenly, snapping a breadstick and taking me completely by surprise. 'I did, over the years.'

'You did?' I can hardly believe my ears. 'You never gave me that impression.'

'Yes. But I was halfway across the world; we'd both started our different lives.'

I can't help thinking that maybe it was for the best. He would have broken my heart when they moved away, if I'd been more involved with him. I can hardly believe he thought about me. If only I'd known.

'So are you enjoying being back in Liverpool?'

'I can't tell you how much. Each day I find a reason to stay here a little bit longer.'

He looks into my eyes and I can't help feeling delighted by

his words.

Our food arrives, and I tuck into amazing gnocchi, with a delicious pesto sauce topped with Parmesan. Luke has a delicious-looking lasagne.

'It's so easy to fall in love with this city all over again. It feels so different from when we left all those years ago; there's a real buzz about the place.'

'There really is,' I agree. 'There's always something going on.'

'You're not wrong. And a couple of the restaurants here would rival anything in London,' he says, tucking into his food.

We declined a starter, having nibbled at some breadsticks, so I choose a tiramisu for dessert, urged on by Luke.

'I've heard the tiramisu here is very good,' he tells me. 'Although I can't personally recommend it. But the waiter did last time I was here.' He laughs.

'Shall I ask for two spoons?'

'You'd share your dessert with me?' He smiles.

Tipsy from the wine, as Luke has only had one glass followed by some water, I'd probably share my bed with him too at this point, but have to compose myself and get that thought right out of my head.

'Of course I would.'

'Thanks, but I think I'll have a cheeseboard,' he says, making me feel less greedy for opting for a dessert.

After finishing our delicious food, Luke grabs the bill and we head out into the frosty night air once more.

'Thanks, Luke, I've had the loveliest evening.' I'm trying hard to keep my voice at a normal level, as I know I tend to talk louder after I've had a few drinks.

'The pleasure has been all mine. I'll drive you home; I'm parked just around the corner.'

Heading to Luke's car, I feel happier than I have done in a

while, and realise that maybe I ought to have a little more fun in my life.

I've been off men for a while now, frightened to let my guard down after being let down by Robbie on more than one occasion, even though I know that's just the way he is, and not all men are the same. I've been on several dates over the past year or so, but have concentrated on Ellie.

She was only fourteen at the time of the divorce, and quite distressed by it. I think she blamed me for the split, but looking back I realise now that I was just the person closest to her, so she aimed her hurt and anger at me. I never went into details with her of why we separated, which may sound strange, but I didn't want her to turn on Robbie. I hoped they would always have a good relationship together.

With hindsight, though, it might have been easier for her to accept our separation had there been a reason, rather than my vague explanation that things had broken down between us and we were no longer happy together. We always reassured her that she was loved, but all the same I know she struggled when Robbie first moved out. In the last year or so, though, she has witnessed for herself Robbie's, shall we say, fickle nature when it comes to relationships. Thankfully, though, their father-daughter relationship has remained intact.

'Do you have many plans while you are over here?' I ask as we head out of the city, and along the small roads that will take us back to the village.

'I'm not sure,' he tells me. 'I'm really loving it here so far. And nice as it is back home, I think I was ready for a change. I'm just taking one day at a time,' he says, not giving much away. 'So what are your plans for Christmas Day?'

Is he about to ask if I would like to spend it with him? Then again, he knows I have Ellie, so I doubt it.

'Family dinner with relatives,' I say vaguely. 'You?'

'I'm spending the day here, with an old friend from my

college days. We've stayed in touch on and off over the years. Anyway, it turns out he's on his own this year too, after recently divorcing. We're having dinner at a restaurant not far from his apartment.'

'Where's your place?' I ask.

'In the Georgian quarter.'

'That's a nice area. Are you close to the cathedral?'

'I am. I've rented a loft apartment that gives an incredible view of it, actually. I have the whole of the top floor of one of those amazing houses. The cathedral is quite something in the evening when it's illuminated.'

'I can imagine.'

I allow myself to think that maybe I won't have to imagine, if things go well between us.

The Georgian quarter is host to many smart Georgian buildings, housing private medical practices and gorgeous houses. One or two critically acclaimed restaurants have also popped up there recently, in the shadow of the Anglican Cathedral. It's in the area of Chinatown too, with its own plethora of great places to eat.

I'm surprised Luke isn't heading home for Christmas, to spend it with his mum and sister, but I guess it's none of my business as to why he isn't.

For a second, I'm tempted to invite him and his friend to my place on Christmas Day, since he's asked how I will be spending it. Then again, it might feel a little awkward for Ellie, having a strange man sitting around the dinner table on Christmas Day, so perhaps I'll ask him over another time. Assuming he wants to see me again, that is.

As we pull up outside the house, I can see the soft light glowing from the lamp in the lounge and the solar lights on the tree outside are bathing the garden in a silvery hue.

'This is your place?' says Luke, casting an admiring glance over the cottage.

'It is. I love living here,' I say proudly.

'I can see why, it's absolutely beautiful. And what a cute village; I always imagined settling down in a place like this.'

'You did?' I'm surprised by his comment, as I had Luke down as a hotshot businessman, heading off all over the world, enjoying a busy life in the fast lane. I was certain a loft apartment in a city would be more his style than a cottage in a village.

'Do you fancy doing this again?' he asks as I'm about to say goodnight and head inside, and my spirits soar.

'That would be really nice.'

'I would have suggested the cinema, but I guess that might not hold much appeal to you.' He laughs. 'But perhaps a trip to the theatre? As it's something I know you love. Have a look and see if there's anything you fancy showing over Christmas.'

I haven't been to the theatre since last year, as it's a little expensive. I think the last time I went to a matinee and it was full of children.

'Oh, I'd love that. I'll see what's on, thanks, Luke.'

'Great, I'll be in touch, then. I've really enjoyed this evening, Sarah. Goodnight.'

He leans over and his lips very gently brush my cheek, and I get a warm, fuzzy feeling inside.

'Night, Luke.'

I float into the cottage as Ellie is just about to head upstairs.

'Hi, Mum, how was your evening?'

'It was lovely, thanks.' I'm trying hard to keep a silly grin from my face.

'So, are you going to see him again?'

'Hopefully, yes. He's asked me out again, maybe to watch something at the theatre.'

'That's nice.' She pauses for a second, before saying, 'Did you know Dad was single again?'

'Really? I thought things were going well between him and Hannah.' I'm surprised by the news.

'So did I.' She shrugs. 'And I liked Hannah.'

'Well, you never know, they might patch things up again.'

'I hope so.' She lingers at the foot of the stairs for a moment. 'Otherwise, where will he go on Christmas Day?'

She leaves the words hanging in the air.

'I'm sure he'll figure something out, he always does,' I say, not liking where this conversation is suddenly heading.

'Could he spend the day with us?' she comes right out and asks, looking at me hopefully.

'No,' I tell her flatly. 'Absolutely not.'

'I knew you'd say that.' Her tone changes as she heads off up the stairs.

'But it's only one day,' she says, turning at the top stair, not able to leave this alone. 'And he is my dad. I just thought it might be nice, that's all. Christmas is supposed to be about family.'

Yes, the family he deserted, I think to myself but bite my lip.

'I know he's your father, and your relationship will always be good,' I tell her calmly. 'But he's my ex-husband, Ellie, and I don't want him here on Christmas Day. I'm trying to move on.'

Ellie considers this for a moment before she heads into her bedroom, evidently still not happy as she slams the door.

I hang my coat up and head upstairs, trying not to let what has just happened ruin a perfect evening. As I settle down to sleep, I find myself smiling at the revelation that Luke thought about me too over the years. Who knew? I drift off with thoughts of Luke and the gentle feel of his lips on my cheek, and fall into a glorious sleep already looking forward to our next date. And also hoping Ellie will put any ideas of having Robbie here on Christmas Day right out of her head.

SIXTEEN

I had put a poster in the window explaining the change of time in the matinee programme on Friday and, thankfully, there were no real objections from the pensioners yesterday, leaving me to float through work the day after my date. I'm not sure what I was expecting, really, but I do know that older people are creatures of habit. As there were no complaints about it, it's one less thing to worry about.

With the day of the children's party upon us, I popped into a party shop in town before work, and now the foyer is decorated with pink and purple Happy Birthday balloons and banners. I've also set a table at the front with some crisps and snacks, and the birthday girl's mum is going to be arriving shortly with the cake that will take centre stage. Jumbo hot dogs are turning over lightly on the rotating grill and Shelley is busy slicing the buns, having made a huge, fresh batch of popcorn earlier.

Five minutes later, a lady with poker-straight black hair and immaculate make-up arrives at the cinema, carrying a cake box that's so big I'm wondering whether she might have picked up a wedding cake by mistake. I also wonder whether or not the simple fold-up table will even bear its weight.

'Hiya, ooh, this looks lovely! I'm Imani's mum.' She smiles brightly. 'Thanks for sorting this, I know it was last minute. You're a real lifesaver. I had Imani's party booked for months, and then the venue goes and floods.' She shakes her head. 'What are the chances?'

'Not a problem,' I tell her brightly. 'We are only too happy to help.'

'It was lucky, actually, because Imani has been wanting to come and watch *The Dog Who Saved Christmas*, but I've been that busy with work...' She chatters away, ten to the dozen. 'The salon has been mad busy with back-to-back appointments, as it always is at this time of year.' She smiles, revealing perfectly straight, white teeth.

I glance at her nails, a work of art in red and greens adorned with candy canes, snowmen and Christmas trees. 'When the other place cancelled, my stress levels nearly went through the roof. Imani was really looking forward to a party with her friends.'

'Well, I'm really glad we could help,' I say again. 'To be honest, we could do with a few more parties; it's been a little quiet of late,' I tell her.

We place the cake in the middle of the table – praying the table won't collapse – and I gasp when she opens the lid. It's a huge castle, sprayed in edible glitter. At least, I hope it's edible.

'Gorgeous, isn't it? I bet you've never seen anything like it before.' She beams proudly.

'I can honestly say I haven't,' I reply, taking in the sparkling work of art.

'Right, I'd better go and collect Imani and her two best friends; the others should all be here by four o'clock. See you soon.' She leaves a lingering waft of expensive perfume in her wake as she disappears.

. . .

The cinema party was a roaring success. We served hot dogs and drinks at the start of the movie, and popcorn halfway through. At the end, Imani's mum returned with the other parents and Imani helped cut huge slabs of cake, which she handed out along with party bags. Everyone sang 'Happy Birthday' and Imani looked suitably thrilled. A guy took some photos and the camera he used looked so impressive, I wondered whether he might have been actual paparazzi. Perhaps he was. Maybe the photos will appear in the next edition of the *Liverpool Echo*. That would really help the cinema.

'Thanks so much, ladies,' says Imani's mum on the way out. 'And if you're in the market for any beauty treatments, here's a ten per cent off voucher.' She pushes a leaflet into my hand.

'Thanks so much.' I glance at my short nails and wonder whether it might be nice to have them done for Christmas. Maybe a sleek green or silver, minus the snowmen.

'And I'll be sure to spread the word.' She winks. 'The kids have had a ball.'

'That would be brilliant, thank you.'

'No problem, thanks again, ta-ra then.'

After cleaning up before the evening film starts at six thirty, Shelley and I have a break and grab a bite to eat.

'Aren't you eating your cake?' asks Shelley. Imani's mum had insisted we both had a slice.

'Erm, I'm not sure I fancy it. It looks radioactive.' I'm staring at the blue and silver mound in front of me.

'Mind if I do?'

'Be my guest.'

Shelley munches on the second slice of cake, as I finish my chicken salad and granary roll. That's after she's polished off a hot dog and an entire tube of Pringles. I don't know where she puts it, she's so tall and slim. Although I suppose you can eat what you like when you're young and active. I kind of wish I'd eaten more junk food at that age, instead of worrying about calories, as it seems nature kindly gives you excess pounds later in life anyway.

I drop Shelley home this evening, which is only a little out of my way. She has no plans with her friends tonight and says that actually, maybe, she had better do a little studying for her upcoming A levels. Between working at the cinema and the social life the students enjoy, she tells me it's quite difficult to make time for revision. 'I don't have the time to be a student,' she once jokingly told me.

Arriving in the village just after nine thirty, I decide to pop in for a drink at the pub, where Jo is in with her daughter Claire. I head to the bar, which has been decorated with swathes of red and gold tinsel and a 'Merry Christmas' banner along the top. I grab myself a drink and join Jo at a table in the corner.

Josh Hunter is standing behind the bar, flirting with Jo's daughter Claire, who is sitting at a bar stool. He's pointing to a strategically placed mistletoe above her head and she's giggling.

'How was Michael Ball?' I ask Jo, settling down with my glass of white wine.

'Amazing. His voice was just perfect. At one point, he stared right at me as he was singing, and I felt like a teenager again. It's a pity he's still with his long-term wife.' She sighs, taking a sip of her red wine. 'Anyway, never mind me, how was your date?' she asks. She still looks ridiculously glamorous sitting here in jeans and a white jumper that shows off her slender figure.

I tell her all about our dinner at the Italian Club and how Luke's offered to take me to the theatre sometime.

'Well, good for you,' she says. 'It's about time you got out there again dating. Ellie's a big girl now.'

'I guess you're right. In fact, she practically said the same thing to me last night when I arrived home. I do worry about her, though.'

I tell Jo all about the pregnancy test.

'Teenagers.' Jo lets out a sigh. 'They are a worry, but Ellie is a smart girl. I used to worry about Claire when she was that age, but she's got things figured out now.'

'How do you feel about her seeing Josh?' I find myself asking, nodding towards the bar. I can't help thinking Claire could do far better than someone like him.

'She's just having a little fun. It's nothing serious, so I'm not worried. I know he has a bad boy reputation, but I also know that if I objected he would probably seem more desirable. I guess you and Ellie just have to talk frankly to each other. Give Ellie the space to make her own decisions, and make sure she knows you will be there if she needs you,' she advises.

'Talking of Ellie.' Jo glances towards the door as Ellie enters, an icy blast following her for a second. I texted her to say I was having a quick drink and to see if she fancied joining me. She declined, so I'm surprised she's showed up.

'Hi, love, do you want a drink?'

I'm about to head for the bar, when my daughter's eyes reach the scene with Josh and Claire, and she declines.

'No, thanks, Mum. Actually, I only called in for your key, I've left mine at home.'

She's been at the house of one of her friends in the village, listening to music and helping her wrap some Christmas presents.

'Right, okay. Actually, hang on a minute, I'll come with you.' I finish my drink and say goodnight to everyone. As we leave, I'm aware of Ellie turning to watch Josh at the bar with Claire, who is throwing her head back and laughing at something he's said. He catches her eye and she smiles, and he gives a half smile back, before returning his attention to Claire.

'Are you okay?' I ask, when we arrive home.

I throw my keys onto a table in the hall and hang my coat up.

'Yeah, why wouldn't I be?'

'I don't know, you just seemed in a real hurry to get out of the pub. I thought you might have stayed for a drink, maybe even had a sample of the curry.'

'I'm not hungry.' She shrugs. 'And I'm not a fan of curry unless it's really mild.'

'Are you sure you're okay?'

To my surprise, she sits on the sofa and sighs. 'It's Josh, he was all over Claire at the bar, wasn't he? He barely even acknowledged me when I thought...'

'You thought what?' Don't tell me she has a crush on Josh Hunter.

'Well, we've been kind of seeing each other,' she says in a small voice.

'You've been seeing Josh?' I ask, aghast. He's the last person I want my daughter seeing.

'I don't know. Kind of. At least I thought so. He never said he was my actual boyfriend or anything, but I thought he liked me.' She avoids my gaze.

'Oh, Ellie.' I try not to give her a lecture. With his sultry good looks and charming manner, I can understand how easy it would be for a girl her age to fall for him. But there's no way she's dating him.

She tells me they have been spending time together at the weekend and I recall Helen saying Josh had sneaked off from his work duties last Sunday, the day Ellie went into Southport.

'Was it Josh you went to Southport with last weekend?' I ask and she nods. 'Oh, Ellie, I thought we'd agreed no more secrets?'

'I know, I'm sorry, Mum. I might as well tell you, it was Josh who came here that night you went out.'

I try to contain my anger. Coming into my house, stealing my vodka and trying to seduce my daughter, the little toerag.

'But it's okay, I won't bother with him anymore. I know he can't be trusted. I kind of thought that anyway, and I saw it with my own eyes tonight.'

'That pregnancy test. It definitely wasn't yours, was it? I have to ask.'

'No, Mum, I was telling the truth about that,' she says and I breathe a sigh of relief. 'Josh did try it on with me more than once, but I said no. That's probably why he lost interest.'

I sit next to Ellie and wrap her in a hug.

'Ellie, I'm so proud of you. And you should *never* be pressurised into doing something you don't want to. Believe me, if you had slept together, he would have lost interest anyway and moved on to the next one. Take it from me.' Judging by his behaviour in the pub this evening, he already has. I truly hope she is telling the truth about not sleeping with him.

'I know. I'm glad I didn't. Thanks, Mum, and I'm sorry for not telling you. I knew you wouldn't approve. Maybe I just didn't want to get into a fight with you about it. I've seen him for what he really is now; I've been stupid.' She buries her face in her hands.

'It's alright. But, please, promise me you'll stay away from him. Apart from anything, he's too old for you. It might not seem like it, but there's a huge difference between a sixteen- and a nineteen-year-old.'

'I realise that now, Mum, and I will.'

'And, please, talk to me. I know I fuss sometimes, but, honestly, I want you to know I'm here for you.'

I think of Jo's wise words, telling me I can only reassure Ellie I am always here for her, and learn to trust her to make her own decisions in life.

'I know, Mum.'

'Right. I'm glad we understand each other. Now, do you fancy a hot chocolate? I think there's some mini marshmallows in the cupboard.'

'Ooh yes, please. Is it too late for pancakes?' she asks hopefully.

'It's never too late for pancakes,' I say as she follows me into the kitchen and I feel pride in knowing what a sensible daughter I have raised, as well as dismissing thoughts of knocking Josh off his motorbike and into one of the roadside ditches in the village.

SEVENTEEN

It's the day of the cinema Christmas party at the Hilton in town and I can't wait. I'm meeting Shelley and the other part-time staff for drinks in town, before we head off for the meal at the hotel. Last year, the food was fantastic, even though we'd kind of expected that it wouldn't be, what with mass catering for large parties over the festive season. As well as the great food, there was a really good band performing, as well as a late disco. I hope we have a repeat of that this year.

I look in the mirror, and decide the dress from John Lewis was definitely the right choice, as it feels good and, dare I say, looks good too. I walk downstairs where Ellie and Izzy, who is staying over tonight, are in the kitchen about to make Christmas cookies. The counter is covered with all the utensils and ingredients in preparation. We bought the Christmas cookie cutters when Ellie was five years old, and she would help me in the kitchen at this time of year, messily decorating biscuits with coloured icing, her little tongue sticking out in concentration as I handed her some sprinkles. The first time we did it, the lid was loose and she poured a whole jar of hundreds and thousands onto one biscuit, and I can still hear the sound of her giggling.

Now here she is making them with her best friend and I can't help feeling sentimental at how quickly the years have rolled by.

Ellie gives a little wolf whistle as I enter the kitchen, and I give a twirl.

'Oh, Mum, you look gorgeous.' She smiles.

'You really do,' adds Izzy.

'Thanks, girls. I must admit I feel really good in this dress. And these shoes are not too uncomfortable. At least not yet. It might be a different story later, when I've had a bit of a dance.'

'You should pop a pair of flip-flops into your bag,' says Ellie, which is what we do when we go to the Grand National in the spring, swapping them with our high heels as we make the trek to the train station.

'That wouldn't be a bad idea if it wasn't so cold. I don't want to risk frostbite.'

'Have a great time, Mum, and don't get too drunk.' Ellie gives me a hug just as I hear the beep of a taxi outside.

Soon enough, I've arrived at a pub in the city centre and I scan the room for the cinema crew. Shelley is seated in a corner with Ed and waves when she spots me. Ed is dressed in a navy suit with a skinny tie, and, with his tousled brown hair, has a kind of rock star vibe going on. Shelley looks pretty in a black dress with shoestring straps, and a necklace with a blue stone at the centre that almost matches the colour of her eyes. I noticed them laughing together when I first walked into the bar and can't help thinking what an attractive couple they make, despite Shelley denying any attraction between them.

'You look nice,' says Shelley, pushing a glass of red wine towards me that she's poured from a bottle.

'So do you, both of you,' I say as I sit down and take a slurp of my wine.

'The others not here yet?' I ask, referring to the students who work part-time at the cinema.

'I'm not sure it's their thing, to be honest. I get the feeling they might just turn up for the free meal later,' Shelley lets slip.

The bar is filled with party revellers, many dressed in outrageous Christmas jumpers. There's a Grinch amongst the revellers and it makes me think of the green poodle I spotted the other day in the village. A bloke wearing a Christmas jumper presses a button, lighting up the Christmas tree on the front of his sweater, to the amusement of his friends in the group.

'You ain't seen nothing yet,' says another member of the party, who looks quite conservatively dressed in a plain blue shirt and a pair of black trousers. Suddenly, he fiddles with his belt and an illuminated robin appears around his groin area and I almost choke on my wine.

'That brings a whole new meaning to Cock Robin,' says someone close by, and the whole bar erupts into laughter.

There's a such a joyful, festive atmosphere in the pub, that we're reluctant to leave, although conversation is somewhat difficult as it's so loud in here, with people frequently bursting into song when a particularly popular tune blares out across the pub.

Finishing our drinks, we head out into the crisp night air, and soon arrive at the entrance to the hotel. We follow the sign in the plush, purple-carpeted reception area that directs us to the function room where the cinema party is taking place.

Entering the ballroom, the first thing we see is the tall Christmas tree that is beautifully decorated and looks stunning. I glance up at the gold stars suspended from the high ceiling, before looking around at the tables set with striking centrepieces of cream flowers and red berries.

As we take our seats, Greg Starr, who the term 'silver fox' might just have been created for, brandishes a microphone and welcomes us all to the annual Starlight Christmas bash.

'Welcome, one and all, to our annual Christmas party.' He smiles, cutting a dash in a dark grey suit with a pale pink shirt underneath. 'I'm not going to stand here too long, as I know you all want to let the party celebrations commence, but I just wanted to say a sincere thanks to every single one of you here this evening, for your hard work and dedication to the Starlight Cinema Group. It hasn't been an easy time for cinemas lately, what with one thing and another, but, thankfully, we've managed to survive another year.'

I find myself hoping we can survive many more years and wonder whether we ought to do more advertising to promote the cinema in the local press.

'So, thank you once more,' he continues. 'It's testament to your hard work and dedication that we're getting through these difficult times.'

A cheer goes up from the assembled crowd, along with a loud whoop from Shelley, and I wonder whether I'm imagining the slightly forced smile on Greg's face.

'And now, that's enough of the work talk, so all it remains for me to do is to wish you all a great evening, and a very happy Christmas.'

'Merry Christmas,' everyone choruses in reply.

Greg sets down the microphone to the sound of applause, and I'm surprised when he joins our table of eight, which includes some staff from another branch as Greg likes us all to get to know one another. When he takes a seat beside me, I spot Shelley and Ed nudge each other.

'I hope the food is as good as it was last year, I'm famished,' says Greg amiably as a waitress appears and offers us a choice of red or white wine. She pours us all a glass, then leaves the bottles on the table. A woman from another cinema in the group is grinning at Greg across the table like a super fan.

'Me too,' I say, thinking I won't be able to move in this dress after I've eaten a three-course meal.

We make small talk about our various plans for Christmas and Greg tells me he is off to Barbados.

'Ooh, lucky you,' I say, taking a swig of wine, which is going straight to my head as I haven't eaten anything yet.

'Not really. It's my brother's place. I'm spending Christmas with them, as my marriage is over,' he tells me matter-of-factly as he takes a sip of his red wine.

'Oh God, I'm sorry, Greg. I had no idea.'

'How could you have? It's been on the cards for a while, I think,' he tells me honestly. 'She's been seeing the gardener. Cliché, I know, although he is extremely handsome so I can see the temptation.' He manages a smile. 'She says I've been neglecting her. Thinking about it, I probably have. She called me a workaholic and I suppose she's right.'

'I'm so sorry. Do you think you can work things out?'

'Honestly? Not really. The kids have grown up and flown the nest and I'm not ready to slow down with work. I built the Starlight Cinema Group from nothing. It's my whole life.' He takes another sip of his drink as our soup starter arrives.

The woman across the table appears to have trained her ears like antennae, and visibly brightens when she hears the news that Greg is newly separated.

After the first course of a tasty broccoli and Stilton soup, the lady admirer – who seems determined to have Greg's attention – downs another glass of wine and winks at him. Greg returns her smile and shifts slightly in his seat.

We get through the second course – turkey with all the trimmings, which is really lovely, succulent and tasty – and by the time we've reached the Christmas pudding, I'm feeling a little tipsy and ready for a good dance. A soon as everything is cleared away, the DJ plays a catchy tune and the lady opposite has dragged Greg to his feet and, loosened up by a few glasses of wine, he happily follows her to the dance floor, looking like he's really enjoying himself.

Greg dances with virtually everyone, leaving his female admirer looking a bit miffed, but he does the same every year, dancing with all the employees from the cleaners to the finance managers. His tie is off and he's having a thoroughly good time, delighting everyone with his nifty moves on the dance floor. They say a good dancer is a sign of a good lover and looking at Greg's moves, I wonder why his wife was with the gardener. Maybe he really was neglecting her.

The DJ is really good, playing some decent dance tunes, along with the usual Christmas songs. He throws a bit of an eighties and nineties mix in to the delight of everyone, all up on their feet. It's a joy to see everyone letting their hair down and having a great time, including me.

Towards the end of the evening, my feet are sore and I flop down onto a chair and glance around for Shelley, who is nowhere to be seen. Deciding I need a breath of fresh air, I head out towards a balcony I can see through a set of patio doors, only to find Shelley and Ed locking lips. I start furtively creeping backwards, straight into Greg Starr.

'Whoops, sorry.'

'No problem. I was just sneaking out for one of these. Fancy joining me?' he asks, producing a cigar from his pocket. 'Although I don't suppose many people smoke cigars now, do they?' He laughs.

'Probably not. No, thanks, anyway. I'll join you outside for some fresh air, though, but not here.'

I guide him to another set of French doors that open out into a small garden area with tables and chairs, where a few people are smoking. A girl in a tiny black dress rubs her arms, complaining it's freezing, as she heads back inside.

'I just didn't want to interrupt a couple outside, getting a bit cosy.' I feel the need to explain, as Greg might wonder why I have dragged him off somewhere else.

'Aah, I see.' He nods and smiles.

It's so hot inside, I welcome the night air, which surprisingly doesn't feel too cold. But then, I have danced the night away. There's a silvery, almost full moon in the black sky that is dotted with tiny white stars. Beyond the well-manicured garden, the sound of party revellers walking past can be heard.

'I'm glad I've got you alone, actually,' says Greg, taking a drag of his cigar, and I wonder what's coming next. I mean he's a handsome man and everything, but he must be pushing sixty. 'I just want to say thank you for how you're running the Little Newdale cinema,' he tells me. 'I see nothing but good feedback from online reviews, commenting on the friendly helpful staff, which is mainly you, it would appear.'

'Thanks, that's good to hear. I love working there, although I do worry that we aren't getting enough customers through the door.'

'I worry about that too. But I think the refurbishment will help. It's what's needed to bring the cinema into the twenty-first century.' He blows a ring of cigar smoke into the air.

'Refurbishment?'

I knew it was probably on the cards, and, of course, I know it's what the cinema needs, yet I can't help feeling the heart will be ripped out of the cinema if it has a modern makeover. But if it's going to survive, I suppose it's the only way forward.

'Yes, I don't think we can put it off any longer,' Greg replies. 'People want reclining chairs, nachos and a variety of hot snacks these days, other than hot dogs.'

'Would the velvet chairs be ripped out?' I ask, already knowing the answer.

'I'm afraid so. But I'm thinking we might leave the back row untouched, as a nod to the cinema's history.'

'That's a nice idea.' I'm relieved that something of the cinema's past can be preserved.

Greg takes a few more puffs of his cigar, before he extinguishes it.

'Actually, we've had a children's birthday party recently,

which was a great success. We're hoping the word will spread around. It could make a real difference,' I tell him optimistically.

'Sounds great. We'll definitely need the leather seats in as soon as possible, then. We don't want the kids being sick over the velvet chairs if they've eaten too many sweets.' He smiles.

Sitting here under the moonlight, I can see the tiredness on Greg's handsome face, despite his outward joviality. It can't be easy breaking up from your wife of so many years and having the strain of running a business too. I hope he has a lovely time in Barbados in the sunshine with his brother.

'Anyway, best head back inside.' He stands up from his chair. 'People will be wondering where I've got to,' he says, although at this point I think most people will be too inebriated to care.

As we stroll back inside, Shelley and Ed are at the bar ordering drinks and I head towards them.

'Oh aye, where have you been, then?' Shelley teases as she spies Greg follow me inside from the garden area.

'I just went out for some fresh air like you did. Actually, maybe not just like you,' I say, recalling her and Ed snogging as I raise an eyebrow.

It's getting late now and most people are beginning to look a little bit the worse for wear. Some have already said their goodnights and headed off in search of a taxi. A woman wearing gold tinsel as a boa around her neck staggers past, almost falling over, and grabs a wine bottle from a littered table and swigs the remains. Her friend grabs her by the elbow and steers her out.

'Great night, wasn't it?' she slurs, smiling at me. I don't recognise her, so she's obviously a new member of staff but I recognise the lady who comes to her rescue, steering her outside.

Greg is in the reception area, saying goodnight to staff as they exit.

'Can we give you a lift anywhere?' I ask Greg, who thanks

me but declines, telling me his daughter is on her way to collect him.

'Sure, okay. Merry Christmas, then,' I say, knowing we probably won't meet again until the new year. Greg is pretty hands-on and calls in to his cinemas several times a year, to keep an eye on things.

Outside, we hail a taxi, and I drop Shelley and Ed off at a bar on the way to my place, as they don't want their evening to end just yet.

'Oh, come on, just have one drink with us?' says Shelley as the taxi pulls up outside a late bar near Matthew Street. I'm a little tired, but what the hell, it's Christmas after all. One more drink can't hurt.

'Go on then, why not? But then I'm off.'

We head inside the bar where a band are playing songs from a stage in a corner, and a crowd are up dancing on a tiny dance floor, others sitting in booths sipping drinks and chatting. We squeeze our way to the front of the bar and soon enough – having managed to find seats at a small table – we share a bottle of wine. The band are really very good, and I find myself tapping my feet and singing along to the familiar tunes they are covering.

Half an hour later, though, I feel a little drunk, slightly regretting not going straight home.

'Right, it's definitely time I left.' I stand up and feel the need to get some fresh air.

Ed and Shelley escort me outside to a nearby taxi rank and tell me they will wait with me until I'm safely in a taxi. Just then I spot two blokes up ahead in the queue, and realise one of them is Luke.

'Luke!' I shout his name, raising my hand and waving wildly.

Luke glances over and makes his way towards me, leaving his friend near the front of the queue. I introduce him to

Shelley and Ed, who look pleased when Luke tells them to go off and enjoy themselves, and that he will escort me home.

'If you don't mind sharing a taxi?' he asks.

'No, of course not.'

Just then, Luke's friend, Andy, shouts over to Luke that it's their turn for the taxi, so Luke grabs me by the hand and we quickly climb into the awaiting cab. I feel a bit guilty when I hear a couple of girls complain that I hadn't even queued up like everyone else.

'How did the cinema party go?' asks Luke as we drive. He's sitting in the back seat with me.

'It was great, actually. I think everyone had a really good time.' I smile, suddenly feeling tired. 'Have you had a nice night?'

'We have. We headed down to the Baltic Triangle for some food. What a place that is.'

The Baltic Triangle is a cool area of cafés and bars, housed in former warehouses in an industrial area of the city.

We chat easily throughout the journey, Andy sometimes turning around from the front seat and joining in. Soon enough we pull up outside my cottage.

'Well, thanks so much for dropping me off. Night, guys.'

I give my dress a little tug, as Luke is accidentally sitting on a part of it, before I climb out.

'I'll walk you to the door. Two minutes,' he tells the driver, who nods.

He walks me up the path and I'm about to head inside when Luke asks me if I have any plans tomorrow.

'Having a lie-in, I imagine.' Suddenly everything feels a little blurry.

'I was wondering whether you would be interested in having a look around the Tate gallery in the afternoon?' Luke asks. 'There's a Lucian Freud exhibition. I don't know if he's your thing, but I really like his work.'

'Actually, yes, I do like him. I like how he captures people's expressions in his portraits.' I'm speaking carefully and slowly, not wanting to appear drunk.

'Brilliant. I'll see you tomorrow. I'm looking forward to it already. I'll pick you up around one. Make sure you wear something warm.' He's smiling at me, and staring at my chest, I can't help noticing. With a feeling of dread, I glance down at my dress and all I can see is my black bra staring back at me.

'Oh my goodness! How long have I been like that?' I ask, feeling like Judy Finnigan at the Brit Awards all those years ago, when her wrap-over dress fell open. I quickly fix the dress, in an attempt to preserve some modesty. 'Please tell me it wasn't like that in the taxi!' I ask with horror.

'It wasn't, don't worry,' says Luke, trying very hard not to smile again.

I realise the tie fastening must have come loose when I pulled at the dress as I climbed out of the back seat.

Luke gives me a peck on the cheek and I can't get inside fast enough.

Standing in front of the hall mirror, I take a peek at the black bra I'm wearing. It's a sturdy, full cup and probably the least sexy bra I own. I kick my shoes off and head to bed, totally mortified at my wardrobe malfunction.

EIGHTEEN

The next day, after a long lie-in and a hearty breakfast, I'm looking forward to heading into town with Luke, although I blush at the memory of me revealing myself to him with the dress disaster and vow not to wear a wrap-over dress ever again. Ellie and Izzy have gone to Izzy's house, so I don't have to worry about introducing Ellie to Luke just yet, which is a relief.

It's a little after one o'clock when Luke calls to collect me.

'Afternoon. How are we feeling?' he asks, a smile playing around his mouth.

'Great, actually. You?' I ask brightly.

'Good, thanks. I'm looking forward to today.'

I invite him in, while I grab my coat and bag.

'Nice place you have,' says Luke, casting an eye around the tastefully decorated lounge. 'Is this an original floor?' he asks, spying the flagstone floor beneath the huge multi-coloured rug.

'It is. It's been down for over two hundred years since the house was built,' I inform him.

'It looks great. Sorry, I can't help noticing flooring wherever I go.' He smiles. 'We sell some incredible tiles that look authentic, but you can't beat the real thing.'

As I step into Luke's car, I think about how lucky I was to run into him again. I enjoy every second of the time I spend with him and wish I knew if he felt the same way.

The dock is a hive of activity, with shoppers walking in and out of the numerous gift shops that are housed in the red-brick buildings, regenerated from the old dock mills. Christmas music is filtering into the streets when the doors of the bars and shops open. I pass my favourite gift shop filled with quirky gifts, that I might go and have a browse around later, after we've visited the gallery.

Pushing the door open of the Tate, I inhale the distinctive smell that belongs to museums and art galleries. It's the smell of polished floors, people and old artefacts, their various scents mingled with fresh coffee from a nearby café.

'I'd forgotten just how peaceful this gallery is,' I say as we move around the large space, stopping to admire the exhibition.

Luke stands alongside me as we study a painting, and his close presence stirs something in me. I long to take hold of his hand and feel it in mine, but instead comment on the picture to distract myself.

'What do you think she's thinking about?' I tilt my head to one side and look at the painting. It's a head and shoulders portrait of a woman lounging in a bed, her arm behind her head. Her expression is quite hard to read.

'Relaxed, maybe? Although she doesn't look particularly relaxed. That's what I like about Freud's work. His expressions are not always easy to read. Genius, really.'

We move around the gallery; all the time I'm aware of his presence alongside me, the hint of his masculine aftershave, the look on his handsome face as he peruses a painting that sets my pulse racing.

'Did you know Lucian Freud once painted a naked picture of Kate Moss,' Luke tells me as we continue around the gallery.

'Oh really? Are you disappointed it's not on display, then?' I tease and he laughs.

'Beautiful as she is, she isn't really my type,' he reveals and I immediately wonder what his type is.

'Is she more your type, then?' I point to a painting of a woman in a yellow dress with a dog on her lap, who has her right breast out.

'Hm, I'm not sure I'd be attracted to someone who exposes herself in public,' he says. 'But then again.' He raises an eyebrow as he looks at me, and I burst out laughing.

After we've finished in the gallery, we head outside into the street and I ask Luke if he would mind taking a look inside the quirky gift shop, and he agrees.

The shop is festooned with all manner of Christmas memorabilia, everything from bottle stoppers to mugs and hand-painted glasses depicting Christmas scenes. There's a dancing snowman with flashing green eyes singing a Christmas tune that looks mildly terrifying. Luke puts on a pair of those glasses that have googly eyes that fall out on springs. I'm looking at something and he taps me on the shoulder wearing them and I burst out laughing.

'Hello, sexy,' he says as the eyes ride up and down on the spring.

'You're an idiot.' I laugh.

In the shop, I spot some pink fluffy socks and a small cardboard cut-out of Olly Murs for Ellie, who is mad about him, so I purchase both items. I also buy a novelty pen saying 'I love Liverpool', thinking it might be something to remind Luke of the city when he heads back to America.

The sky has darkened when we exit the shop, the lights from the dock twinkling across the River Mersey, giving it a magical feel. Couples stroll by linking arms and I long to slip my arm through Luke's, yet somehow I hesitate. I've had little more than a peck on the cheek from Luke since we met, even though he confided that he fancied me as a teenager. He certainly isn't giving much away as an adult, though.

'Do you fancy dinner at the pub tonight?' I ask Luke as we head to the car. 'I fancy a curry, which is now on the menu all weekend.'

'Actually, yes, I've barely eaten today. I could murder a curry.' He smiles as we walk along in the chilly night air.

NINETEEN

It's just after six when we pull into the village. I've texted Ellie, who is going to join us for dinner at the Penny Farthing. Izzy is coming too as she's sleeping over again tonight.

'I'm looking forward to this; it's ages since I've had a nice curry,' says Luke. 'It won't be turkey, though, will it?' He grins.

'I don't honestly know. Although, truthfully, I hope not. There will enough of that over Christmas.'

We park up at my house and walk the short distance to the pub, with Izzy and Ellie in tow. Ellie asks Luke about living in America, telling him how she would love to live there one day.

'It's not all like it is in the movies, you know,' he tells her. 'Although I suppose it does have its charms.'

When he tells her he lives in Florida, her mouth falls open. 'How could you not love living there? All those beaches. Have you ever seen anyone famous?' she asks.

'As a matter of fact, I have,' Luke tells her as we walk. 'Ozzy and Sharon Osbourne. My company supplied flooring for their new home. Oh, and Tom Jones,' he adds as Izzy and Ellie look suitably impressed.

Inside, the pub is far busier than usual and we grab a table in a cosy nook, after I've sad hi to people. Helen dashes over when she spots me.

'Hi, guys. I've got three curries on the menu tonight,' she gushes. 'Lamb, veggie and chicken.'

I introduce Helen to Luke.

'Good to meet you, Luke. It was Sarah that gave me the idea for the curry nights,' she tells him with a newly found sparkle, I can't help noticing. She is quite literally sparkling tonight in a silver-sequined top, black trousers and some mulberry lipstick that matches her hair.

'I'm so pleased for you, it's busy in here this evening.' I glance around at the full tables as well as people propping up the bar, sipping beer.

'I know, it's brilliant, isn't it? I'm thinking of having a quiz night too,' she tells me with excitement in her voice.

'I'm definitely up for that. I've watched so many catch-up episodes of *The Chase*, I just might be unbeatable.'

Our food when it arrives is absolutely delicious. Luke and I opt for the lamb that is melt-in-the-mouth tender and so tasty, and Izzy and Ellie have the vegetable curry, with chips and rice.

'I really enjoyed that,' says Luke, having finished every mouthful of his meal.

'Me too. It's about time we had some decent food on the menu here in the pub. It's what the village is crying out for,' I say and Ellie and Izzy agree as they finish their meal.

After we've eaten, the girls ask if they can head back to the cottage to watch Netflix.

'Sure. We'll just have another drink here and walk back shortly,' I tell her.

'Are you staying the night?' Ellie asks Luke with the directness that only comes from a teenager.

'Ellie!' I'm shocked by her question.

'What? I'm only asking,' she says.

'No,' Luke says very definitely and, even though I didn't

imagine he would be, I feel a pang of disappointment that clearly the thought had never even crossed his mind.

'So, tell me all about Kay,' I say when we've ordered another drink and settled in. 'I would absolutely love to see her. Do you think I should text her and tell her I've bumped into you? Unless, of course, you've already told her.'

Is it my imagination or does he look a little uncomfortable when I mention contacting her?

'She's away at the moment,' he says vaguely. 'I'll be in touch with her soon, though, and I'll be sure to tell her I've run into you.' He smiles now, although he declines to give me her phone number.

'I can't tell you how happy I was to have run into you, Sarah.' He looks at me with those gorgeous brown eyes and I forget about everything else. Maybe talk of his family can wait, even though I'm dying to know more about Kay and what she's been up to.

We round off the evening with a warming mulled wine and when we head out into the dark evening once more, I ask him if he would like a coffee.

'I'm going to have to call a taxi too, I'm over the limit now.'

We're standing outside the cottage, beneath the star-studded sky, when he circles his arms around my waist and draws me to him and I feel almost light-headed. My teenage crush, who these days is still the most gorgeous bloke I've ever seen, is standing here outside my house.

'Of course, you could always stay if you like? I mean, I have a spare room, I—'

Suddenly his lips are on mine and my head spins as his gentle kiss deepens, until he's kissing me with a passion that leaves me breathless.

'Wow, I wasn't expecting that,' I find myself saying when we pull apart.

'I've been dying to do that all evening,' he admits. 'I hope it's okay.'

'Of course it's okay. Are you coming inside, then, or do you want me to be the subject of gossip in the village?' I ask as he moves in for another kiss.

'There's no one about,' he says a little breathlessly just as a bloke from one of the nearby cottages walks past with his dog.

'Evening,' he says, before moving on.

'Evening.' I almost giggle like a teenager who's been caught outside her house snogging, before she heads inside.

Ellie and Izzy are downstairs watching television in the lounge when we enter.

'Hi,' says Ellie, shuffling along the couch for us to sit down. Izzy, who was stretched out on the opposite sofa, sits upright.

'What are you watching?' I shrug off my coat, feeling the warmth from the cosy log burner wrap me in a hug.

'That Harlan Coben drama I told you about. It's brilliant, Mum, you should definitely watch it.'

'I might do. I thought you'd be watching a Christmassy film.'

It makes me think how much she's grown up since last year, when her favourite movie was *Home Alone*, that she must have watched dozens of times.

'There's loads of time for Christmas films. I'm off school, remember.'

'Of course.' I smile. I'm looking forward to spending some time with her over the Christmas holidays.

'Does anyone want a drink?' I ask.

'Are you making hot chocolate?' Ellie asks hopefully.

'I'm sure you've deliberately waited until I've come home to make this for you,' I say.

Izzy laughs. 'My mum says that to me too.'

'Of course not. But honestly, Mum, this episode is so good

we didn't want to miss any of it. And yours is always nicer than mine.'

'Yeah, right. Never heard of a pause button?'

Luke follows me into the kitchen and I put a pan on the stove and fill it with milk.

'I don't suppose you want a hot chocolate too?' I turn to Luke.

'No, but I wouldn't mind a coffee. I'll make it,' he offers, heading to the coffee machine. 'Do you want one?'

'I will, but decaff for me thanks or I won't sleep.' I point to two clear canisters on the side containing the coffee. 'The one with the silver top is the decaff.'

'And then I'd better phone for a taxi,' he says, filling the machine. 'I'm over the limit, but I'm hoping Andy will drive me over in the morning to collect my car.'

We finish our drinks, Luke chatting to the girls about school and life in general, and before long, a taxi arrives outside the cottage and I walk him to the door.

He leans in and gives me a final kiss. 'I'll see you in the morning?'

'I look forward to it. Night, Luke,' I say before I close the door and glide inside.

TWENTY

Luke collected his car this morning and he and Andy stopped for a quick coffee. Now I'm driving into work and pass Frances from the flower shop, wrapped up warmly in boots and a navy quilted coat with the hood up, walking through the country lanes.

'Morning, Frances, is everything okay?' I ask as I wind my window down.

'What? Oh, hi, Sarah. Yes, I just felt the need for a walk to clear my head this morning, before I open up the shop.' Her smile looks forced, in contrast to the usual ray of sunshine that is normally Frances Flower, as Ellie calls her.

'Okay, well, have a good day,' I tell her and I drive off, hoping all is well with my friend.

Ed is standing talking to Shelley when I arrive at the cinema.

'Hi, Ed, are you doing overtime?' He's not due in until later this afternoon for his shift.

'Hi, Sarah, no chance of that.' He laughs. 'I've just called in to see Shelley for a minute to show her my new wheels,' he tells me. 'Well, my mum's old ones, actually, as she's just bought a new car, but wheels are wheels. I passed my driving test,' he says proudly.

'Oh, that's great news, congratulations.'

'Cheers. Right, see you later then,' says Ed, who's dressed in jeans, a black roll-neck jumper and a parka.

'Are you two going out together now, then?' I ask as I take off my coat and hang it up.

'Kind of,' Shelley says as she threads some bags of Maltesers onto a metal stand. 'I like Ed, he's cool but...' She pauses for a moment. 'I don't want to be getting serious with anyone right now. I'm hoping to go to university next year.'

'And the world is your oyster?'

'Something like that.' She shrugs. 'Plus, I've applied for Durham University; their art degree is second to none, apparently. It's a bit of a hike from here, so it would never last between us.' She picks up some bags of Revels that she places alongside the Maltesers.

'Perhaps you should just see how things go. People's relationships can survive long distance, I suppose.' I can't help thinking about when Luke heads back to America. Even though we are not actually a couple, I dare to dream that we soon will be.

'I know they can, but I'm realistic enough to know ours probably wouldn't. I do like him, but I get the impression he's keener on me. I don't want to hurt him.'

'As long as you're honest with each other and don't make any promises, I'd say just take one day at a time and enjoy yourselves,' I advise.

'That's exactly what we're going to do, and now that he has a car, we're off to Blackpool tomorrow to watch a band one of his mates is in. They're performing at a small theatre up there. I want to see the lights on the promenade too, before they finish.'

'That sounds great, I'm sure you'll have fun.'

That's another memory I have, of me and Robbie taking

Ellie to see the Blackpool lights when she was a young child, spending a fortune in the arcades one year when Robbie was determined to win a giant snowman for Ellie. Sometimes, we would stay over at a bed and breakfast and take a bracing walk along the seafront the next morning after a hearty breakfast.

'Oh, and I know it's only a week before Christmas,' says Shelley, 'but could we do another kids' party on Thursday? Would you believe I overheard someone having a conversation at a bus stop yesterday, saying her daughter wants a birthday party but she couldn't find anywhere at such short notice. So, I kind of waded in and suggested the cinema.'

'Of course, yeah, great. More money through the tills can only be a good thing. Well done, Shelley, you should be on commission.'

'Maybe I'll just take one of these?' She grins, lifting a mini tub of ice cream from a small freezer.

'Go on, then, you've earned that. I'll put the money in the till.'

The matinee is busy this afternoon with the regular pensioners, as well as a few younger couples. Thirty-six people in total, which is great for a matinee. They are here to see a special screening of *It's a Wonderful Life*, an enduring classic that is always popular whenever it's screened around this time of year.

During my shift at the cinema, I go over last night standing outside the cottage. I relive the feeling of that kiss, that sends shivers down my spine just thinking about it. I wanted Luke to kiss me so badly, and was thrilled when he did. I wonder what his plans are? Perhaps he's having a lovely time in Liverpool with someone he knew in the past? Maybe that's exactly how I should be thinking about it too, to dispel any notion of anything developing between us. Especially as he will be heading back to America soon.

'Penny for your thoughts?' Shelley asks.

'What? Oh, I don't know, miles away thinking how complicated relationships can be.'

I tell Shelley all about my date with Luke, and how I'm not sure if it's going anywhere.

'Didn't you just tell me to take it one day at a time?' she reminds me. 'Maybe you ought to take your own advice.'

'You're right, of course. I definitely don't think I could do a long-distance relationship, though. You could say my experiences with Robbie have left me a little mistrusting of blokes.'

'Not all men are the same. And if someone's going to cheat, they will. No good stressing about it,' she says, with all the wisdom of someone much older.

'That's so true,' I say. Even so, I can't help feeling cautious when it comes to new relationships.

'Oh and talking of Robbie, do you think I'm being unreasonable not having him around for Christmas lunch?' I ask Shelley, keen to get a young person's perspective.

'Why on earth would you have your ex around for Christmas?' She looks puzzled.

'Ellie wants him to come.' I sigh. 'It seems things are over with his current girlfriend and Ellie is feeling sorry for him. She tried to guilt trip me into inviting him, saying something about Christmas being about family.'

'But he cheated on you and broke your family up,' says Shelley, with her usual candour.

'Exactly.'

'So, no, I don't think you're being unreasonable. I get Ellie wanting her dad there, of course I do, but things seem to be going well with Luke and you wouldn't want to jeopardise that, would you?'

'I absolutely wouldn't. Thanks, Shelley.'

'No probs.'

It isn't long before the film has ended, and the crowd exit

the cinema; some of the customers are dabbing at their eyes with a tissue.

'Oh, it gets me every time,' says one of our regulars.

That evening, I drive home and I'm so tired, I don't feel like cooking, so I call in to the Hot Pot café to see if they can do a couple of takeaway portions for me and Ellie to enjoy at home. I'm trying to spread my custom equally between the café and the pub when I eat out.

Jo is sitting at a corner table, nursing a coffee and dressed in a Christmas jumper and navy jeans, as well as her trademark red lipstick. Her dark hair is softly curled and falling at her neck. Jo is the last person you would imagine wearing a Christmas jumper and I can't help commenting.

'We hosted a pensioners' Christmas party today, as the heating broke in the community centre,' she explains. 'I thought I had better get into the Christmas spirit. One thing I will say for the jumper is that it's nice and warm. It seems everything in life has a redeeming quality.' She smiles. 'So what can I do for you?'

'I was hoping to take a couple of hot pots home for me and Ellie.'

Jo springs up and heads behind the counter, filling two plastic containers with the tasty hot pot, along with two little pots of red cabbage.

'Thanks, Jo, this will hit the spot tonight. Oh, by the way, have you seen anything of Frances today?' I ask.

'It's funny you should ask that. The flower shop was closed this afternoon and it never closes early,' she says, handing me my change. 'Why do you ask?'

'I'm not sure. I saw her out walking early this morning and when I said hi, she didn't seem her usual cheery self,' I confide to Jo. 'Although we all have our off days, I guess.'

'That's true, but it is unusual for the shop to close early,' Jo agrees. 'Well, I'm sure it will be open tomorrow. If not, I have her mobile number; I'll give her a call.'

'Good idea. Thanks, Jo, see you soon.'

Outside, Josh Hunter is handing a helmet to Claire as they prepare to go out on a ride, so it seems she has finally succumbed to his charms, and I can't help wondering what Jo thinks about that. Claire says hi as I pass, as Josh roars the bike into life, the noise thundering around the courtyard before they speed off.

'Mm, I enjoyed that.'

Ellie takes her plate to the sink and fills the bowl with soapy water. 'You should ask Jo for the recipe.'

'I think it's a closely guarded secret. A bit like Betty's hot pot in the Rovers Return.'

'Who's Betty?' she asks, and I think of the generation gap. She just about knows that the Rovers Return is in *Coronation Street*, as she never watches the soaps. It's all Netflix or the Disney Channel for youngsters these days.

'Do you want to help me make a Christmas cake?' I ask Ellie after we've washed up and I've tidied the kitchen.

'Haven't you normally done that, like, weeks ago?' she says, surprised that I'm only just thinking about making one.

'Yes, but I've been busy. And, to be honest, some of the shop-bought ones are so good I wasn't going to bother this year, but I know my aunt and uncle will appreciate it.'

'Your Christmas cake is the best, though, Mum. Dad always said it never compared to anything you could find in the shops.' She reminds me of his comments every Christmas, and the memory of Robbie enjoying a slice of Christmas cake after Christmas lunch has old feelings rising to the surface.

'It's a pity he can't come for Christmas,' she says wistfully. 'Especially as you're baking a cake this year.'

'Oh, Ellie, not this again, please. He's not going to be sleeping on the streets. He has lots of friends,' I tell her gently.

'It won't be the same, though, will it?' she mutters under her breath.

'I'm sure he'll be alright,' I try and reassure her. 'And you know he will see you over Christmas.'

'Suppose.' She shrugs. 'Maybe we can save him some cake for when I see him, then.'

'That's a good idea.' I smile. 'And I'm sure the cake will be fine; I'll just have to hold off from adding brandy to it every few days.'

Normally, I would bake the cake at least three or four weeks before Christmas Day but with less than a week to go, it will just have to do.

'Alexa, play "Driving Home for Christmas",' says Ellie, throwing up a not-so-happy memory. Robbie had been working away, and he drove home for Christmas from South Wales in a blizzard. He told me the song kept him going, the thought of not making it home to us spurring him on. I think Ellie was about eight years old at the time. It was also around the time I discovered he'd cheated for the first time, whilst he'd been working away, so the song that once brought a smile to my face now fills me with annoyance.

'I'm not keen on that one,' I say. 'Alexa, play a medley of Christmas songs.'

'Hey, I was listening to that,' protests Ellie, but soon enough we're singing at the top of our voices, 'And the bells were ringing out for Christmas Day', as the kitchen fills with the scent of fruit and spices.

A while later, the cake is in the oven, and the timer set for two hours, so we settle down and watch *The Great Christmas Bake Off*, with a hot chocolate and a mince pie. I glance at my phone as the flames flicker in the log burner, only now allowing myself to look forward to Christmas Day.

TWENTY-ONE

The next day, Robbie has arrived to take Ellie away for a few days, having surprised her with a hotel break to Alton Towers. At least he isn't sleeping on the streets. They'll be back before Christmas, just in time for the recital of *A Christmas Carol* at St George's Hall.

Ellie has bounded down the stairs full of excitement, carrying her holdall.

'I can't believe I'm going to Alton Towers at Christmas! This is the best present ever,' she says as she bounds upstairs again to grab her travel bag, and I hope the Doc Martens boots and Soap and Glory products I've bought her won't prove disappointing by comparison.

'That's a nice surprise,' I told Robbie, when he'd phoned last night. 'I believe Alton Towers at Christmas is wonderful. Ellie will be thrilled.'

'The rides aren't open, but the indoor pool is, and there's that Winter Wonderland thing I thought Ellie might like,' he tells me.

'Is Hannah not going with you?' I ask.

'No,' he says vaguely, not revealing that they have split up. 'I thought it might be nice for me and Ellie to spend some time together, and it might be nice for you too, having a few days to yourself. Ellie told me you're seeing someone.'

I wonder when he turned into this thoughtful person.

'I am, although it's early days.' I'm not about to discuss my blossoming friendship with Luke. Especially when I have no idea where it's heading myself.

After hugging Ellie goodbye, I head off for my shift. On the way, I call into the courtyard to see if the flower shop is open. Frances is standing behind the counter, and greets me with what I perceive once more to be a slightly strained smile.

'Morning, Sarah, how's things?' she asks as she artistically arranges some flowers in a vase.

'Good, thanks. How about you?'

'Oh, you know, fine, apart from being worn out, that is. It's been non-stop here lately, not that I'm complaining, of course; things tend to go a little quiet after Christmas.'

'Until Valentine's Day,' I remind her, when the shop is usually packed out.

'Of course, yes. Romance is alive and well.'

'Anyway, I can imagine how busy you are at this time of year, but don't neglect yourself,' I tell her. 'Actually, are you free for a coffee later?' I ask. I can't help thinking there is something on her mind, but then, maybe she is just simply exhausted.

'Er, no, not really, to be honest. I have to be somewhere this evening. Another time, though.'

'I'll hold you to that. Right, I'll see you later.'

I buy a pretty, pointy-leafed poinsettia plant before I leave.

'Thanks, Sarah.'

'And remember to take some time for yourself,' I tell her and she nods.

'I will do.' She plasters a smile on her face and I can't help noticing that it doesn't quite reach her eyes.

. . .

The following morning, I wake early and open the door to a fresh covering of dew on the grass outside. I had a restless sleep last night, as I often do when Ellie isn't home, and I heard every creak of the stairs or whistling wind from the trees outside. Wrapping my cardigan tightly around me, I head outside to the front garden to pour some seeds into a bird feeder, and, to my delight, there's a red robin sitting on the fence close to the gate.

'Good morning,' I greet the robin and head towards it, fully expecting it to fly off but it stays put.

'Hey there. I imagine you're looking for some of these?' I shake the box of seeds before filling a nearby feeder. 'I imagine it's hard finding worms in the frozen ground, isn't it?'

The robin stares right at me, then pecks at the seeds, before flying off into the distance. Some people think that a visit from a robin is a message from a loved one who has passed. Although I don't actually believe that myself, it does always make me think of Mum and Dad, so in some ways I guess it's true.

'Don't be a stranger,' I call after it, wondering if I'm losing the plot chatting to birds in the garden.

Seeing the robin this morning has lightened my mood a little, as I still haven't heard from Luke and, with a slightly heavy heart, wonder whether I will again.

Shelley is blowing her nose into a tissue when I arrive at the cinema, before she wraps her hands around a cup of something.

'Morning,' she says, her voice thick. The scent of lemon is spiralling from her cup.

'Have you got a cold?'

'I'm full of it,' she says. 'I've run antibacterial wipes over the door handles, but I'm not sure I should serve the oldies today.' She sneezes loudly into a tissue.

'I agree. In fact, I'm not sure you should be here at all. I can probably manage on my own; why don't you get yourself home?' I suggest.

'Are you even allowed to be here on your own?' she asks.

'Probably not.'

'In that case, I'll just sit in the office with my Lemsip, away from everyone. I'm fine, really. I'll just stick around in case you need any sort of backup.'

'You mean in case the kids throw something into the hall again? I think I'll cope.'

'I don't mind, I actually don't feel too bad. Maybe I can tidy the stockroom or something?'

'Well, okay, but after the matinee, finish your shift and I'll call one of the other part-timers and see if they want any extra hours.'

'Have you got anything planned for later?'

'Yep, a long bubble bath, a glass of wine and the final chapters of a book I'm reading. Ellie's gone away for a couple of nights with Robbie to Alton Towers.'

'Ooh, nice. I've heard there's a gorgeous woodland walk around there that's all lit up with candles and statues along the path.'

'Yes, it's a Winter Wonderland, I think. There's a Christmas market too. She was really excited.'

Shelley sneezes loudly into a tissue so I despatch her to the office at the back of the reception area.

'Shout if you need me,' says Shelley, before disappearing into the office, clutching her drink.

'I will do.'

We're showing *Elf* this week, so I expect the evenings may be busy in the run-up to Christmas, but I'm not sure if *Elf* is really the pensioners' cup of tea, but then they often surprise me with their film choices.

The film is starting in ten minutes; a dozen or so people have filtered through the door, including a couple of dads with young children and I wonder if they're single parents taking their children out over the Christmas holidays. Robbie once bemoaned to me that cinemas, bowling alleys and fast-food restaurants were full of weekend dads, and I remember thinking at the time that it was entirely his choice to join their exclusive club.

I turn my back to grab some paper coffee cups from a cupboard, and when I turn back, two men are standing at the counter.

'Two tickets for *Elf*, please,' says Luke, smiling broadly.

'Luke, what are you doing here?' I can't believe he's standing in front of me.

'I'm here to watch the film. It's my favourite Christmas movie.'

'Actually, it's one of mine too.' I laugh.

Andy is busy gathering a selection of snacks for the movie. He has so many sweets, I can't help thinking he's following Buddy the Elf's high-sugar diet.

'Oh, and two bags of popcorn, please.'

'See you in there,' says Andy, juggling the stack of sweets and popcorn. 'You grab the coffees. Nice to see you again, Sarah.'

'Of course, I didn't come here purely to watch *Elf*, even though it is my favourite Christmas film,' Luke tells me as I hand him his coffees. 'I came to see if you are free this evening.'

'I might be,' I tell him, not wanting to appear too eager as he pings his card against the reader.

'Well, if you are, do you fancy going for a drink? I could meet you at the Penny Farthing in your village, if you like,' he suggests.

The relaxing evening I had planned has happily gone right out of the window.

'I could do, but I actually won't be home until around nine.'

'Great, shall we say nine thirty then.' He smiles and I'm already looking forward to this evening.

'Enjoy the movie.'

I check in on Shelley, whose head is resting on the desk on

her rolled-up sweatshirt, so I quickly order a taxi and send her home. After that, I call one of the students who happens to be free, and will arrive in half an hour.

The rest of the afternoon passes quickly, and when Luke exits the film with Andy, I'm chatting to a member of staff and explaining something about the till, so he waves and mouths 'see you later', then he's gone.

It's good to see the cinema a little busier and tomorrow we have another children's party. If we can host more parties, I vaguely wonder whether or not it will be necessary to remodel the cinema, yet I know deep down that the work will probably go ahead. Even one of our regulars mentioned last week that the seats probably weren't doing her arthritis any good, as she rubbed her back on the way out. I have to concede that in many ways it will be nothing but a good thing for the locals to have a modern, comfortable cinema on their doorstep, although it's still tinged with sadness.

As I lock the doors later that evening, I head home, feeling butterflies in my stomach at the thought of spending the evening with Luke.

TWENTY-TWO

I have a quick shower instead of the lingering bath I had anticipated and dress in a burgundy woollen dress and some black tights. It's absolutely freezing outside now, frost covering the trees and grasses in the early morning, and a mist that descends in the late evenings. I'm thankful the pub is literally a two-minute walk away, and when I arrive Luke is already seated at a table, with Helen standing chatting to him with a tray full of glasses, en route to the bar.

'Here she is,' she says with a smile. 'Ooh, close that door quickly,' she continues as an icy blast briefly enters the cosy pub lounge. Glancing around, it's good to see quite a few people in, some eating food. Obviously the curry night was a great advert as to how good the food in the pub can be.

'Sarah, good to see you.'

Luke stands and kisses me on the cheek. He's wearing a stylish navy coat, a burgundy scarf tucked inside that matches the colour of my dress.

'I thought we would have one in here, then drive to a little place I know not far from here. I'm sure you're familiar with it. It's called the Scandi Kitchen.'

'No, actually, I'm not sure I do know that place. Is it new?'

'Pretty new. Andy tells me the food is brilliant. That is, if you don't mind eating a little later?'

'Not at all.' I smile, thinking it lucky I only ate a salad earlier. He never mentioned going out to eat.

'It's built in a log cabin style, modelled on a Norwegian-style bar, I think,' continues Luke. 'Think fairy lights, mulled wine and would you believe there's even a hot tub at the rear, but you have to book that.'

'I hope you haven't,' I say and he laughs and says no, he hasn't.

'Well, it sounds magical.'

We each opt for one of the speciality beers the pub currently has on offer called Old Nick, which is a chocolate porter with berries that is quite delicious. It's so cosy in the pub, both of the fires have roared into life, that I'm almost loath to head back outside, but looking at the handsome Luke, I'd be prepared to go anywhere with him.

Luke was right about the restaurant being a short drive away, as literally a few minutes later, we have stepped out of the car and stand looking at the front of the cute building. Its wooden frontage has a row of coloured fairy lights stretched out along it, and fake snow on the roof with a Santa clutching a chimney on the top that makes me smile.

'Oh, wow, this looks charming,' I say. I could almost be in a ski resort.

Inside, it definitely makes me think of après-ski times I enjoyed as a teenager with my friends, when I had a skiing trip to Austria with school. Although under the watchful eye of the teachers, we had alcohol-free fruit wine.

The wooden interior is cosy and inviting, with a log burner in one corner, and blonde wooden tables. There's a huge fir tree next to the bar, covered in all manner of decorations. Dotted around the restaurant are free-standing Christmas gonks that really do give it a Nordic feel.

A pretty waitress takes our coats and hangs them on a wooden stand near the door, before taking our drinks order.

'This is a real find.' I glance around at the other diners, mainly couples, sitting at tables with red candles in the middle of the chunky wooden tables.

'How has your day been? I noticed you were alone when we came to the cinema today,' says Luke as he pours us a glass of Glühwein.

'Shelley took ill, so I sent her home. Luckily, I managed to get cover and it was pretty quiet. Although maybe lucky is the wrong word. I always worry about whether the cinema will survive with so few customers.'

'I'm sure it will. Cinemas everywhere are struggling these days. I've heard even the big chains are half empty after the initial release of a film; everything is streamed so quickly.' He reminds me of a fact I'm only too aware of.

'You're right. So how about you?' I change the subject. 'Is everything all tied up with your uncle's estate now?'

'Yes,' he says as we both peruse a menu.

'Actually, talking of estates, I saw your old family home the other day. It's up for sale,' I tell him, taking a sip of my drink.

'Really? Well, whoever moves in there won't regret it, I'm sure.' He smiles. 'Oh, and Kay sends her love.' He takes me by surprise as he mentions her name.

'You spoke to her? I won't lie, I kind of got the impression you didn't want to talk about her when I asked.'

'I suppose you were right.' He sighs. 'We had a bit of a falling-out, but everything's okay now. She was thrilled to hear that I'd bumped into you. She wanted to know all about what you'd been up to.' He doesn't reveal what the falling-out was about, and I don't ask.

'That's wonderful! You can give her my number if you like; I'd love to find out what she's been up to.'

'Already have done.' He smiles. 'I thought it would be okay.'

'Of course it is.'

My mind flits to Kay, and all the wonderful times we had at the amateur dramatics. There was a lady there who was completely miffed when I got to play Frenchie once – just like I had at school – in a production of *Grease*, even though she was about fifty years old and could have hardly played a girl in high school. I think it was more to do with the fact I'd landed a major part after only being a member of the society for a few weeks.

Thoughts of those days come flooding back and I recall the letter Kay sent me, telling me she would be appearing in *Chicago* on Broadway and it all seems like another lifetime away. I can't wait for her to fill me in on the intervening years.

We dine on a delicious, warming veal casserole, with buttery mashed potatoes and red cabbage. I'm almost too full to manage a dessert, but there's a Toblerone cheesecake on the menu that I just can't resist, so I order two spoons and Luke – even though he tells me he isn't really a dessert man – manages a few mouthfuls and says it's very good.

'What a wonderful find,' I tell Luke as we climb into his car and head back to the village. 'I feel as though I've just been to Iceland, I really do. I must tell Ellie about this place; she would love all those gonks. Oh, and the Toblerone cheesecake. Toblerone is her favourite chocolate.'

'What's she up to this evening?' Luke asks.

'She's away with her father for a couple of nights.' I tell him all about them heading to Alton Towers as we drive, and the thought suddenly occurs to me that I have the house to myself.

'I bet she will love that.' He smiles.

'Oh, she definitely will. Robbie always comes along and manages to bring all the fun stuff with him,' I can't help saying.

'I guess that's what absent parents do,' says Luke. 'They

turn up and take the children out to do all the fun activities, while the other parent does the day-to-day stuff.'

That I can definitely vouch for. Robbie wasn't the one who consoled Ellie when her teenage hormones kicked in and she blamed me for the divorce, or cried when she fell out with her friends, or when she found her schoolwork too difficult. I consoled her when she sobbed the evening our beloved dog Toby died and Robbie was on holiday with his latest squeeze. Despite everything, I'm pleased they have a good relationship together. I would never turn her against her father, as the future will determine whether or not the relationship stays as strong when she becomes an adult, but I don't want to influence that.

My tummy turns over in anticipation as we drive, as I wonder whether Luke will accept an invitation to come inside for coffee. Will he think I mean something entirely different, and, truthfully, am I hoping there will be more than coffee?

Inside, we shrug our coats off and I light my Christmas Yankee Candle and head into the kitchen to fetch us both a brandy, that we drink from balloon glasses in front of the fire.

'I've had such a lovely evening, Luke, thank you,' I tell him as we sit beside each other on the comfy leather sofa. I've kicked my shoes off and stretch my feet out in front of the fire in front of me.

'You look beautiful in front of that fire. I like the way the light catches your hair.'

He gently runs his fingers through my hair and I feel my stomach flip. I sip the last of my drink before he takes the glass from my hand and places it on the coffee table. Then he locks eyes with me and eases me gently down onto the couch, kissing me deeply, and my heart is telling me there's absolutely nothing I want more than to be in this moment. Despite the feelings I'm experiencing, though, a few seconds later something stops me from letting things go any further and I sit upright.

'Are you okay?' asks Luke, slightly concerned he has done something wrong.

'Wonderful. I'm just worried things are going a little too fast,' I tell him truthfully.

'Who says they need to go any further? Can't we just snog like teenagers?' he says, before pulling me towards him and draping his arm around me. He runs his fingers up and down my arm affectionately, before he kisses the top of my head.

'You don't mind?'

'Of course I don't mind. Don't get me wrong, I'd like nothing more than to drag you upstairs and ravish you. God, ravish? I sound like a Victorian gent or something.'

'A gentleman would never say such a thing,' I joke and we both laugh.

I pour us both another drink and we spend the rest of the evening talking; sometimes I curl up and rest my head on Luke's shoulder, sometimes we kiss again, just like teenagers. And it feels so right.

Before long, I'm shocked when I glance at the clock and it's almost one o'clock in the morning. I stifle a yawn.

'Do you want to stay?' I'm aware Luke is over the alcohol limit. 'In the spare room, if you don't mind.'

'I'm not sure I could control myself, knowing you're in the next room,' he says, snuggling into me. 'But of course I don't mind. I'd phone a cab, although I am really comfortable here.'

'It's been a while since I've slept with anyone,' I explain. 'I don't want to rush things. I hope you understand.'

'Of course I do,' he says gently.

'But it's freezing out there and you could be waiting ages for a taxi to arrive.'

'That's true. And I'm so comfortable, I might just stay here, if you grab me a quilt.'

I head upstairs and return with a duvet and some pillows.

'Maybe I'll just stay here for a while too,' I say, snuggling under the covers with Luke and perhaps it's the wine, or the toasty warm room, but soon enough, we both fall fast asleep in each other's arms.

TWENTY-THREE

The next morning, Luke makes coffee as I prepare us a bacon sandwich in the kitchen.

'I really enjoyed last night,' says Luke as he reaches for my hand across the kitchen table. 'It was so good talking to you and finding out a bit more about you.'

'Same here,' I say, happy with the decision I made about not sleeping together, even though every fibre of my body was telling me otherwise. I still don't know of Luke's future plans and I don't want to get my heart broken all over again.

'What time do you finish work tomorrow?' Luke asks as he washes our coffee cups at the sink.

'Not until closing. But I might be able to switch to one o'clock. If Shelley is feeling better, I might be able to swap shifts with her admirer.' I smile to myself, thinking of Ed.

'In that case, do you fancy taking a ferry across the Mersey in the afternoon?'

'In this weather, are you mad?' Outside, the sky has turned that haunting grey shade, streaked with pink, and I'm convinced it might snow later.

'Probably. But there's something really exhilarating about sailing in cold weather. As long as you're all wrapped up against the elements. We could have a hot chocolate in New Brighton. It's years since I've been there. Andy said it's changed quite a bit.'

'It has had some regeneration since you last lived here,' I tell him. 'There's a bit of a funfair there, and some nice cafés along the front. They've modernised the area quite a bit. I don't think many people take the ferry in the winter, though. Only the mad ones.'

I recall taking Ellie over the water as a child, but only in the summer months where we would purchase a bucket and spade and she would play happily for hours on the small beach there, building sandcastles with Robbie. I'm still not convinced about a freezing cold sail, but there's always that hot chocolate to look forward to at the end of it, I suppose.

An hour later, I realise I need to shower and get ready for work.

'I should probably make a move too. I have a few things to do today. I'll pick you up from work tomorrow. Let me know if you manage to switch shifts.'

As I'm driving through the village, just after ten thirty, a woman flags me down, clearly in a panic.

'What's up?' I ask.

'Have you seen a black cockapoo on your travels?' she asks me breathlessly.

'What? No, I haven't. What's happened?'

'A dog's only gone and escaped from the salon.'

She must be a new dog groomer, one I don't recognise.

'Oh no. How?'

'I obviously hadn't closed the door properly, and I took a phone call mid groom. I put my scissors down, answered the phone, and the next thing the door opens and he's off. Oh God, what am I going to tell my client if I can't find him?' I can hear the panic in her voice rising.

'Right, let's stay calm. He can't have gone far, and he's probably headed for the farmers' fields. Hop in.' I've already opened the passenger door.

'Thank you!' Her cheeks are flushed as she's obviously been running around the village searching for the dog, who is called Oscar.

Driving along, we spot a dog bounding over a field, but as we draw closer we spot the dog's owner a few yards behind brandishing a lead and realise it isn't Oscar.

'Let's go round again in a loop; keep your eyes peeled.'

I'm cutting it fine getting in to work but it's only a short drive and I can't leave the groomer in this state.

'He can't have got far.' I try for a reassuring voice, as we drive. 'It's only a small village, and he'd stand out like a sore thumb walking along one of the main roads.'

'That's what I'm worried about, though. He's quite an expensive breed and there's a lot of dog theft about lately. He's a gorgeous boy; I really hope he's alright.' She looks as though she might burst into tears. 'If I don't find him, my reputation will be in ruins. It's my first day at the parlour today too.' She lets out a deep sigh.

I'm beginning to feel like it's a futile task when, as we approach the pub, we notice Helen petting a dog outside. 'Oh thank God.'

'Grab his collar, don't let it go,' the groomer yells at Helen, who is feeding the dog a titbit of food.

'Oh, it's one of yours? I found it in the yard, mooching around. I mustn't have locked the gate properly.'

'Thank you *so* much.' The relief is written all over the dog groomer's face as she attaches a lead to the dog and crosses the road to the grooming parlour.

'Poor girl,' I say to Helen. 'She's only just started the job. I imagine it wouldn't go down too well losing an animal on your first day.'

'Gosh, can you imagine? Good job you were there to help.'

'That's true. Actually, are you busy tonight?' I ask Helen. 'I know it's short notice, but are you up for a girls' night round at mine? Ellie's away and it's ages since we've had one. I'll cook some carbonara.'

'I'm definitely up for that; I love your pasta. It's usually quiet on a Thursday evening at the pub,' says Helen.

'Great. I'm heading to work now, so could you ask Frances and Jo too? Shall we say seven at mine?'

'Looking forward to it. Do you want me to bring anything?' asks Helen.

'Just yourself, maybe some red wine as I only have white in the fridge,' I tell her.

'Will do. See you later, Sarah, and thanks.'

One of the things I love about living in the village is how easy it is to make friends. Funnily enough, it's one of the things Ellie can't stand about village life, saying how everyone knows everyone else's business and she can't wait to move to the city when she's older, which saddens me a little. I never felt that way when I was her age, although I guess times have changed a lot.

Once again, I wonder whether it may take a few more years for Ellie to appreciate just how lucky she is to live in a place like this. The cottage will be her future inheritance after all, although I can see how tempting the bright lights of the city are when you're young. Ironically, many people crave the country-side when they are a lot older.

In between film screenings, I'm just making a batch of fresh popcorn, when in walks Greg Starr. I nudge Ed as he approaches and his eyes widen.

'Greg, what a pleasant surprise,' I tell him. I'm glad Shelley isn't in today. I could imagine her removing some hidden treat from under the counter in case he conducts an inspection of some sort.

'Hi, Sarah.'

'You remember Ed from the Christmas party; he's one of our part-time students.'

'Of course, how are you, Ed?' Greg extends his hand and shakes it warmly.

'Fine, thanks,' Ed replies, looking a little nervous.

'What are you studying at college?' asks Greg.

'Geography. I'm hoping to study it further at university.'

'Interesting. I imagine that might inspire you to travel.'

'Yeah, I've been saving up to do just that. This job has been brilliant for me.' Ed smiles.

'Glad to hear it. And good luck with your studies.'

'Thanks,' says Ed, rearranging some sweets in an effort to look busy.

'So, what brings you here?' I ask Greg when he's finished chatting to Ed.

'I just want to take a good look around the place. Remember I told you of a renovation? It's pencilled in for the first week in January. The cinema will close for a week.'

'It will close?' I ask, although I'm not sure how I thought it could remain open in the middle of a refurbishment.

'Don't worry, you will be paid your wages in full,' he reassures me. 'But we need it doing sooner rather than later. There are some blockbuster movies out in February. If the Roxy has any chance of competing with the larger cinema complexes, it has to look fresh and modern,' he explains.

'I understand that,' I reluctantly agree.

'We'll be running an advertising campaign too,' he tells me, and I can't help thinking maybe there should have been a bit more of that with the current cinema. I suppose nothing stays the same in life, and change and innovation is essential in order to survive in an ever-changing world.

Greg has a look around the cinema with the surveyor who has just joined him, after using the bathroom, and I listen as they talk of the new seating system and lots of photographs are taken. They glance up at the Victorian ceiling with the magnificent plaster rose at the centre.

'Please tell me that's going to stay,' I can't help saying as I glance at the beautiful plasterwork.

'Pending another survey, yes, it will. It's something of the cinema we can preserve, plus replacing the ceiling would be a massive undertaking,' Greg reassures me. 'There will be new carpeting, reclining chairs and spotlights set into the flooring. The stage is going; there's no need for that anymore.'

I stare at the front of the auditorium with the heavy red curtains. Years ago, the stage would have been used for entertainment, when a pianist would play for the crowd before the film began. Probably better than the endless advertisements today.

'The sound system will be updated too,' Greg says, summing up his appraisal. 'The last one has been in place since the late nineties.'

'We can only hope this all works. Will the price of the admission need to be increased?'

'Not necessarily. The costs can be absorbed from one of our busier cinemas, although there may be a small increase. Nothing like the major chains, though,' he informs me. 'Anyway, Sarah, I would like to personally thank you for being at the helm of this branch so loyally over the years. And the idea of hosting children's parties is a great thing. I know Christmas is almost upon us, but maybe in the new year it's something you could advertise in the local press. It can't do any harm.'

'No, it can't, that's a good idea, and something I was thinking about, actually. We have a party in this afternoon. Twenty children.'

'That's wonderful. It's a pity I didn't arrive a bit later to see how it all works.'

'Are you sure about that?' I say doubtfully 'Twenty overexcited kids?'

'Maybe not.' He grins. 'Anyway, we'd better be making a move.' He glances at his watch.

I walk Greg and the surveyor to the door.

'Bye, Sarah. Hope the party goes well. I'll keep you updated with news of the refurbishment.'

It's surprising how all children's parties are different. The last one, with the sugary cake as large as a wedding cake, was in stark contrast to the party this afternoon that had a low-sugar, gluten-free ensemble. The children had names like Phoebe and Sebastian and the snacks consisted of platters of carrot sticks, hummus and low-salt crisps. They were all so well behaved it almost didn't feel like a children's party, and I hoped they were having a good time. The kids deposited every bit of paper from their snacks into the bins, and every one of them said thank you as they left, telling me how much they loved the film with huge smiles on their faces. Jeremy, the birthday boy, said it was the best party he had ever had, never imagining he would ever have a private screening of a movie just for himself and his classmates. Don't get me wrong, the kids from Imani's party were a great bunch too, polite and very well behaved – considering the amount of sugar that had been consumed – although the cinema did look like there had been an explosion of the popcorn machine inside the auditorium.

'Goodnight, Ed, thanks for coming to the rescue for the kids' party,' I tell him as we lock up and leave. *Elf* is still proving popular and I'm hoping there will be more families here over the Christmas holidays.

'Not a problem. The extra money is always useful. Shelley

will be gutted she missed out on the kids' party, though.' He grins.

'Actually, I don't think she will. There weren't enough sugar products,' I say and he laughs.

'True story. Night, Sarah.'

TWENTY-FOUR

After a quick change, I'm sipping a glass of wine in the kitchen when the doorbell rings.

Jo is first to arrive, looking sensational as per usual, wearing a pair of black trousers and a blood-red blouse that matches her lipstick. She's brandishing a bottle of champagne. She kisses me on both cheeks as she walks inside.

'Thanks for the invite; it's been a while since we had a girls' night. Although, actually, I think it's probably my turn.'

'Don't worry about that. I thought Francis would have arrived with you. And champagne!' I say, clocking the bottle of Moët she's carrying. 'What's the occasion?'

'Do we need a reason? It's nearly Christmas, after all. Oh, and Frances isn't coming as she said she had something on this evening.'

'I hope she's alright. I don't think she seemed her usual sparkly self when I last saw her. What do you think?' I ask.

'Maybe not, but when I asked if she was alright, she told me she was just tired. Which is entirely believable at this time of year as she's rushed off her feet,' Jo reasons.

'She told me the same thing. Even so, I hope she's alright. Perhaps we ought to take her a small gift from us all to cheer her up.'

'Good idea. As long as it's not flowers.' Jo smiles.

A couple of minutes later, Helen arrives carrying red wine and brandishing a dessert. 'A home-made pavlova,' she says proudly.

'Oh, perfect, I love a pavlova.'

I usher them into the kitchen and pop the delicious-looking pavlova that's loaded with red berries into the fridge.

'How are we both this evening?' I ask as they sit around the large kitchen table.

'All good, thanks, although some toerag has stolen the charity box from the bar,' Helen says with a deep sigh.

'Oh no, that's awful.'

'I know. They probably thought there would be few quid in it, being around Christmastime, but it had only been emptied last week. They'd be lucky if there was a tenner in it. All I can say is, if they genuinely need the money, then God bless them.'

'That's very forgiving,' says Jo as she pops the cork on the champagne.

'It's Christmas, the season of goodwill. On the other hand, if they haven't stolen it out of necessity, I hope they catch an STI over the festive season.'

My friends asks me how things are going with Luke.

'Really good. Great, actually, but I don't want to fall for him,' I tell them, wondering if it might be a little bit late for that. I grab some champagne flutes and Jo pours us all a glass of fizz.

'Why not?' asks Jo as she takes a sip of her drink. 'Life is for living.' She winks.

'I know, but I'm just not exactly sure of his plans,' I explain. 'He lives in America and he's a bit vague as to when he's heading back.'

'Maybe you could persuade him to stay a bit longer,' says Helen, before sniffing appreciatively at the carbonara I have just placed down on the table in a huge white dish, telling everyone to help themselves.

'Maybe. I suppose I'll just have to wait and see how things turn out.'

'Ooh, this carbonara is even better than the last one,' says Helen. She makes an appreciative noise as she eats.

'I'll second that,' says Jo. 'I can never quite get the sauce right.'

She helps herself to some salad, but avoids the garlic bread that Helen and I happily tuck in to.

'So why did you say Frances couldn't make it this evening?' I ask as I pour us all a glass of wine, having polished off the champagne.

'Something about an appointment somewhere, but she was vague about it,' says Jo. 'I must admit, I did wonder what type of appointment she could be attending in the evening. You're right, I think we should all arrange to visit her together and take her a gift.'

'And drag the truth out of her,' says Helen with her usual candour.

Frances, who is in her early thirties, lives with her mother in one of the five sandstone cottages in the village. Her mother purchased it when Frances opened the shop in the courtyard. She'd just broken off an engagement with her fiancé at the time and was happy to move in with her mum, a sprightly widow in her late sixties. She's had a couple of boyfriends since, but says she is far too busy with the shop and early mornings at the flower market to even find the time for a boyfriend. I don't suppose she would find one anyway, unless she actively searched for one. Single men aren't exactly in abundance in the village.

Helen tells Jo all about the escaping dog this morning.

'Gosh, I'm glad it turned up. Imagine having to tell an owner you'd lost their dog.' She takes another sip of wine.

We're finishing dinner, and I'm just taking the gorgeous-looking pavlova from the fridge, when there's a knock on the front door. I'm surprised when I see Frances standing on the doorstep.

'Fran, hi! Come on in!'

'I know I've missed dinner, but I need a large glass of wine.' She waves the bottle of red wine she is carrying.

The girls are thrilled to see Fran as she enters the kitchen, where I immediately pour her a drink and she eyes the pavlova in the centre of the table.

'Oh, my goodness, that looks incredible. At least I haven't missed dessert.'

'There is actually a bit of carbonara left, but it's not so good if it isn't eaten straight away.'

I point to the slightly congealed remains in the dish.

Her smile has returned and she looks like the sunshine once more.

'Honestly, I'm fine. Wine and dessert will do.'

'I'm so glad you're here, Fran, we were all worried about you,' says Helen as she cuts a slice of the pavlova and slides it across the table to her.

'I know you were and thank you. All of you, I really appreciate it and maybe you were right to be concerned. I know I've been a little evasive lately, but I was worried about something.' She takes a glug of her red wine.

'Worried? What about?' I ask.

'I found a lump in my breast. And I ignored it, too frightened to go to the doctor,' she tells us and there's a hush in the room. 'Anyway, I finally plucked up the courage to see a doctor. I've just had the results back from the investigation.'

'And?' says Helen, placing her hand over Fran's.

'I can breathe again.' She smiles. 'A benign lump.'

'Oh, Fran, that's wonderful.'

We all instinctively go to her, and suddenly there's a group hug and Francis stifles a sob.

'Oh, you're all so lovely. I'm so lucky to live here. And I'm sorry I never confided in you all; I just wanted to know what I was dealing with first.'

'Of course you did,' I tell her. 'And you're here now, that's the main thing, isn't it?'

Fran nods as her eyes moisten with tears.

We enjoy the fabulous pavlova, drink wine and finish the evening off with a Tia Maria coffee in a tall glass mug.

'I'm glad everything turned out okay, Fran, but maybe you ought to take a little time out. When was the last time you had a holiday?' asks Jo. 'All work and no play is not good for anyone.'

'Three years ago. And you're right, I do need a break. Maybe I'll take one in January when it's quiet at the shop.'

'Barbados is lovely in January,' says Jo. 'Me and Vince cele-brated a wedding anniversary there one year. It was wonderful.'

'Do you know, I have always fancied the Caribbean,' says Fran. 'Maybe I'll give that some thought. I'm sure Mum would love to join me too, she's been banging on about me going on a cruise with her, but cruising isn't really my thing.'

We carry on catching up, with a healthy amount of giggling, and all too soon I'm seeing everyone to the door and thanking them for coming.

'Thanks, Sarah. It's been a great evening,' says Fran as they leave. Squeezing me tightly, she continues, 'Exactly what I needed. It's good to know I have such great friends.'

'My place next time,' says Jo. 'We can peruse the takeaway menus.' She laughs.

Jo openly admits to disliking cooking in the evening, espe-cially after being in the café all day. We normally order in when we visit her place, a handsome Victorian red-brick semi, and no one minds.

As I close the door, I think of Fran's words and realise she's not the only one who is lucky to live here and have such amazing friends. I also feel truly blessed.

TWENTY-FIVE

'Oh, Mum, it was amazing,' Ellie gushes as she tells me all about her time at Alton Towers, practically the minute she walks in the door.

'Everything about it was brilliant. It didn't matter that the rides were closed; the waterpark was open and the Winter Wonderland was magical. And the food was all yum.' She chatters away excitedly.

Robbie is sitting opposite me at the kitchen table, sipping coffee, and seemingly in no hurry to leave after dropping Ellie off.

'It sounds really lovely. I can imagine those illuminated forest walks really being something.'

'You could have come with us,' says Robbie, looking at me and smiling.

I'm about to say, *why on earth would I do that?* when I notice Ellie glancing between us and smiling. I realise, not for the first time, that no matter what has gone between us or how long we have been separated, Ellie would like nothing more than for us to be together as a family again. I wonder whether children, no matter what age they are, always harbour that desire deep down? My mind often flits to a time in the future, a graduation ceremony, maybe even a wedding, where we will both be expected to attend. I have to reluctantly admit, though, I don't think Robbie will ever let Ellie down when it comes to being present for the important things in her life.

'I don't remember being invited,' I say jokingly. 'Although I'm not sure I could have taken the time off work anyway.'

'You might prefer it in the summer when the rides are open,' says Robbie, a mischievous look on his face. 'I'll provide the sick bucket.'

'Very funny.' I pull a face at him, and he laughs. Robbie is referring to a time he persuaded me to go on a roller coaster and I was violently sick at the end of it. He never let me live that one down.

'You won't get me on a roller coaster again in a hurry.' I shake my head.

'Or the waltzer, Mum,' Ellie reminds me. 'I remember you staggering when you got off them that time we went to Blackpool for the day.'

'Oh, I did, didn't I? I'm sure the people in the gift shop thought I was drunk.' I giggle at the memory.

'Right, I need to be getting ready for work.' I stand, hoping Robbie will take the hint, and thankfully he does as he drains his coffee.

'See you soon, gorgeous.' He kisses Ellie on the top of the head and crushes her in an embrace.

'Bye, Dad, and thanks,' she says, resting her head against his chest for a second before he departs.

'Is it okay if I go and stay at Izzy's tonight?' asks Ellie.

'Sure, but I'd maybe avoid going into town unless it's quite early. There's lots of Christmas parties this week and some people might be a bit the worse for wear,' I warn her.

'No, were just going to stay in and chill. Her mum and dad are meeting friends for dinner or something.'

'Okay. And don't forget it's the recital of *A Christmas Carol* at St George's Hall tomorrow evening.'

'Ooh, is that tomorrow? I'm looking forward to that; I haven't seen Jess and Zak for ages.'

'You haven't, have you? It will be nice to have a catch-up.'

It makes me realise how busy people's lives are, and how Christmas is the ideal time to reconnect.

'And just so you don't worry, 'cos I know what you're like,' says Ellie, but smiling. 'Izzy's mum is going to pick me up from here around four o'clock.'

'That's great.'

She crosses the room and hugs me. 'I'll put a wash on before I go to Izzy's. All the stuff I wore at Alton Towers,' she tells me, before she heads upstairs.

'Okay, who are you and what have you done with my daughter?' I ask and she laughs.

Ellie's room tends to have clothes strewn around or piled up in corners, and I constantly have to remind her to put any washing in the basket on the landing. Maybe she's growing up a tiny bit, I think to myself. And looking at her, once more I'm quite proud of the woman she is becoming.

TWENTY-SIX

'I'm glad you're feeling better.'

'Thanks. I haven't had a bad cold like that in years; I hate being sick.' Shelley pulls a face.

When I arrived at the cinema, she was chatting to Ed. Who isn't supposed to be on shift yet.

'Can't keep away from the place, hey?' I tease Ed, then wish I hadn't as he goes bright red.

'Just seeing if Shelley fancies a spin later, now that she's better. Anyway, see you later.'

Ed's wearing his long parka with a black roll-neck jumper beneath. His floppy hair is almost covering one eye.

'You two seem to be getting along well,' I comment, even though Shelley told me she isn't after anything serious with hopefully going to university.

'I suppose we are.' She smiles. 'He was absolutely lovely when I wasn't feeling well; he even called around with a bunch of flowers one night. My mum was well impressed.' She smiles again. 'And he knows I like to read, so he bought me a couple of paperbacks and dropped them off too. He said he took a chance on what he thought I might like, and his choices were spot on.'

'That's really thoughtful. And quite romantic too, really. I've never met a man who has brought me a book.'

'Me neither, until now,' she says with a look of affection on her face.

I've swapped half of my shift with Ed, who's returning later, as I've unbelievably agreed to go on a sail on the Mersey with Luke to New Brighton. He texted me earlier as I was about to leave for work, to finalise when and where he's collecting me and I told him that, thankfully, Ed was happy to step in. I say thankfully, but let's see how I feel later after I'm bordering on hypothermia. I've brought a woollen hat, scarf and thick boots with me today, as well as a chunky jumper, ready for when Luke collects me.

All too soon, Ed is back for the afternoon, happy to be working with Shelley, I think.

'Thanks for this, Ed. I hope you two have a nice afternoon. Oh, and I've counted those packets of sweets.' I wink, and Ed looks mildly embarrassed.

'I've never taken anything without putting the money in the till,' he tells me sincerely.

'She's talking to me.' Shelley laughs. 'Although to be fair, I've been paying too, despite the rubbish wages. I don't want to be contributing to the cinema going bust.'

'See you later, guys. Don't forget to lock up.'

'I won't, now go and have fun freezing to death on the ferry.'

'Cheers for that.'

Outside, Luke is leaning against his car, dressed in dark jeans and a thick bubble jacket. Even in a woollen hat he still manages to look stylish and effortlessly sexy, like a model in an outdoor clothing catalogue.

'How are you?' He walks towards me and kisses me lightly on the lips and I feel a bolt of warmth even on a day like this.

'I'm good, thanks. How about you?'

'Fine, are you ready for this, then? Ready to blow away the cobwebs.' He rubs his hands together enthusiastically.

'Ready to be blown away more like,' I say but can't help laughing at his enthusiasm all the same.

There's literally five people on board, including a retired couple wrapped up for an Arctic mission. We get chatting and they say they are crossing the water to spend Christmas with their daughter and each have a pull-along suitcase.

'We could have driven through the tunnel,' the woman tells us, 'but it feels like more of an adventure this way, and hubby's an old seafarer, so any excuse we get out on the water.' She laughs.

Her husband is chatting to the ferry's captain on the sailing deck, whilst his wife glances at the scenery all around, clutching a warming cup of tea from a flask. I can't help admiring their adventurous spirit, especially at their age. There's a bloke around the same age as Luke, staring out to sea and not really engaging with anyone, lost in his thoughts. I wonder what his story is? We all have one. In my imagination, he's just out of a relationship and is heading across the water to see friends. Or maybe he's collecting a son or daughter. Of course, he could have simply been shopping in Liverpool, yet he has no shopping bags.

We've disembarked now and I tell Luke about my thoughts on the single guy as we walk.

'Or maybe he's just committed a crime and is heading off out of town,' I suggest.

'There are faster ways to flee than on a leisurely river cruise,' Luke replies, laughing.

'Ah, but it's not the first place you would think of looking, is it? Especially in this cold weather.'

'No, I suppose not. So, you like people watching and guessing their stories, do you? What do you reckon people would think about us?' he asks.

'I'm not sure really. I'm not even sure I know what to make of us.' The words I've been thinking are out of my mouth.

We're walking along the promenade and Luke stops and stares at me.

'What do you mean, you don't know what to make of us?'

'I mean, it's really nice and everything, I really love spending time with you, but...'

'But?'

'Well, I don't know what to expect from this relationship. Is it even a relationship?' I ask honestly, surprised by my own directness.

We pass a little fairground where the sound of children's laughter can be heard coming from a carousel, alongside a stall selling hot donuts, drinks and crêpes. Luke doesn't immediately answer my question, and soon we are in front of a cosy-looking pub and we head inside and find a table. The pub is warm and welcoming with a Christmas tree at the entrance and a thick holly and ivy garland stretched across the fireplace. It's not long before we are tucking into tasty Brie and cranberry sandwiches and warming mulled wine.

'So, are you going to answer my question?' I ask finally, feeling emboldened by the mulled wine.

'I was coming to that.' He fixes me with his gorgeous brown eyes. 'What you said made me think. I haven't been entirely fair with you, have I?'

'Not really.' I'm wondering what he is alluding to. 'For all I know, I could be just someone you're happily having a brief fling with while you're over in England on business.'

'Is that what you really think?'

'I'm not sure. I know your life is in America, so I assume you will be heading back there after Christmas, and I'm just wondering, what then?'

In a way, I'm annoyed with myself for allowing myself to develop feelings for him. My life before he arrived was relatively uncomplicated. Despite the trials of raising a teenager, post-Robbie, and the uncertainty over the cinema, everything was ticking over nicely. His presence here took me completely off guard.

'Well, the first thing I have to tell you is that I'm not sure when I'm heading back to America,' he reveals. 'I've loved everything about being back here in Liverpool. I think I've fallen in love with the city all over again. Maybe even not just the place.'

His eyes lock with mine as he reaches across the table and takes my hand in his.

My heart is thumping in my chest at his words. Is Luke trying to tell me that he's fallen in love with me?

'But I may not have been entirely honest about one thing, though.' He sighs.

'What's that?' I ask, the expression on his face making me dread the answer a little.

'Remember I told you about a relationship with a woman back home? The one that didn't work out?'

'Yes.' I wonder what's coming next.

'She's my wife.'

'You're married!' I raise my voice so loudly the couple at the next table turn and look across at us both, probably thinking they are witnessing some dramatic love triangle.

'Soon to be divorced,' he says. 'In fact, the divorce should have been finalised, but she was dragging her feet signing the papers. Sorry I didn't say anything; I didn't want you running a mile,' he says quietly. 'Not when I've only just run into you again.'

His words sound so sincere, yet I'm filled with confusion. Why didn't Luke tell me he was separated? I'm divorced too, so I would have completely understood. But perhaps he's right, if I knew he was in the throes of divorce maybe I wouldn't even have entertained the idea of a future for us.

Not that I was ever certain about that, given the miles between us.

I try to be reasonable. He's almost divorced after all, and did say his ex was the one who was dragging her feet, so clearly Luke is the one who is keen to press on with the divorce. I paint on a smile, trying to hide how much this has shaken me.

'Maybe you should have told me sooner,' I say eventually. 'Is there anything else you have failed to mention, such as, do you have any children?'

'No.' He shakes his head. 'Which is probably a blessing, really. Oh, Sarah, I realise how this must sound and I'm sorry I wasn't completely truthful. But for me, the marriage was over a long time ago,' he reveals.

I'm still reeling, but I try not to let the news of his marriage spoil things. After another drink, we take a wander around the little Christmas market, where I buy some Stollen and a cute little hand-carved wooden jewellery box, that I think will make a nice Christmas gift for Cassie. The smell of a hog roast filters from a stall and a bunch of people are crammed inside a wooden bar strung with lights, drinking German beer.

Fortified with mulled wine, the journey home on the ferry doesn't seem quite so cold and I quite enjoy the sail, once more marvelling at the city waterfront and its striking buildings as we approach the Pier Head. There are around a dozen passengers heading back to Liverpool, in a festive mood, chatting animatedly and laughing. When we disembark the ferry, and head towards the car park, Luke takes my hand in his and a warmth floods through me and any confusion I might have disappears. For now, at least.

TWENTY-SEVEN

The next morning, I'm getting ready for work when my phone rings. The caller display shows an unknown number, which I often ignore as it's generally someone trying to sell me something, but today I take the call.

'Sarah, is that you?' A woman with an American accent is on the other end of the phone.

'Yes.'

'It's me, Kay.'

'Oh, my goodness, Kay! How are you?' I'm thrilled to hear the voice of my old friend on the other end of the phone.

'I'm good, thanks, how are you?'

'I'm really well. Gosh, Kay, it's so good to hear from you.'

'You too. Luke gave me your number. I've been meaning to call but wasn't sure when would be the right time. Are you free to talk?' she asks.

'I am. I'm getting ready to go to work, but I have a little time.'

Which is true, as I always allow myself more time than I need in the morning as I'm an early riser.

For the next ten minutes, Kay tells me all about her life in America, filling me in on the missing years.

'So, tell me all about you. How is life treating you?' she asks.

I give her a brief rundown of my life in England, which doesn't sound half as interesting as her life by comparison, and reminds me of one of the first conversations I had with Luke.

'Luke has told me how thrilled he was to run into you,' she tells me.

'Really? He said that?'

'Of course. He talks of little else during our conversations. At least we are on better speaking terms now. I'm afraid we had a bit of a falling-out,' she reveals, echoing what Luke told me.

'I'm glad you're speaking again,' I say, not asking what the falling-out was about, but she tells me anyway.

'We argued over his ex-wife, which, of course, wasn't his fault, but she kept calling around to my house asking where he was. Sometimes she was drunk. I told her he had gone overseas, but I don't think she believed me. I told him it wasn't fair that Mum and I were dealing with his ex, while he swanned off to England.'

'But he was here to deal with your uncle's estate?' I enquire.

'He was, yes. Which could have been wrapped up in several days, but then he decides to stay. His ex, Jane, can't seem to accept the break-up, even though she cheated on my brother. More than once,' she reveals.

'She cheated on him?' This is something Luke certainly didn't mention to me.

'She did.' She lets out a sigh. 'She hurt him a lot. I think he tried to make things work, but she was never right for him. I think he had been unhappy for quite a while.' I recall Luke saying the marriage had been over in his mind for a long time.

'She's quite unstable, to be honest,' Kay continues. 'I think Luke thought that marriage might have given her the stability she craved, but it would appear it didn't. She wasn't prepared to give up her partying ways, which often led to infidelity.'

'Oh, my goodness, poor Luke.'

'I know. When he first filed for divorce she seemed accepting of the situation, but lately she's been drinking and behaving erratically, turning up here at my house or next door at Mum's at all hours, demanding to know of his whereabouts.'

'I'm sorry you've had to deal with that; it can't have been easy for you.'

'It wasn't. Especially with Mum recovering from a recent hip operation.'

'Luke mentioned that. How is she doing?'

'Pretty good, actually. Stronger every day, though she could have done without the drama of Luke's ex turning up on the doorstep. Thankfully things have calmed down a little now, after I issued her with a restraining order.'

'That sounds awful. I'm glad things have quietened down, though.'

'Me too. Anyway, Luke tells me he is staying in England for a while and I realise he has every right to go where he wants. He was the injured party in the marriage.'

We chat for a while longer, as I try to process what I have just been told. Luke had been cheated on by his wife, so he must have been hurting recently and yet I had no idea. And he's told Kay he is staying in England for a while.

'Oh, Sarah, it's been so great talking to you,' she says as we wrap up the call. 'And I would love to see you. Maybe I'll take a trip to England and see you and my brother in the near future.'

'I would absolutely love that, Kay,' I tell her, hoping that she really means it.

We finish the call with promises to stay in touch and I'm thrilled my old friend has made contact with me.

That afternoon at work, I go over the conversation with Kay, still shocked that Luke's ex-wife has been giving his family a hard time, demanding to know where he is. I also remember him telling me the marriage had been over for him for a long time, and can't even imagine what he must have been going through emotionally.

My shift goes quickly; it's been a fairly busy day at the cinema. Tonight, it's the recital of *A Christmas Carol* at St George's Hall with Cassie and the children, and I'm really looking forward to it. I'm actually quite glad I'm not seeing Luke this evening. I need time to mull over how things are going between us and what the future might hold. And I think Luke does too.

TWENTY-EIGHT

Ellie and I take the train to Cassie's house in Allerton, where she has prepared a tasty hot buffet in her spacious kitchen and I present her with a Christmas flower bouquet, courtesy of Francis at the flower shop.

'Oh, thank you so much, Sarah, you shouldn't have. They're absolutely gorgeous.'

'Just a little thanks for the food, and for driving us into town this evening.'

She takes the pretty red and cream floral display from me and arranges it in a large vase. We feast on chicken wings, hot curries and lots of little food parcels, samosa style, as well as home-made mince pies with buttery, melt-in-the-mouth pastry. I present her with the Stollen I bought at the New Brighton Christmas market and she accepts it gratefully, offering to slice it up and serve it, but I tell her to keep it for another time as there is already enough food to feed an army here and we've already sampled the delicious mince pies. Jess takes Ellie to see her newly decorated bedroom and Zak stands for a few minutes, not sure whether to follow them upstairs or not.

'So how are things, Zak? Are you still into your gaming?' I ask him as he grabs a handful of peanuts from a bowl.

'I don't do it as much as I used to,' he says. 'I've joined a gym with some of the lads from college, so I go there quite a bit now.'

'I think girls are more of an interest to him now,' James whispers, when Zak heads to the lounge with Ellie and Jess, who have returned from upstairs. 'I'm glad he's joined the gym, though. He was spending too much time in front of that computer screen, in my opinion.'

'A lot of kids are into their gaming, although I guess it's all about balance,' I say, thankful I don't have a son I have to drag from the Xbox every now and then to take some exercise. Ellie's never really been into gaming, as she prefers watching movies and reading.

After finishing the delicious buffet, we head off. Half an hour later, we've parked up in town and climbed out of Cassie's seven-seater people carrier, and are ascending the steps of St George's Hall.

'Gosh, it's such a splendid building, isn't it? It takes my breath away every time I come here,' says James.

'It is,' I say, staring at the wonderful building, recently featured in a new Batman movie.

We take our seats inside as excited whispers can be heard around the hall that looks hauntingly pretty, with strategically placed candles in sconces all around the room. When everyone has taken their seats, we are respectfully asked to switch off our phones and asked to refrain from taking photographs during the recital. Soon, the lights are dimmed and a pair of heavy red velvet curtains slide open at the front of the room to reveal a stage bathed in candlelight in all its glory. A hush descends all over the hall as the recital begins.

'Marley was dead.' Gerald Dickens has appeared on the stage, dressed in full Dickensian attire, including a green velvet waistcoat. The scene in the background is of a lounge with a leather chesterfield chair, a fireplace against a red-flock-wallpa-pered wall, and a dark-wooden bookcase.

From the moment Gerald steps onto the stage, he has the audience in the palm of his hand, with his deep, velvety voice. It's an incredible one-man show, with Gerald taking on the voices of the main characters in the play effortlessly, showing a true talent that has us all marvelling. There are some swift scenery changes too, from Scrooge's counting house to Bob Cratchit's home, each one evoking vivid memories of the movie. The scenery is exactly how I had imagined it in my mind's eye when I read the book when I was younger, even though the film version didn't exactly match up to the images I had conjured up. Then again, I've only watched the black-and-white version with Alastair Sim. No wonder Ellie was a bit spooked when she was little.

It's a glorious reading of the story, with plenty of humour, pathos and even audience interaction at various points. At the end of the recital, there is rousing applause from the audience, who are all on their feet.

'Oh, I really enjoyed that,' I say as we descend the steps of the hall and say our goodbyes, before Ellie and I head to the train station, a short walk away. I politely decline a lift home from my friends as they would have to drive half an hour out of their way, when the train will have us home in no time at all. We can then pick up a taxi for the short ride to the village.

'You should come and have a sleepover one weekend. In fact, you should all come. We could have a games weekend,' suggests James, who loves his games and is quite competitive as I recall.

'Not Monopoly?' Zak rolls his eyes, but he is smiling. 'Although, I actually don't mind really as I am the undefeated champion,' he declares proudly.

'Sounds like a challenge,' says Ellie, which it probably is as she always wins when we play Monopoly at home.

'Don't forget the Logo game. There's a new edition out; we should buy it,' says Jess.

'That's a great idea, I love the Logo game. We will definitely have to arrange something,' I agree, thinking that a games evening with my friends sounds like a wonderful idea.

We say our goodnights with lingering hugs, Zak giving the briefest of hugs and looking slightly uncomfortable doing so, which isn't unusual for an eighteen-year-old boy, I guess.

It's a little after ten o'clock when we arrive home and, pulling my phone from my pocket, I consider texting Luke, but I decide against it. He knows I am out for the evening, so maybe I will give him a quick call in the morning. It seems odd for Luke to be spending Christmas Day with his friend Andy, although now I realise why Luke is not rushing to return home to America for the festive season, as he's going through a messy divorce. I just can't help feeling slightly disappointed that he didn't tell me, but then he's explained that I might have run a mile had I known the truth, even though I'm pretty sure I wouldn't have.

There's just a couple of days until Christmas now, and I feel like I have so much to do and not enough time. But I remind myself that a lot of people feel this way and that everything is under control and, actually, there is nothing to worry about. I have all Ellie's presents wrapped and hidden away in boxes beneath my bed and I'm collecting a fresh turkey from a farm close by tomorrow, as it's Christmas Eve, along with some fresh vegetables. I'm mentally going over everything when I realise I have forgotten to buy some Christmas crackers, which I will need to pick up from somewhere. The Christmas cake will be iced tomorrow evening and I will make a batch of mince pies with Ellie before we head to the local church for the Christmas Eve carol service.

I did think about buying Luke a gift, but wasn't sure whether or not he would have been embarrassed. We haven't discussed gifts, or even been together very long. Are we together, as in, a proper couple? I'm not even sure, but I considered buying him something as a thank you for taking me out and being so generous paying for our meals. I realise I'm completely overthinking this and suddenly feel a bit mean for not having a gift for Luke. Perhaps I'll buy some whisky, which he mentioned he enjoys at Christmas. I do hope Luke enjoys Christmas Day and like to think that at least some of his plans include spending some time with me over the Christmas holidays.

TWENTY-NINE

'Have you forgotten your key again?'

I prise myself from the sofa, where I'm watching an episode of *Jamie's Best Ever Christmas*, and open the door of my pretty cottage to find Ellie standing there. Only she isn't alone.

'Thanks for this, Sarah, and it's only for a few days, I promise. I'll be out of your hair after Christmas.'

I widen my eyes in surprise and glance at my daughter, who is biting her lip and twirling a strand of her long blonde hair around her finger. Robbie, with his curly brown hair and twinkly blue eyes, kisses me on the cheek, before carrying his large leather holdall into the hallway, beaming like a schoolboy.

'What the hell, Ellie?' I hiss.

'Sorry, Mum, I kind of said he could stay for Christmas.' She shrugs her shoulders as she follows him inside.

'You did what?' I can hardly believe my ears. 'You know I never agreed to this.'

'I know, but you wouldn't want him to be sleeping on the streets over Christmas, would you?'

I count to ten before I give her an answer. My ex-husband on the doorstep at Christmas! That's just about all I need.

THIRTY

It's Christmas Eve and I still can't believe Robbie has pitched up here to join us for Christmas Day. I'm mad at Ellie for doing this behind my back, but tell myself that it won't be for long and if it makes her happy, then perhaps, strictly just this once, I'll go along with it.

I spend the morning dashing about cleaning the house from top to bottom, whilst Robbie has settled himself in front of the television, giggling at reruns of *The Vicar of Dibley*, the one where the vicar eats several Christmas lunches. I'm in the kitchen with Ellie, grabbing a coffee whilst she unloads the dishwasher.

'I can't believe it's Christmas Eve,' she says, joining me at the kitchen table, sipping from a bottle of flavoured water she's pulled from the fridge. 'And I'm sorry I never told you about Dad.'

At least she has the good grace to apologise.

'I won't lie, I was mad at you for going against my wishes, but he's here now, so let's make the best of it.' I muster up a smile.

'Thanks, Mum. And it's only for a day or two. I told you he would be spending it on his own otherwise and no one should spend Christmas Day alone. He is my dad, after all,' she says in a small voice, managing to make me feel guilty, even though he isn't my problem.

'I know.' I sigh, trying not to sound heartless. 'I just wasn't expecting this. I don't want a fight on Christmas Eve, but I told you I didn't want your dad here for Christmas Day, yet you went ahead and invited him anyway.'

'Sorry. I'm sure it will all be okay, though.' She at least has the decency to look a little sheepish.

'Go and give your room a going-over.' I hand her a duster, some polish and a bin liner. 'And bring some glasses and cups down. We seem to be missing some from the kitchen.'

'Sorry, Mum, yeah, I will.' She disappears into her room as I run the hoover over the stairs and landing carpet. When I switch it off later, I hear Robbie shouting to me from downstairs.

'Do you want a hand with anything, Sarah?' he asks. I'm about to say no, when I head downstairs.

'Actually, yes,' I tell him, wondering why the heck I am running around like a headless chicken as he lounges in front of the TV munching on a box of mint Matchmakers. If he's going to stay here at such a busy time, he can blooming well pull his weight. 'Maybe you could go and collect the turkey and vegetables from the farm shop. Oh, and pick up some Christmas crackers from Tesco Express too; I completely forgot to buy some.'

'Will there be any crackers left?' he asks doubtfully. 'It's Christmas Eve,' he says, as if I need reminding.

'There were tons the other day,' I tell him. 'Maybe buy those first, then go to the farm. Just in case the car is stolen with our Christmas lunch inside,' I say and he laughs and says things like that don't happen in small villages.

'You can't be sure. The charity box was stolen from the pub the other week, apparently,' I inform him.

Robbie heads off, giving me a break from his unexpected presence. As I finish the cleaning, Ellie emerges from her room, with four mugs and two glasses on a tray. One of them is my Mother's Day mug that she bought me last year and I hope there isn't green fungus growing in the bottom of it.

'Don't worry, I've rinsed them,' she says, as if reading my mind. 'I just forgot to bring them downstairs.' Luckily, she has a sink in her bedroom.

'Okay. Here.' I hand her the hoover and she hands me the tray that I head downstairs with. This time tomorrow, I'll be entertaining my family for Christmas lunch, which now happens to include Robbie. Deep down, I suppose Ellie's right; I wouldn't like anyone to spend Christmas Day alone. It wouldn't feel right.

I just hope Luke doesn't expect to be invited in this evening after I've been out with him for a drink. I wonder why I don't want to tell him about Robbie turning up with Ellie, even though it's perfectly innocent and only for a few days. I wish things were different, and that I had sent Robbie packing, but I know it would have upset Ellie. I guess there is nothing I can do now, but just get on with things.

The food is packed away, and Robbie bought two boxes of crackers, so Ellie has placed some on the Christmas tree, just like she did when she was a little girl.

'Oh, and I got these.'

Robbie hands Ellie some chocolate tree decorations in purple foil, that he helps her to tie around the branches of the tree, both of them laughing together as the fire crackles in the log burner. Anyone observing this scene would assume it's a

happy family preparing for Christmas morning. I feel a pang of
regret for what might have been. Before realising I am just being
sentimental at this time of year, and remembering that Robbie
proved to be the most unreliable, unfaithful partner a girl could
have the misfortune to meet.

I head off to work for the matinee, and one and only screening, at the cinema today. *Elf* is still showing, and no doubt it will
be filled with overexcited children, being taken out of the house
for a couple of hours before darkness falls. It's just wonderful
watching the children heading into the cinema with broad
smiles and exiting the screening with even wider ones.

'Merry Christmas, Shelley.'

I take a box from my bag and hand Shelley a gift.

'What did you do that for? I haven't got you anything.' She
looks a little embarrassed.

'And I wouldn't expect you to. Anyway, it's only something
a little silly,' I tell her as she opens the box. Inside is a sparkly
keyring with a photo of her and Ed on the cinema night out at
Christmas.

'Ah that's brilliant, thanks, Sarah.'

'I thought it was a particularly lovely photo of you both so I
got it made into a keyring. Especially as things seem to be going
well between you.'

Shelley steps forward and crushes me in an embrace.

'I feel bad now, so here you go. I know you are a bit partial
to these.'

She hands me a large bag of Revels and pops the money into
the till.

'That's just perfect.' I smile. 'I think I've eaten the Quality
Street I bought for Christmas. I'll never buy tins of chocolates
so early again,' I vow.

When the film is over, and all the families have gone, full of
festive spirit, Shelley and I say goodbye. I lock the cinema for

four whole days, relishing the thought of reading books in front of the fire and taking long winter walks. Greg Starr insists on closing the cinemas for several days over Christmas, saying the staff deserve a well-earned break with family, which is very generous of him. Once upon a time, the cinema only closed for two days, but was practically empty until the new films were released in the new year, which prompted the decision to let the staff take an extended holiday.

It's just after seven o'clock and the mince pies have been made, along with some orange shortbread – courtesy of a Jamie Oliver tutorial on a cookery channel – and the last of the presents have been wrapped. I've bought small gifts for my aunt and uncle, and a box of Belgian chocolates for my newly separated cousin. I don't like leaving anyone out, so I've even bought a box of Liquorice Allsorts for Robbie that I know he's partial to, and a bottle of Liverpool gin from Ellie. Just like Santa, I've made a list and checked it twice and I think everything is under control. Time to breathe and enjoy a small gin and tonic before I get ready to go and meet Luke.

Robbie and Ellie tell me they will peel some vegetables whilst they watch a film later and I'm grateful that it's one less thing to worry about tomorrow.

I dress quickly and just before eight, I head to the Penny Farthing, where Luke is already waiting for me and my heart lurches. He looks wonderful in a pale-blue cashmere jumper and jeans, his brown leather jacket thrown over the back of a chair.

'Sarah, you look wonderful.' Luke kisses me on both cheeks as his eyes roam over me and the short black dress I'm wearing. I can smell the delicious scent of his aftershave.

The pub is busy this evening, everyone in a jovial mood,

chatting in groups as Christmas songs can be heard in the background. Jo is sitting at the bar talking to Helen, and they say hi as I enter the room and join Luke. It's a bit of a tradition that everyone gathers and wishes each other well on Christmas Eve, before attending midnight mass. Not everyone in the village heads to the church, but it's something I always enjoy.

We join my friends near the bar, yet I feel on edge, wondering whether Robbie might walk into the pub at any minute. I wonder if I ought to tell Luke he's spending a few days with us at Red Robin Cottage. Then again, Robbie did say he would be watching a film and peeling the vegetables in preparation for tomorrow so why would he turn up here? He knows I've gone out to meet Luke, but I never said where we would be heading.

'I hope he knows how lucky he is,' Robbie had said when he'd learned I was seeing someone. That irritated the hell out if me, as I thought it a pity he hadn't considered himself lucky before ruining things between us. I told him so.

Just after nine thirty, Luke glances at his watch and tells me he ought to be making tracks.

'I imagine you won't want to leave Ellie alone for too long on Christmas Eve. In fact, I thought she might have joined you here,' he says.

'She's wrapping presents for her friends. I told her I wouldn't be long,' I say; my heart is thumping as I feel as though I'm lying, even though Ellie was searching for wrapping paper earlier, saying she had to wrap a gift for Izzy. At least Luke hasn't asked to call in at the cottage and wish her a merry Christmas in person.

'Well, wish her a merry Christmas from me.' He smiles.

'I'll be sure to.'

Outside the pub, Luke draws me close to him.

'Merry Christmas, Sarah.' He presses his lips down onto mine and my head spins once more, as I lose myself in the moment beneath the inky, starlit sky on Christmas Eve. 'I hope you have a lovely day with your family.'

'Enjoy your day with Andy. Merry Christmas, Luke.'

He kisses me again and as we stand, wrapped in each others arms, it's as if we are the only two people in the world. I wish I could stay in this moment forever.

'I'll call you tomorrow,' he promises when we finally break apart.

As he drives off, I think about tomorrow with mixed emotions. I want it to be the best day for Ellie, and I'm looking forward to seeing my aunt and uncle. Later, I will go and light a candle for Mum and Dad at the Christmas church service, and hold them in my thoughts for a while.

Christmas has always been my favourite time of year, but having my ex-husband around the table was certainly not something I had planned for.

The church service was beautiful, and I mull over the vicar's words and how he explained that all of the world's ills could be overcome if people just showed love to one another. Maybe I ought to show a little more tolerance towards Robbie, as the vicar echoed Ellie's statement about Christmas being the season of goodwill.

'I love going to church on Christmas Eve,' says Ellie. 'No one really goes much these days, do they? I know none of my mates at school do,' she muses as we walk the short distance to the cottage.

'Maybe they don't have a church close by. It's nice that we have one in the village for special celebrations. And I like the church at this time of year. I guess it reminds us of the real reason we actually celebrate Christmas.'

I link arms with Ellie as we walk back to the cottage. It's ten thirty now, the service having been moved forward in recent years from the original midnight mass to deter inebriated people who would call in on their way home from a night out.

'And I'm glad Dad is staying for Christmas. I think this will be the best Christmas ever,' says Ellie as we walk up the path to the cottage. I hope she's right.

THIRTY-ONE

Robbie has peeled vegetables that are sitting on the stove and the turkey is in a large pan in the fridge, stuffed and ready to be popped into the oven tomorrow morning.

'You could cook it on a low heat overnight,' suggests Robbie as I'm checking a few last things in the kitchen.

'Not a chance. I want to be awake when the oven is on. What if there was a fire in the middle of the night?'

'You have fire alarms, don't you?'

'I do but it's not going to happen. I couldn't relax knowing the oven was on whilst I slept.'

'Maybe not overnight then, but did you know there's an app you can link to Alexa to switch your oven on when you're not there?' He pushes on with his idea. 'I think it's just with slow cookers, though. Handy if you're out for the day and there's a meal waiting when you get in.'

'I'd rather be home when I'm cooking. How can you check and baste the turkey if it's cooking throughout the night?'

'It might actually be better. Technology is there to make life easier. Slow cooking probably means it won't be dry, like it can be,' says Robbie, seemingly have turned into an expert on the subject.

'Are you saying my turkey is dry?' I push past him to retrieve something from a drawer with a little more force than I intend.

'What? No, course not. You're a great cook, really. I'm happy you've invited me for Christmas lunch.' He smiles a little sheepishly.

'I didn't invite you,' I remind him. 'I'm doing it for Ellie.'

'Sorry, of course, I know that and I'm grateful. I know you're seeing someone now anyway. I'm happy for you, Sarah, I really am. I hope he treats you right.'

He's quiet for a moment. 'Anyway, it is Christmas Eve; shall we have drink? I brought this with me.'

He brandishes a bottle of good brandy, but I decline. Brandy loosens me up a little too much and I don't want to be here with Robbie feeling mellow and relaxed.

I'd prefer to be doing that with Luke.

'Thanks, but I think I'll stick to wine,' I say, pulling a bottle from a wine rack built into the kitchen units.

'Is there anything else you want me to do?' asks Robbie as I lift the lid from the cake tin containing the Christmas cake and the spicy aroma hits my nostrils.

'You've made a Christmas cake?' Robbie rubs his hands together. 'Your Christmas cakes are the best.'

'I did. I was going to buy one from a shop, but I enjoy doing it and I know my aunt and uncle will appreciate it.'

Robbie stands next to me, and peers inside the tin at the cake that has white peaks of icing to resemble snow and figures of skaters with a small Christmas tree at the centre. His presence next to me feels familiar, yet wrong at the same time. Robbie has spent the last year with another woman, and I've been getting to know Luke and daring to hope that we might have some sort of future together. I quickly place the cake back in the tin and make some distance between us.

'Right. I think that's everything sorted. I'm going to have this drink, then turn in for the evening. I like an early start on Christmas Day.'

'Yes, I remember.'

We take our drinks into the lounge as the last of the logs glow in the burner, and Robbie flicks the television on. After the silence stretches for a little longer than comfortable, Robbie starts to tell me he might stay up for a short while as he's not sleepy, just as Ellie reappears downstairs to say goodnight. Together, Ellie and I head upstairs, leaving Robbie swirling the brandy around in his glass, and I can't help thinking what a fool he has been. He could have been here enjoying a normal Christmas Eve in the bosom of his family, instead of being here as a guest I never invited.

THIRTY-TWO

'Merry Christmas!'

Ellie has bounded into my bedroom wearing a pink fluffy dressing gown dotted with white stars. She sits next to me on the bed and wraps me in a hug. Robbie is hovering in the background with a mug of tea that he quickly places on the bedside table. It feels strange Robbie being in the bedroom, but thankfully he wishes me a merry Christmas, then disappears downstairs.

'Can we open our presents before lunch?' Ellie asks. Normally, we will open one gift then save the others until after we've eaten, enjoying the anticipation.

'Well, okay, maybe as we are having guests. Perhaps save a couple for after lunch, though, when we hand gifts to our guests.'

'Okay,' she says excitedly.

We pad downstairs to find Robbie in the kitchen, making scrambled eggs on toast.

'I thought we'd need a decent breakfast as it's only early, and dinner won't be until around three.' He turns to face me with a spatula in his hand. 'Am I right in assuming that? You always used to time it for the Queen's Speech on telly. Is that still the case?'

'I guess so. Old habits die hard. And thanks for making breakfast.'

I try and bite my tongue watching Robbie make a mess in the kitchen, using just about every pan and utensil. He pops some thick granary bread into the toaster.

'I'll make us some coffee,' I say, firing up the coffee machine.

Sitting in the kitchen eating breakfast and sipping coffee – fresh orange juice for Ellie – I try to relax but I feel something is missing, and, of course, I know it's Luke. I'm also mad at myself for not being honest with him about Robbie being here, but then, would he have understood? How would I feel if he told me he was spending Christmas Day with his ex-wife? I could kick myself for not inviting him over now, where we could have all behaved like grown-ups and eaten Christmas lunch together.

After breakfast and with the first of many baking trays for Christmas lunch in the oven, Ellie opens her gifts, her eyes widening when she sees her shiny black Doc Martens boots. She quickly removes her slippers and tries them on and walks around the lounge.

'I'm not sure they quite match the pink fluffy gown,' I tell her and she laughs and says she can't wait to go for a walk later and try them out.

'Thanks, Mum. I never thought I would actually get these.' She squeezes me so hard I can barely breathe. She is thrilled with all of her presents, and squeals with delight at the Olly Murs cardboard cut-out. After she's opened her gifts from me, Robbie hands her a present.

'Oh, Dad, thanks. How did you know?' She slips the Thomas Sabo bracelet onto her wrist, before squeezing him too.

'A little bird might have told me.' He winks at me.

'Oh, and I've got presents.'

Ellie rummages beneath the tree and, to my surprise,

presents us both with a gift. Mine is a gorgeous silk wrap, Robbie's a bottle of aftershave.

'Ellie, how thoughtful. I didn't expect this. Where did you get the money?'

I admire the grey silk wrap that really is very pretty.

'I'm running low on this aftershave, thanks, Ellie,' says Robbie. 'But how did you afford it? Have you got a job you haven't told us about?' He smiles.

Saturday jobs are hard to come by, but Ellie does occasion-ally do some babysitting in the village.

'I've been saving my babysitting money since September,' she confirms. 'And any bits of money you have both given me. Plus, I got them in the sales.' She smiles, looking pleased with herself.

'Well, thank you. It's really generous of you; I love my present.' I give Ellie a hug.

In the past, Ellie has asked for some money to buy Robbie a small gift, which I always give her, so I'm so proud she has managed to do this by herself this year. It's another reminder of how quickly she is growing up. I think I'll keep the Liverpool gin for myself now, as Ellie has bought Robbie something with her own money.

'You won't be wanting that box of Liquorice Allsorts now,' I tease Robbie.

'Give them here! There my favourites. I don't have anything for you, though,' he tells me.

'And I wouldn't have expected anything.' *From you*, I think to myself. Keeping it civil in front of Ellie, I continue. 'Besides, you've already made a contribution towards the food.' Which he has, and I'm grateful for.

'Well, that's only fair. Anyway, here you go. Merry Christmas.'

He plucks a white flower from a pretty display in a chunky vase and hands it to me and I can't help smiling.

I do a quick tidy of the room, placing all the wrapping paper in a bin liner ready for recycling and Robbie and Ellie laugh at me and tell me to relax.

'I will do when this room is a little tidier. Oh yes, and when I've showered, dressed and cooked the Christmas lunch.' I try not to sound sarcastic, as I do love Christmas Day. It is bloody hard work, though.

'Relax, we're here to help too, you know. And the veg is all prepped,' Robbie reminds me.

'You're right. And thanks for that. Maybe you could put the breakfast things in the dishwasher, while I go and grab a shower.'

'Not a problem.'

Robbie is so eager to help, I can't help thinking that if he had been a bit more like this when we were together, our marriage might have stood a chance. But then, there was the small matter of his infidelity, I guess.

After I've showered, I head into my bedroom and pick my phone up from my bed only to discover I have a missed call from Luke, and my heart sinks. I dial voicemail, and listen to Luke wishing me a merry Christmas and saying he hopes we can meet up soon. I quickly return the call, but to my disappointment, it goes straight to voicemail. I wish him a merry Christmas and say I hope he enjoys the day with Andy. Then I get dressed. He knows I am preparing Christmas lunch for family today, so maybe he will call me back this evening.

The kitchen is filled with wonderful smells as I open the oven door and check on the turkey and ham that are gently roasting inside. A tray of carrots and parsnips will soon be added to cook slowly and some green vegetables steamed. The stuffing is prepared, chestnut with sage and onion, and some bread sauce from a packet for Uncle Bernie, who is the only person I know who still eats it.

Just after one o'clock, the doorbell rings and looking at

Uncle Bernie is just like looking into the grey eyes of my father and it saddens and comforts me at the same time. I welcome our guests inside and, having settled everyone with drinks, we're sitting on the sofas chatting.

'The room looks really lovely,' says my cousin Heather, who, I have to say, looks relaxed and stylish, caramel highlights in her shoulder-length hair and wearing a pretty blue wrap-over dress. She looks a lot happier than she did when she was married to Joe.

'Thanks. I always go all-out at Christmas,' I say proudly, looking at the shimmering tree and tasteful decorations in my favourite traditional colour scheme.

'The grave looks lovely too,' says Uncle Bernie, helping himself to some peanuts from a bowl on the coffee table. 'We've just been and left some flowers.'

'I know. Countryside Flowers always do a wonderful display. And I like to think that Mum and Dad are always with us.'

'They are.' Auntie Jean nods, a quiet woman who has always been so kind. She's a good listener, my uncle being the talkative one. I remember her always being so loving and patient, especially when I was a child.

Robbie heads to the window and admires Bernie's car, and a conversation about cars ensues. Heather and Jean follow me into the kitchen as I go and check on lunch. They both offer to help, but I think everything is under control.

'You're a wonderful cook, just like your mum,' says Jean kindly, as Ellie takes Heather upstairs to show her the Olly Murs cut-out and her new boots. 'I still miss your mum and our long chats. She was the best sister-in-law I could have wished for.' She sniffs.

'I know, I miss Mum and Dad too. It can be hard at Christmastime but you're family. I'm lucky to have you both.'

Jean clears her throat and pats me on the arm 'You're a good girl, Sarah. I know your mum and dad were really proud of you.'

'Thanks, Auntie Jean.'

'I must admit, I was surprised when Sarah told me you were coming for lunch,' says Uncle Bernie to Robbie, as we take our seats around the dinner table.

'Oh, right. Well, me and Sarah are mates now, and I think it's nice for Ellie having me here,' replies Robbie, with a smile on his face. He glances at Ellie, who is giving Uncle Bernie an evil stare, as Auntie Jean nudges him.

'She always liked having you here, before you buggered off,' Bernie mutters under his breath, his words still audible, to me at least, but maybe that's because I'm sitting closer to him.

'Wine, anyone?' I pour drinks in an attempt to diffuse any growing tensions. I didn't expect Uncle Bernie to be so vocal with his thoughts, especially after chatting about cars with Robbie earlier. Thankfully, the wine seems to mellow the mood around the table and Bernie says no more on the matter over dinner. Although I'm not sure why Robbie shouldn't hear the truth. Ellie did like having him around; Uncle Bernie was right about that.

Dinner is a wonderful affair, the food delicious and the jokes in the crackers actually very funny. The fortune-telling fish tells me I will find a new love. In response, I hear Uncle Bernie say it's only what I deserve after the last bloke, and this time Robbie definitely hears him.

'Yes, I know I was a prick, Bernie, you don't need to have a go.'

Bernie shrugs and takes a sip of his wine.

'Let's not have this conversation around the Christmas table,' I say firmly, throwing Robbie and Uncle Bernie a look. 'Anyway, it's time for the Queen's Speech now.'

I stand and switch the television on. We respectfully listen to the Queen's Speech as we always do, and I offer people dessert, but we're all far too stuffed for Christmas pudding. Uncle Bernie says he will just have a little breather and half an hour later, we've devoured Christmas pudding and custard – Ellie having hot chocolate fudge cake and ice cream – and are slouched around on sofas in a food coma.

'Ooh, I've forgotten about the Christmas cake,' I say, and Uncle Bernie's ears prick up.

'Is it home-made?' he asks.

'It is, and the best you'll ever taste,' says Robbie, almost proudly.

'Ugh, please, I feel sick,' says Ellie.

'It's not that bad.' I smile.

'I mean, I'm just too stuffed to think of food.' She clutches her stomach. 'How can you even mention cake?'

'I don't think I could manage any right now, but I'll take some home, if that's alright,' says Uncle Bernie. 'It will go down well with a cup of tea later when we watch the Christmas episode of *Call the Midwife*.'

'Of course! Take a big chunk; I'll only eat it all otherwise,' I tell him and Robbie looks slightly disappointed. If he thinks he's going to sit around here for the next few days, munching on Christmas cake, he can think again.

Later, as we load the dishwasher, Heather comes over and thanks me for the invite.

'I can't tell you what a lovely day I've had, Sarah,' she tells me as we sip a coffee, while everyone else is in the lounge watching a Christmas film. 'Although I was worried earlier that things were going to kick off with my dad and Robbie. Dad has trouble stopping his thoughts from coming out of his mouth.' She shakes her head.

'I suppose he's always been that way, hasn't he? At least you know where you are with him.'

'That's true. To be honest, I was dreading Christmas Day, so thanks again. Who wants to be at home with their mum and dad at forty-two? What a saddo.' She laughs. 'But I said Joe could stay at the house until he finds somewhere to rent,' she tells me, answering the question in my head as to why she has left the family home. 'He literally had nowhere to go, and I thought it might be nice to spend some time with my parents as they're getting on in years now. Anyway, he has somewhere fixed up for January, so I'll be moving back home then,' she reveals.

'I'm glad you're getting on with things. And you look really well.'

'Thanks.' She smiles. 'So what's the story with Robbie?' she asks and I tell her all about Ellie inviting him over when his relationship ended.

'Despite me telling her I didn't want him here.'

'Ouch. When's he leaving?'

'Soon, I hope. He's not short of money, Ellie just didn't like the thought of him being alone on Christmas Day. And it has been nice for her, having him here, I suppose.'

Heather tells me she manages a fashion store in the city centre, and asks if I think Ellie might be interested in a Saturday job.

'Would she ever! They're really hard to come by. I think if you offer her one, it might just be her best Christmas present ever.'

'Brilliant. I'll have a chat with her later.' She smiles and I wonder why we stop spending time with our cousins when we grow up and go our separate ways. They are some of our first friends and I remember going to the beach with Heather as a kid and on holidays to North Wales. As if reading my mind, Heather tells me we should meet up sometime for lunch.

'I'd love that,' I tell her, really meaning it. 'Let's not leave it too long.'

Uncle Bernie has woken from a snooze, and tells me he might just have a small piece of Christmas cake with a cup of tea before they head on their way, at almost seven o'clock. We've had a great afternoon playing charades and a drawing game that had us all in fits of giggles as the drawings were so awful. Apart from Heather, who obviously has a creative streak and was the easy winner of the game with her easily identifiable sketches.

My heart is filled with love when I wave my family off, and Ellie was beside herself with joy when Heather told her to fill out an online application form for a weekend job at the fashion store in Liverpool One.

'Wait until I tell Izzy I have a Saturday job too!' she says excitedly. Izzy works in her mum's hair salon every Saturday sweeping up and making tea for clients and always has a little more money to spend than Ellie.

'I love Auntie Heather. Why don't we see her more often?' asks Ellie.

'Busy lives, I guess, but I'm hoping we will be able to spend more time together. We're going to organise a lunch meet-up, although you'll certainly see more of her if you work in the shop,' I remind her.

The last time we got together was actually two years ago when we attended a family party in a restaurant and Joe embarrassed Heather by drinking too much and falling over and knocking into a waitress carrying some drinks. I'm pleased to see how well she's looking and moving on with her life since their split.

After everything has been tidied away and the place looks a little more normal, I slip upstairs and change into a pair of comfortable pyjamas. Downstairs, I glance at my phone to check for any messages, but there are none apart from some GIFs of flashing Christmas trees from my friends in the village wishing me a merry Christmas. I don't know what I was expecting, really; Luke did call me this morning after all and I left him a message. Even so, it would have been nice to hear his voice before I head to bed. I pick my phone up and think about calling him, but decide not to as I don't want to come across as needy. I'm sure we will speak tomorrow.

Just after nine o'clock, Robbie carries a cheeseboard into the lounge on a tray, loaded with various cheeses and grapes.

'Anyone hungry?' he asks, placing the tray on the coffee table. Surprisingly, I am a little peckish even after the feast of earlier today.

'I am a bit, but not for that.' Ellie turns her nose up at the cheeseboard and heads off to the kitchen in search of a different snack. I follow her to grab some chutney and gasp at the state of the kitchen, wondering how someone could make so much mess cutting up some cheese.

Ellie gives us both a hug before heading to her room to have a Skype call with Izzy to chat about their day and show each other their presents.

I pour us both a glass of wine and talk turns to his relationship.

'So, what happened between you and Hannah, then?' I ask as I sip my wine.

'A misunderstanding.' He sighs.

'A misunderstanding?' I frown, almost certain that there is something more to it than that.

'Yep. I went on a stag do with a couple of mates and stayed out all night,' he explains. 'Hannah got it into her head that I'd spent the night with someone, but I'd crashed at a mate's. I was wasted.'

'And why didn't she believe you?' I ask, wondering if it wasn't the first time he'd given her cause for doubt.

'Dunno. Bloody Facebook, probably. I was tagged in a few photos that someone had taken and there was a couple with a woman who had her arms draped around me. I don't even know who she was, we just got chatting to some women in a bar and having a laugh. Nothing happened, honest.'

'It isn't me you need to convince,' I remind him.

'I've tried but she doesn't believe me.' He sighs. 'It's a shame because I thought things were going well between us.' To my surprise, he actually sounds genuine.

'Maybe she doesn't trust you. It's hard to be in a relationship with someone you don't trust.'

No one knows that more than me.

'I know. And I'm sorry, Sarah. I know I behaved like an idiot when we were married.'

'You can't turn the clock back. But at least we're civil to each other now.' I smile, hesitating to use the word 'friends', as I don't want him turning up here every time he has a drama in his personal life.

We chat for a bit longer, perfectly pleasantly and with no emotional talk and just after ten thirty I stretch my arms out and yawn loudly. 'Well, that's me, then, I'm off to bed.'

'There's a James Bond movie starting in a minute. If you fancy it.'

'No, thanks, I'll leave you to it. Night, then.'

'Night, Sarah. And thanks for today, it's been great.'

I've enjoyed today too, but tomorrow I need to ask Robbie about his plans to move on. There's no way he is going to outstay his welcome.

THIRTY-THREE

The next morning, I open the curtains and gasp. An overnight snowfall has blanketed the garden and the farmers' fields beyond. I nip to the bathroom and notice Ellie's bedroom door is tightly closed, meaning she hasn't surfaced yet. I can't wait to see her reaction when she sees the snow. She's always loved it.

Downstairs, Robbie is in the kitchen listening to the radio and sipping coffee.

'Morning, you're up early,' he says, glancing at the clock that shows just after seven thirty.

'I know. I was wide awake. I think it's because I had a really deep sleep last night.'

'Have you seen the snow outside?' he says, walking to the window.

'I know, Ellie will be thrilled when she wakes.' I smile as I can imagine her screaming and running downstairs.

'She certainly will.' He grins as he pours me a coffee. 'Do you want any breakfast?'

'Gosh, no, thanks. I'm still stuffed after that late supper.' I don't add that I would quite like the kitchen to remain tidy for a while.

'I thought we might go for a walk later, what do you think? Then maybe we should make a huge snowman in the garden. Do you remember that snow family we made one year...' Robbie is chatting away ten to the dozen like an excited child.

I do indeed remember the snow family. Mum, dad, two kids and even a snow dog. It stayed freezing that year for over a week and the snow figures stood in the garden like an extended family. Ellie cried when the temperature dropped and, one by one, they slowly melted away. I hope Robbie doesn't harbour any ideas about doing that again, as I'm hoping he will be on his way tomorrow, now that Christmas is over.

We sip our drinks and I do a bit of tidying around and an hour later, as I expected, there's an excited shriek and Ellie comes bounding down the stairs.

'Have you seen the snow! Can we go sledging on the hill?' she asks excitedly.

The hill – as it is simply known as locally – is on a field nearby and the first snowfall will, no doubt, have families pulling sledges from their sheds and heading over there as we speak.

'Oh, yeah, I'd forgotten about sledging on the hill,' says Robbie, sounding just as excited as Ellie.

When Ellie dashes upstairs to get dressed, I turn to Robbie.

'So, what are your plans tomorrow, then?' I rinse my coffee cup at the sink.

'I'm not sure. I'll probably check into a bed and breakfast or something. I'll soon run out of money, though.' He sighs.

'Well, you can't expect to stay here indefinitely.' I turn and face him. 'I agreed to you coming for Christmas, and now it's over. It's not fair if Ellie gets used to having you around again.'

'I know, and I'm grateful for that. Maybe I can crash on a mate's couch for a bit now that Christmas is over.' He looks at me with puppy-dog eyes. 'It's murder trying to find a flat around here.'

Ellie returns to the kitchen, kitted out for a day in the snow, and gulps down a bowl of cereal, whilst I have another coffee and curse the situation I find myself in.

'Can I have the key to the shed, Mum?' asks Ellie, and she and Robbie head off to retrieve her red sleigh. We bought one several years ago, just before an unexpected snowfall, thankful that we did as there were none to be found in shops anywhere for miles around.

'You two go, I have things to do around here today,' I say and Ellie looks disappointed.

'Aw, Mum, don't you want to come with us? It won't be the same without you.' She pulls a face.

I'm almost tempted to tag along, but don't think it's right for us to be playing happy families again. Plus, I want to phone Luke.

'No, really, you go and have fun.' I paint on a smile. 'You know sledging isn't really my thing, clumsy clot that I am. Text me when you're about to head home and I'll have some hot chocolate ready.'

'Okay.' She brightens. 'Right, Dad, are you ready?'

'Pretty much. Good job I found my old walking boot in the shed,' says Robbie, glancing at the sturdy grey boots on his feet.

As they head off to the hill, I take a deep breath and call Luke. I'm not sure what I'll say if he asks me about Christmas Day and not for the first time I wish I'd just told him the truth about Robbie being here.

To my disappointment, the call goes straight to voicemail once more, so I nip upstairs for a shower. It's barely ten o'clock and I'm not sure what to do with myself, so I decide to call Frances and ask her if she fancies going for a walk.

'Sarah, hi. I thought you'd be over at the hill with Ellie; I know how excited the young ones are when it snows.'

'She's gone with Robbie,' I tell her. 'And don't worry if you don't fancy a walk; I might just call in on you anyway and say hi if you're not busy.'

'Actually, I would love a walk,' she tells me enthusiastically. 'Mum has just opened a huge jigsaw that she's going to settle down with for the day. I've gorged on so many chocolates, a walk is probably exactly what I need right now.'

'Brilliant. See you in ten minutes.'

The village looks beautiful covered in snow, just like a scene on a tin of Christmas shortbread. The church looks resplendent, its roof looking as though it has been dripped with white icing. I say good morning to people in their front gardens with young children, already building snowmen, the children giggling excitedly.

As I pass Jo's cottage, her garden looks pretty, the bushes covered in snow and stone sculptures dotted about. A metal dog is poking its nose through a thick coating of snow. Jo has closed up the café for a couple of days and gone to spend Christmas with her sister in Cheshire.

Arriving at my friend's cottage with its red-painted front door with a wreath on the front, I shake the snow from my boots and step inside the cosy lounge to wish her mum a merry Christmas.

'Oh, hi, Sarah love. Did you have a nice day yesterday?' asks her mum, Carol.

'I did, thanks. You?'

'Ooh, lovely. We went to my niece's; it was a wonderful day, wasn't it, Fran?'

'It was,' agrees Frances. 'We had a great time but I'm never going to eat again for a week. Sally is such a great cook.'

'I'm glad you had a nice day. I had family over too. I suppose that's what Christmas is all about.'

I glance at the picture on the box of the jigsaw, showing an old-fashioned sweet shop, jars of sweets all lined up on shelves.

'Enjoy your jigsaw,' I say as Fran and I are about to set off.

'I will. Much as I enjoyed yesterday, I've been looking forward to doing this with a nice cup of tea. Although, looking at that picture makes me wish I had a bag of sherbet lemons beside me.' She laughs.

Walking along the main street, we turn right down a country path, walking in the tractor grooves. It seems farmers' work never stops. The temperature has warmed a little since the snowfall and, after a short while, I remove my hat and stuff it into my coat pocket.

'It's so peaceful here, isn't it?'

A watery sun is breaking through the clouds and I can't help wondering how long the snow will last on the ground. Maybe it's good that Ellie and Robbie spend the day sledging, and soon enough he will be on his way when the snow thaws. I tell Fran all about Christmas Day and how I feel dishonest not mentioning to Luke that my ex-husband was joining us.

'I had a missed a call from him on Christmas morning, but I haven't spoken to him since. I have a niggling feeling he isn't that bothered about contacting me again but... but maybe I'm being paranoid,' I tell her as we walk. We pass hedgerows bursting with winter berries, and a blackbird swoops down and picks at something, before flying off.

'Maybe you're overthinking it,' she tells me as our feet scrunch through the fresh snow. 'He knew you had family over yesterday, and it is only Boxing Day morning. I'm sure he will be in touch soon.'

'Oh, Fran, you're right. I probably am overthinking things.'

He may even have overdone it on the whisky with his friend yesterday and is feeling a little fragile. It's still quite early in the day, I remind myself.

'Relationships can be so complicated, can't they? I was spared the angst when I was happily single,' I lament.

'Being single has its merits, but don't you ever feel lonely?'

asks Fran as we walk past a clough, ash trees draped in snow on its sides.

'I can't honestly say that I do. I'm busy with work and I have Ellie to look after. Beside, after Robbie, I find it a bit hard to trust men, if I'm honest,' I tell her.

'I can understand why, but... well, I have been feeling a bit lonely lately, so I've decided to dip my toe into the dating scene,' Fran tells me. 'I've been on Tinder.'

'You have?'

'Yeah, I realised it's been years since I've been involved with anyone. I'm so busy at the shop and looking after Mum, taking her shopping and so on. I realised I have a bit of a boring existence. Anyway, I'm meeting someone tomorrow.' She smiles. 'Just for coffee in town.'

'Fran that's great. I'm really pleased for you. Meeting in a public place is probably a good idea too.'

'I thought so. Until recently, I'd been happy enough on my own but since the lump, well, I thought it's about time I grabbed life with both hands. Life is for living, isn't it? None of us know how much time we have. The business takes up most of my time, as I said, and much as I love Mum's company, I know she won't be around forever. It's time to make a life for me, I think.'

We take a right turn past a narrow river, the surface covered with thin ice, and soon enough a farmhouse comes into view, the green tractor that made the tracks in the path we walked along parked outside. A sheepdog comes running to the front gate to greet us as we pass.

'Morning,' says a lady wearing green wellingtons who's clearing a snowy path with a shovel. 'He's a friendly soul, don't mind him.'

Fran pets the dog, who wags his tail wildly in appreciation.

Moving on, we pass houses and fields that are redundant squares of brown earth in the winter, bursting to life with bright yellow rapeseed in the summer months. After walking for over an hour, we head back towards the village, where we see people walking up the hill carrying their sledges. As we approach the scene, we see children whizzing down the hill, scarves flailing behind them and excited squeals. I spot Robbie sitting on a nearby bench, glancing at his phone.

'Mum.' Ellie, who is at the top of the hill, poised to slide down again, waves over.

Robbie taps a message out on his phone, then looks up and says hello to us both.

'Fancy a go, then, girls?' He nods towards Ellie, who is scooting down the hill on her sledge, arms outstretched.

'I think I'll pass.' Fran laughs. 'I think I've done enough exercise for one day.'

'Coffee at mine, then?'

'Lovely, thanks, Sarah.'

'We'll probably be back shortly. I'm getting a bit cold standing around,' says Robbie. 'I've had a few goes on the sledge but we could probably do with two. I'll pick up another one if I see one when I'm out and about,' he says.

Back at the cottage, I make Fran and I coffee and we sit in the kitchen, hands wrapped around the steaming grey-glazed Emma Bridgewater mugs.

'I've just remembered I have some Christmas cake left. Would you like some?' I offer.

'Sarah! I'm trying to be good after yesterday. Is it your home-made one, though?' she asks, her resolve weakening.

'It is. And it's Boxing Day. Still officially Christmastime in my book. What was that you said about living life?'

'You're right, stuff it, go on then, but just a small slice.'

Fran makes appreciative noises as she sinks her teeth into the cake. 'All those calories burned off, and now this.'

'We've earned it.'

I even have a piece myself, and, though I say so myself, it's really very good.

Half an hour later, Fran is about to leave and I hear a text on my phone. I rush to read it, hoping it might be Luke, but it's Robbie telling me he and Ellie will be home in ten minutes. It's strange for him to be using the word 'home'. It's no longer Robbie's home. I hope he doesn't get any ideas about thinking otherwise.

'Thanks for this morning, Sarah; it was just what I needed.' Fran wraps me in a hug. 'And if you have no plans tonight, I might pop into the pub for a drink around seven. There's always a few in on Boxing night.'

'Sounds good,' I say, thinking I probably will head over there.

It's after lunchtime time and, with a sinking feeling, I realise Luke hasn't returned my call from this morning, or even messaged me. Maybe it's time to get on with my life here. Starting with a drink in the pub this evening with my friends in the village.

THIRTY-FOUR

Robbie and Ellie return a while later, and after a warming hot chocolate, they walk into the lounge and settle down for a game of cards. Robbie asks if there is any Christmas cake left, and I happily give him the very last of it, so I won't be tempted to polish it off myself.

'You don't mind if I just hang around here today with Ellie, do you?' asks Robbie, positioning himself on the sofa next to her with the Christmas cake for him and a selection box for Ellie. 'I'll be out of your hair tomorrow,' he says, taking me completely by surprise.

'No, of course not. And really? You've got yourself fixed up somewhere, then?'

'I'm going back to Hannah. It seems she wants to give things another go,' he says, a huge grin on his face.

'Wow. How come?' I ask, intrigued by the latest turn of events.

'Maybe she missed me at Christmas.' He smiles. 'Although the real reason is, it turns out someone from the night out saw me getting into a taxi with the mate I crashed with, bearing my story out. Her dad wasn't as ill as she thought, plus her brother is staying with her parents for a bit, so she's driving home from Scotland this afternoon. I'll see her tomorrow.'

'I'm glad you and Hannah are back together,' says Ellie, unwrapping a chocolate bar. 'I was worried I wouldn't see you if you didn't have a place and I couldn't stay over,' she says and Robbie hugs her.

'I'd still come and see you here, though, you know that. You'll always be my little girl.'

Ellie isn't the only one who's relieved that Robbie has made things up with Hannah, as even though he's Ellie's dad I don't want him rocking up here whenever he feels like it.

Later that day, I'm in the kitchen when my phone flashes and I see a text from Luke. He's replying to the text I sent this morning, saying that he had a nice Christmas and hopes I did too. The message seems perfunctory, with no suggestion of us meeting up again and I can feel the memory of the wonderful time we spent together slipping away from me. Did I imagine the connection I felt with him? I'm relieved now that at least I didn't sleep with him and feel utterly confused as I head to the pub with a heavy heart.

'You look like you could do with that.' Fran is sitting at the bar chatting to Helen. She nods to the glass of wine that is there waiting for me. She looks pretty tonight, in jeans and a gold-coloured top that matches her golden curls.

'I do,' I say, taking a long gulp of wine.

'Shall we grab a bottle and take it over there?' I point to a snug that has just become vacant.

'I'll bring it over.' Helen smiles. 'I'll join you for a drink shortly, before we get busy. Well, I can only hope we do.'

'So what's up?' asks Fran as we sip our wine. 'I'm guessing Luke still hasn't been in touch?'

'He has, actually, but now I feel even worse.' I sigh. 'He politely told me he had a nice Christmas in response to my text and hoped I did too. That was it.'

'Did you text back?'

'Yeah, something like, yes, I did, thanks. I never said much else as I could almost feel the chill from the other end of the phone. My finger was hovering over the call button, but in the end I never bothered. I still haven't heard from him.'

'You could try asking him what's wrong, you know. I mean it doesn't add up, does it? You seemed to be getting along so well. He owes it to you to explain why he's had a change of heart.'

'You're right. I will call him, but not tonight. I'll try and get hold of him tomorrow when Robbie leaves.'

I tell her all about Robbie moving back in with Hannah.

'I bet you're relieved about that, hey?'

'Just a bit.' I roll my eyes. 'I mean, we get along okay these days, but that doesn't mean I want him under the same roof as me. There's no chance we would ever get back together.'

'You're certain of that?' she asks.

'Absolutely. Maybe I could have forgiven him if he'd cheated once and bitterly regretted it. Actually, even then I'm not sure that I would. But he's a serial cheat. I could never go there again.' I shake my head.

'Definitely for the best, I'd say. As long as Ellie has a good relationship with him that's the main thing, I suppose.'

Helen joins us a few minutes later, and I fill her in on the conversation and we all chat about Christmas and some of the gifts we've been given and Helen proudly shows off a lovely watch from Paul. Talk of Christmas gifts makes me think of the expensive whisky I have for Luke and the 'I love Liverpool' pen. I wonder how I could have got things so wrong.

Chatting with my friends, I try and put all thoughts of Luke out of my mind and a while later, a band appear on a tiny stage in the corner of the pub. Jo turns up having returned from her sister's after the snow had thawed, telling us over the music that she was worried she'd be stuck there if it snowed again.

'Much as I love her, her place is like a madhouse,' she reveals. 'Three kids, two dogs and a lunatic cat.' She laughs. 'A couple of days was more than enough.'

'The band are great, aren't they?' says Fran, tapping her feet and having a good time.

After a bit more wine, we're all up dancing with most of the pub as the band do a rendition of a popular rock song, and I can feel the stresses of life melt away.

'Well, that turned out to be a great night,' I say as we walk along, me feeling slightly tipsy as we step outside into the cool night air. Jo and Fran walk me back to my cottage at the end of the road, before walking back together, their houses literally being across the road from each other.

'Enjoy your coffee date tomorrow,' I tell Fran. 'Let me know how it goes.'

'I'll be sure to. Goodnight.'

'How was the pub?' asks Robbie, sitting up from a lying position on one of the couches; Ellie is on the other sofa. A pile of snack wrappers are on an occasional table in front of her.

'Busy. The girls were in, I had a few glasses of wine.' I'm aware I have huge grin on my face.

'Are you drunk, Mum?' Ellie is studying me with a grin on her face.

'Nooo, just merry.' I'm grinning inanely again. 'Starving, though, is there any cheese left in the fridge?'

'A bit, yes. Shall I get you some?' Robbie jumps up. 'And maybe I'll make you some coffee,' he adds, raising an eyebrow.

'Decaff for me.'

'Yes, I know.'

I realise there's a lot Robbie knows about me, having spent so many years together.

I kick my shoes off and sit back on the sofa next to Ellie, as

Robbie returns to the lounge with cheese, crackers and coffee. I ask them about the film they watched this evening, and they ask about my evening at the pub.

'You should have come.' I direct this at Ellie.

'No, thanks. Watching the oldies get drunk and dance isn't my idea of a good night.' She laughs.

'Less of the oldies, if you don't mind.' I wag my finger at her, suddenly feeling a little the worse for wear. I finish the last of the cheese, when I'm suddenly struck by a bout of hiccups.

'Oh dear. I think it's time I headed to bed.' I take my plate into the kitchen and grab a bottle of water from the fridge to take upstairs with me.

As I'm about to climb the stairs, Robbie grabs me gently by the wrist and I turn to face him.

'Thanks for everything, Sarah, I mean it.' He looks at me with his handsome face and attractive blue eyes and, for a second, I wonder what he's thinking before I pull myself together. He's moving back in with his girlfriend tomorrow and I've had a little too much wine.

'It's fine. And I'm glad you've made up with Hannah. Goodnight.'

'Night, Sarah.'

It's just before eleven o'clock when I settle down in bed, giving a final glance at my phone but there's no messages and my heart aches for Luke.

THIRTY-FIVE

Robbie is up early and has soon packed his large holdall and is hugging Ellie at the front door.

'See you next weekend.' He kisses the top of her head, and I can't help noticing she holds on to him for quite a long time and the familiar, yet irrational, guilt of us no longer being a family rises to the surface once more.

'You okay, love?' I ask later that morning as she's curled on the sofa texting someone.

'Yeah, fine, Mum.' She smiles. 'I'm just texting Izzy. Is it okay if I go and stay at hers tonight?' she asks.

I was kind of hoping we could have a girlie night together, maybe a board game, but, of course, she stayed home last night, so is probably dying to see her friends.

'Of course you can. I'll drop you off later.'

Thankfully, the snow has all but completely melted and the roads are free from ice.

Upstairs, I'm sorting out some washing, happy to see that Ellie has deposited her clothes in the washing basket once more, when my phone rings.

'Luke! How are you?' I'm so thrilled to hear his voice at the other end of the phone.

'I'm good, thanks. How are you?' he asks.

'I'm fine, it's really good to hear from you.' I feel a sense of relief flood through me. I wasn't sure when he would be in touch again.

'Is it?' he asks and I find myself puzzled by his question.

'Of course it is. I was worried there was something wrong. Although, of course, I know you did call on Christmas morning. I was downstairs,' I explain. 'I returned the call but it seems we kept missing each other.'

'Listen, Sarah, I was wondering if we could meet. Are you free this evening?' His tone is very matter-of-fact.

' I am, yes. And I'd love to meet up.'

'Great. Is it okay if I call around about six?'

'Six o'clock is good.'

A while later, after hoovering upstairs and putting a wash on, I lower myself into my scented bath, unsure of how the meeting this evening with Luke will turn out. I'm thrilled he called me, but I can't help thinking of how flat his voice sounded and wonder what's on his mind.

After lunch, I drop Ellie off at Izzy's, who lives around a mile away from the city centre, and decide to drive into town and have a quick look at the sales. Walking through Liverpool One, I glance at the staircase that leads to the chain cinema, where groups of young people are heading to watch a film and wonder whether the Roxy will ever see such numbers through its doors.

The shop windows are emblazoned with huge posters advertising massive discounts and I wonder whether I might find something with a voucher I was given by my aunt and uncle. Cassie thinks the sales are a waste of time, suggesting shops wheel out all of the rubbish from their storerooms. I think half the time it's true, especially as I'm inside a shop browsing some of last season's autumn dresses, in impossibly tiny sizes. In another department store, I spy a nice black blazer that looks like good quality with a thirty per cent reduction. I slip it on and it fits like a glove. As I'm debating whether or not to buy it, my phone rings and it's Cassie.

'Hi, Cassie, I was just thinking about you. I'm in town at the sales. I've just dropped Ellie at her friend's.'

'Are you going to be there for a while?' she asks. 'I have to return a Christmas gift, so we could meet for a coffee.'

'Great. I'll meet you at Leaf on Bold Street in around half an hour?'

'Okay, see you in a bit.'

I purchase the blazer, along with some pretty new under-wear, briefly wondering if anyone other than me will ever see it. Passing the perfume shop, I head inside and treat myself to a new bottle of perfume, just my usual one that I'm running low on. I'm thrilled to find that there's a discount on that too.

We're seated inside Leaf enjoying a warming latte coffee in a tall glass and a slice of delicious carrot cake, despite me trying to stay off sugary treats. As Cassie reminds me, we are still in the Christmas season and diets begin strictly in January.

'Why do the things that are bad for us taste so good?' I finish the last crumb of cake in satisfaction.

'Cakes aren't necessarily bad. Especially that one, it's got vegetables in it,' she says, making me laugh. 'Besides, everything in moderation is the key.'

'There's been nothing moderate about my eating habits these last few days, but I know it's still Christmas,' I say, feeling a tiny bit less guilty.

I tell Cassie all about my Christmas and how, despite how much I enjoyed it, I'm pleased Robbie has gone on his way, and she tells me all about her Christmas Day.

'James bought me this.' She shows me a pretty silver

bracelet. 'And some new running gear, which I'd mentioned I needed. He bought me the wrong size, though.' She laughs. 'That's what I'm returning to the shop today. I haven't been a size ten for at least five years.'

'Ah well, that means he still sees you in exactly the same way as when you first met. How romantic.' I smile.

'Talking of romance, how are things going with the handsome Luke?'

'I haven't a clue, to be honest.' I sigh as I sip my coffee. 'I thought everything was going really well, but he seemed a little cool on the phone earlier. I'm seeing him this evening, though, so we can have a proper talk.'

'I'm sure everything will be fine. You both had separate plans at Christmas, and he knew you were spending it with family. Maybe he didn't want to come off as being a bit pushy.'

'I get that. I was worried about that too, and seeming needy ringing him. Oh God, I don't know, I'm out of practice.'

We spend another hour browsing the sales, Cassie still moaning at the rubbish on offer, that is until she spots a pair of boots in a shop window that she ends up going inside to see, trying on, and buying.

'Enjoy the rest of your time off work,' she tells me as we're about to head off in different directions. 'I hope everything works out with Luke. See you soon. Ooh and we must do that games evening. I'm back in work tomorrow, but we'll sort something.'

As Cassie walks off, I realise how easy it is not to follow through with plans when life gets busy. There's a good chance the games evening will be postponed for a while, once Cassie and James go back to work, especially with James's irregular shifts.

Back home, I feel a nervous anticipation for my date this evening, and spend the next couple of hours doing some tidying around and trying, unsuccessfully, to read a few chapters of the book I'm currently reading. Abandoning the book, I glance through the window from the dining room into the front garden, and I'm pleased to see a robin sitting on the garden gate.

I head out with some seed, and, to my delight, the robin hops over to the bird feeder, once I have filled it.

'It's good to see you,' I say as it pecks at the food. 'I wonder what you think about relationships, hey? Although I've read you don't have so many complications, as I've heard some birds mate for life. Or at least until the little ones fly the nest.'

The little robin, cocks its head to one side as if taking in every word. The sight of the robin in the garden never fails to make me smile and I feel lighter when I head back inside. No matter what happens in my personal life, I know how lucky I am to live here.

Just before Luke arrives, I text Fran and ask her how her Tinder date went. She tells me it went well and that they chatted easily for two hours and have arranged to meet again. I send her a thumbs up emoji and that I'll speak to her soon.

At a few minutes to seven, I hear the sound of Luke's car and glancing outside, see his blue Mercedes parking up. I wasn't surprised to see Luke had chosen a stylish car to hire during his stay in England. I realise I still haven't been to the place he's renting in the Georgian quarter and wonder if I ever will? My heart is beating fast when I check myself in the hall mirror and open the front door.

'Luke, hi.'

'Hi, Sarah. Can I come in?'

'Of course you can.' I usher him inside.

I'm expecting the usual kiss on the cheek, but to my disappointment he steps straight into the hallway.

'Can I offer you a drink?' I lead him into the kitchen, thrilled that he's here, yet feeling like he might be here to tell me he's heading back to America.

'A coffee would be good, thanks.'

I place his coffee down in front of him, a decaff latte for myself.

'Let's take these through to the lounge.' I place the cups on a tray, with a plate of the orange shortbread I'd made and almost forgotten about, and he follows me.

'Luke, is everything alright?' I ask him, my heart beating wildly, unsure if I want to hear the answer. I've been over and over the time we spent together, and apart from him telling me about his divorce, can think of nothing that may have caused a problem between us. Unless he's decided to reconcile, although given the details of their separation, I would find that highly unlikely.

'I'm not too sure.' He looks me in the eyes. 'Sarah. Is there anything you want to tell me?'

'What about?'

'About you spending Christmas with your ex. It's your business and I don't mind, of course, but with you not mentioning it to me, I kind of thought it was an issue.'

'Oh, Luke, I'm so sorry.' I suddenly feel so stupid. 'I've beaten myself up about not saying anything, but the truth is I thought you might have got the wrong idea about us if I'd mentioned Robbie being here.' I realise I'm talking too quickly. 'Ellie surprised me a couple of days before Christmas. He had nowhere to go, as his girlfriend had thrown him out. Ellie didn't want him to be alone, and he was in the house before I knew what was going on. It definitely wasn't planned or anything.'

'So, there's no unfinished business between you two? Because if there is, I would rather you told me now.' He searches my eyes with his.

'No, Luke, there is nothing between us. Ellie literally turned up with him here on Christmas Eve. I had absolutely no idea she was going to do that.'

'And where is he now?' he asks, taking a sip of his coffee.

'He's actually made it up with his ex, thank goodness.'

'You're happy about that, really? There's absolutely no way you want to get back together with him.'

'Luke, of course I don't! I've told you, I did it mainly for Ellie. She was worried about her father spending Christmas Day alone. I'm so sorry, but whatever gave you the idea that I want to get back with Robbie?'

'I called over on Christmas Day.' He pauses for a moment.

'You did? But I thought you were spending the day with your friend?' I say, completely surprised by what he has told me.

'I did, but we ate earlier than originally planned, so I nipped out after lunch to bring you a gift, before we got started on the whisky. I was going to quickly give it to you, then be on my way.'

'So what happened?'

'I did knock on the front door, but there was no answer,' he explains. 'I glanced through the dining room window and saw you all sitting together. I kind of assumed the bloke sitting next to Ellie was your ex.'

'Oh, Luke, I wish I'd told you Robbie had turned up. I regret that more than anything now.'

I'm disappointed I never heard him knock at the door, and curse the fact that I never got the broken doorbell fixed. I suppose it did get quite noisy around the table, all of us laughing and talking. Plus, the television was on in the background during the Queen's Speech.

'And I'm not the jealous type but...'

'But what?'

'Well, you appeared to be holding hands across the table.'

'What? Holding hands. No, not at all. Are you sure that's what you saw?' I can't believe what Luke is telling me. I'm racking my brains as to how he could possibly have observed that through the window.

'So I figured, maybe you were getting back together,' he continues. 'Two years isn't that long to be apart, especially when you have a child together. Christmas can be a very nostalgic time for people. I thought it best to maybe leave you alone for a while to figure out what you wanted.'

'I remember!' Suddenly I think of the scene around the dinner table that Luke must have observed.

'We were pulling crackers and Robbie got one of those fortune-telling fish in his cracker. I held my palm out and he placed it on it. I think it said something about finding love. He knows I've been seeing you; he was laughing about it.'

'Really?'

'Yes, I made it very clear that I was seeing someone,' I insist, thinking of all of the instances I'd moved to put more space between me and Robbie through the day. 'And I'm not the only one who wasn't happy about him being there. You should have heard the comments from my uncle.'

'Sounds like I might have got things very wrong.' He looks slightly embarrassed.

'You certainly did.' I stand up from the chair and sit down beside him on the sofa.

'I'm sorry if I left you a bit confused, Sarah, but you can see how it might have looked. And I wouldn't want to stand in the way of a family reconciling.'

'I do not want to reconcile with Robbie, not in a million years,' I reassure him once more.

'Is that right?' Luke puts his arm around me and draws me to him.

'Absolutely. Besides, someone else has been occupying my thoughts these past couple of weeks.'

'Oh really?'

I can smell his scent as he moves closer, my heart thumping.

'Really.'

'Well, that's alright then.'

Suddenly his lips are on mine and we're sharing a gorgeous, thrilling kiss that I want to go on forever.

'I can't tell you how relieved I am to hear you say that,' says Luke as we break apart and sink back into the sofa.

'Me too. I was worried you'd had a change of heart about us.'

'Never. It killed me not to speak to you but I had to give you some space. I was kind of prepared for you not getting in touch with me again.'

'And there was I thinking it was *you* who had had a change of heart. What are we like?' I snuggle into him.

'Oh and I have something for you. The gift I never managed to give you on Christmas Day.'

He goes into the hall and retrieves something from his coat pocket, before handing me a small black box.

'For me?' I'm completely surprised and touched.

'I hope you like it.'

I slowly lift the lid of the box and when I open it fully, I gasp. Sitting on a velvet cushion is the most beautiful brooch of a robin, glittering with red and white stones.

'I wasn't sure if brooches were just a thing with older ladies,' he says. 'But I couldn't resist buying it when I spotted it in a vintage shop near my rented apartment.'

'Luke, it's absolutely gorgeous!'

'I'm glad you like it. The rubies are real, but the diamonds are paste,' he says, smiling. 'So don't go pawning it, thinking it will set you up for life.' He laughs.

'As if I would. I love it.' I turn the brooch over in my hand, the stones glinting as they catch the light through the window. 'And although, admittedly, I don't generally wear brooches, I will certainly wear this. In fact, I've just bought a new blazer and it will look stunning on the lapel.'

'In that case, would you like to go out to dinner with me sometime?' he asks.

'I would love to. And I actually have a little gift for you too.'

I nip upstairs and return with the whisky. I purchased it from a specialist shop in town and hope he likes it.

'Thank you, you shouldn't have bought me anything,' he says, taking the whisky from the bottle bag. 'But I'm glad you did. This is an impressive single malt. Brilliant choice.'

'Oh and there's something else in there, just a silly little thing,' I say, pointing to the bottle bag.

Luke pulls the pen out and a huge grin spreads across his face, as he sees the 'I love Liverpool' pen.

'Just something to remind you of here, when you're back in America,' I tell him.

'Well, that's really thoughtful of you,' he says, before moving in for another kiss. 'But I have to tell you, I'm in no hurry to leave here.'

'I'm so happy you're here, Luke.' We're sitting on the sofa together, cuddled up, staring into the flames of the fire.

'So am I, not to mention relieved. I needed to talk to you and, of course, I wanted to give you your gift. But I also wanted to ask you something. Do you have any plans for New Year's Eve? As I'm having a party,' he asks.

'You're hosting a party at your rented accommodation?' I ask in surprise.

'It's pretty spacious, actually, easily room for a dozen or so guests. Andy will be there, as well as a few other people I'd like you to meet. Bring Ellie too of course' he adds. 'She might like it, as there will be one or two other young people there.'

I'm amazed Luke has managed to arrange a New Year's Eve party at such seemingly short notice, as he never mentioned anything about it the last time we met up.

'Actually, I think Ellie said something about a party at Izzy's, but I'll need to confirm that her parents will be there first, before I agree to it. If I'm happy with the arrangements, I would love to come to your party.'

'Wonderful. The bedroom has a really gorgeous view,' he

says, locking eyes with me and making my insides do a somersault.

'That sounds wonderful. I'll look forward to it.'

'I meant all of the bedrooms, including the guest rooms. It will be impossible to get a cab on New Year's Eve,' he quickly adds, maybe not wanting to take anything for granted.

'I'll look forward to it. I usually just go to the pub on New Year's Eve, but I'd much rather spend it with you. And New Year's Eve also happens to be my birthday, although maybe it's one I'd prefer to forget this year.'

'Why would you want to do that?' Luke looks surprised.

'Because it's my fortieth.'

'Of course! A special occasion, then. That really is something to celebrate.'

I wonder why Luke said 'of course', as I hadn't mentioned my birthday before, and wonder whether or not he may have remembered it from when we were younger.

Luke glances at his watch. 'Sorry, I have to be somewhere in half an hour, but I'm glad you can come over on New Year's Eve. I'll be in touch; I have one or two things to organise for the party over the next couple of days.'

At the front door, he kisses me and I feel the familiar butterflies in my tummy. I'm also thrilled by the news that Luke is going to be around for a while longer.

THIRTY-SIX

It's the day before New Year's Eve, and I'm back at work to a surprisingly busy matinee, packed out with families. I can't help thinking about all of the money parents must have spent on toys for their children, yet here they are treating them to an afternoon at the cinema. It would appear kids have to be constantly entertained these days. Not that I'm complaining. Business at this time of the year is more than welcome. I do notice that the sales of chocolate is pretty slow, though, popcorn being more popular, so maybe kids are still working their way through their selection boxes. Perhaps they've sneaked them in under their coats.

'So, how was your Christmas?' asks Shelley and I tell her all about Robbie turning up, as well as Luke getting hold of the wrong end of the stick.

'Ooh, sounds like an episode of *EastEnders*,' she says, idly flicking through a magazine once the film has started.

'Nothing quite so dramatic, thank goodness. How was your Christmas?'

'Yeah, really good, thanks. My grandparents came to our house for dinner, and Grandad handed me and my sister an envelope after dinner and I got the surprise of my life. There was a thousand pounds inside,' she says as she turns over a page of her magazine.

'Wow, that's really generous.'

'I know. He said we'd get some inheritance when he passes away, but thought we might like it while we're young to have some fun with it. Typical of Grandad, he's always been fun-loving, the type to grab life with both hands.'

'Well, I think that's lovely. What will you do with the money?'

'I'm going to Barcelona in January. I was going to go on my birthday in March, but as the cinema is closing for a week in January, it seemed like a good idea to go then, so Ed can come too. He's saving like mad now, as he said he doesn't want me spending a single penny of my grandad's gift on him. He's so sweet.'

'So things are going well, then?'

'They are for now, but I don't like making plans for the future too far in advance, what with university and everything,' she says casually, but I can see she has completely fallen for Ed.

The afternoon passes in a flash and we're soon standing outside in the crisp night air about to head home.

'Any plans for tonight?' asks Shelley.

'Not a single one,' I say, suddenly feeling overcome with tiredness. I guess it's been a busy few days, being Christmas, not to mention my emotions being on a roller coaster. I'm looking forward to nothing more than a hot bath and a few chapters of the book I've been struggling to find the concentration to read.

That night, I finish the orange shortbread, after eating a healthy stir-fry. The biscuits probably cancelled out all of the goodness, but at least they were home-made, and contained some orange peel. I smile to myself as I think of Cassie saying a similar thing about the carrot cake containing vegetables.

After dinner, I make myself comfortable on the sofa with a

hot chocolate and my book. This time, I find myself completely absorbed in the story and, after finishing my drink, I decide to take my book up to bed. I snuggle down into my comfy bed, thinking about what an eventful Christmas it's been. All things considered, it's been pretty good. I think about Ellie and how she was worried about not seeing Robbie if he had nowhere to live, and it's made me appreciate that I don't know half of the concerns she must have in her head. Maybe I ought to ask her a little more about how she's feeling, even though she would probably just shrug and tell me that she's fine.

As I switch the bedside lamp off when I struggle to keep my eyes open any longer, I feel happy that everyone's okay. Robbie has patched things up with Hannah and I'm so happy to have cleared up any misunderstanding with Luke. I can hardly wait to see him again at the New Year's Eve party.

THIRTY-SEVEN

I wake early, before heading downstairs to sit with a coffee. I'm just sending Helen a quick message about my change of plans tonight, when Ellie phones me just after nine o'clock wishing me a happy birthday, telling me she will be home in an hour. Apparently, there's been a change of plan, and she's no longer staying at Izzy's for the New Year's Eve party.

'Hi, Mum.' An hour later, Ellie has walked in and the first thing she does is give me a hug and wish me a happy birthday as she pulls a card from her bag.

'Thank you, Ellie.'

'I'll just go and get your present.' She races upstairs excitedly, and returns with a gift wrapped in rainbow paper, with a gold bow in the middle.

'Ellie, thank you.' I rip off the paper and my eyes widen in delight when I see the picture in front of me. It's the African scene I admired in Ellie's folder, beautifully framed in dark wood.

'You did say you liked it. I hope you really did.' She smiles.

'Oh, Ellie, I love it! How thoughtful of you. It's going to

have pride of place on the wall in the dining room.' I place the picture down and give her a lingering hug.

I tell her about the party Luke has invited us to this evening. 'So what happened with the party at Izzy's?' I ask.

'Her mum cancelled it as she's not feeling too good, although I heard her parents having a massive row last night,' she tells me, and I hope Izzy is alright.

'I'm sorry to hear that. In that case, do you think Izzy would like to come to the party with you? I'm sure Luke wouldn't mind.'

'Wouldn't he? I actually think she'd love to. I think she might like to get out of the house, as all her mum and dad seem to do is argue.'

I imagine Ellie and Izzy sitting in her room, Ellie empathising with her friend, telling her how crap it is when parents fall out, and I wonder if Izzy is worried that they might divorce.

'That's settled, then. As long as it's okay with her parents, of course.'

'I'm sure it will be. I'll give her a call now. Thanks, Mum.'

I get ready for my short shift at work, and when I head downstairs, Ellie tells me Izzy's mum will drop her off here shortly. As I'm about to leave, Izzy arrives and her mum gets out of the car and asks me if she can have a word.

'Thanks for this,' she tells me as the girls head inside. 'Izzy's dad and I are having a few problems at the moment,' she confides. 'He lost his job recently, so I cancelled our New Year's party. It was going to cost us quite a bit of money, which we can't afford given the circumstances. We had a huge row about it last night.'

I don't tell her that Ellie had told me all about the row.

'I'm off to return a load of booze, which luckily the super-market is prepared to take back. He'll thank me for it come New Year's Day. At least I hope he will.' She manages a smile.

'I'm sorry to hear about your husband's job. And Izzy is more than welcome to join us for New Year's Eve. In fact, it's probably a blessing as I'm sure Ellie will enjoy the party more if she has a friend with her.'

'Well, thanks. And happy New Year,' she says.

'Happy New Year to you too. I hope everything works out for you and your husband.' She heads off down the path.

'I'm going to work now; help yourself to anything in the cupboards. I'll be back around three after the matinee, and Luke will be collecting us for the party at eight,' I tell the girls as I'm about to leave, just as the postman arrives and hands me several cards in pastel envelopes. I quickly open the cards from family members and Cassie, and place them on the fireplace. Just then, Cassie calls to wish me a happy birthday and says that she will call over in a day or two.

'Where is the party, Mum?' Ellie asks.

'In the Georgian quarter at the place Luke is renting.'

'Is it a posh do? I'm not sure what to wear,' says Ellie.

'I doubt it, love, it's a house party,' I tell her, suddenly wondering if it will be a grand affair, and worrying if the dress I'm thinking of wearing will be okay. I think I'll give my Christmas party dress a miss, unless I reinforce it with a load of safety pins.

'Let's go and have a look through your wardrobe,' says Izzy and the two girls bounce upstairs.

Arriving at work, I'm glad the cinema is showing a matinee only today, as it will still give me time to get ready for this evening. As I expected, there aren't many customers through the door today and Shelley and I spend most of the shift chatting.

'What are you doing tonight, then?' I ask Shelley, after we've tidied around and refilled the sweet counter.

'We've got tickets to a club in town. Ed's mate is playing

with his band. I'm dreading it, though,' she tells me as she sucks on a lollipop.

'Why?'

'I just hate New Year's Eve; you can never get a taxi home,' she grumbles. 'Last year, me and some friends walked home from town and got hounded every step of the way by drunken wankers,' she tells me.

'Well, at least you'll have Ed with you this year, so at least that isn't likely to happen,' I reassure her.

'Suppose so. I'm not that fussed about going out as we'll be going to Barcelona for a few days soon.'

'Oh yes, of course. Well, have a great time and happy New Year.'

Shelley and I hug each other outside the cinema. 'And be safe,' I tell her.

'I will, you too. See you next year,' she says, which sounds really strange, but it's true. Especially as we have an extra week off work when the cinema refurbishment gets under way.

Back home, I rifle through my wardrobe, deciding on a red dress that I bought last year, but haven't actually worn. I think it will look good with my new black blazer, and the adorable red robin brooch.

'I've decided to wear this, what do you think, Mum?'

Ellie appears in my room, with a cute black-and-white pinafore and a black felt hat. She puts the hat on and does a little pout in the mirror.

'That looks lovely,' I tell her.

'And really cool. The jeans and top I've brought don't look half as good.' Izzy pulls a face.

'Borrow something of mine, if you like,' says Ellie. 'I've got another pinafore in burgundy; it will look nice with that pretty white blouse you've brought with you worn underneath it.'

'Oh great. Let's have a look, then.'

The girls head back to Ellie's bedroom, and it takes me back to when I was younger, sitting in Kay's room, whilst she rifled through her clothes, which were all stylish and expensive-looking. Sometimes, when I particularly admired something she would toss it over and tell me to keep it, saying she never wore it. It was lucky we were around the same size, just as Ellie and Izzy are. I'm going to give her a call on New Year's Day and wish her all the best. And who knows? I might actually save up and go and visit her in America one day.

As I cross the landing to walk downstairs, I can hear the sound of music coming from Ellie's room and can imagine them dancing around, trying on outfits and posing in front of the mirror.

Once we're all changed and ready, I suddenly start to feel a little anxious about meeting some of Luke's friends, and consider having a small gin and tonic to quell the nerves. The girls have had a squirt of my perfume and the lounge is filled with a floral aroma, as we are sitting around listening to some music, the girls sipping cherry cola.

It's over half an hour before Luke is due to arrive, and I'm about to head into the kitchen for that gin, when there's a knock on the door. When I open it, I'm stunned to find my friends in the village standing in front of me on the doorstep.

'Surprise!' they say in unison, brandishing gift bags and a Happy Birthday balloon.

'Did you really think we would forget your birthday?' says Helen, being the first to step inside, followed by the others.

'And not just any old birthday, but your fortieth! You kept that quiet,' says Francis, as she hands me the most beautiful bouquet of flowers.

'Oh, girls! What a surprise, thank you so much!'

Along with the flowers, there's a bottle of champagne, a cake and a gorgeous silver bracelet dotted with my birth month stones of turquoise. I slip it onto my wrist and stretch out my arm to admire it.

'I can't thank you enough, it's absolutely gorgeous, and what a surprise seeing you all here! How did you know it was my fortieth?' I ask, and I notice Jo smiling over at Ellie.

'Let's get that champagne open, and toast the new year early,' I say heading into the kitchen for some glasses.

'Go on, then. I can't stay long, I've nipped out while it's quiet in the pub, before the madness starts later,' says Helen. We pour champagne and as we clink our glasses together, Fran proposes a toast.

'Here's to a great new year. I hope we all enjoy good health, wealth and happiness. But mainly health,' she says. 'Wealth isn't much use without that. Here's to us.'

'To us,' we all say, raising our glasses.

'That was a wonderful surprise,' I say to Ellie and Izzy when my friends leave, and I feel completely overwhelmed with love. 'And when did you let it slip that I was forty this year?' I ask.

'Can't remember.' She shrugs. 'I think it might have been at the curry night.'

Soon enough, Luke has pulled up outside the cottage, and I feel a little calmer now after that glass of champagne. He looks wonderful as he steps out of the car, wearing a gorgeous navy suit, a blue-and-white patterned shirt beneath it, open at the neck.

'Hi, ladies, may I say you all look particularly lovely this evening,' he tells us as he steps onto the flagstone floor of the hall and kisses me on the cheek. 'Oh, and happy birthday.'

I'm glad I've chosen the red wrap-over dress as it's a perfect fit and very flattering.

'You may indeed. You scrub up pretty well yourself,' I tell him.

'Thanks.' He smiles. 'Shall we get going, then?'

I grab my blazer from the hall with the little robin on the lapel and Luke notices it.

'You're right, that looks really nice on that jacket, and the red matches your dress. You look stunning,' he whispers in my ear as the girls walk in front towards the car, and his comment thrills me.

As we drive out of the village, talk turns to Christmas gifts and Ellie shows him her Doc Martens, which she's wearing this evening with her pinafore and heavy tights. 'Very nice.' He glances over his shoulder for a second to the back seat. I recall Izzy's mum saying her father had recently lost his job, and worry she may not have got much, but she lists several nice gifts, including a new bike. I guess her parents bought her presents in plenty of time, as her father has only recently lost his job.

After a while, I realise we're heading out towards Crosby, rather than driving towards the city centre and the Georgian quarter, but maybe Luke just wants to avoid heavy traffic. There are groups of people walking along, some in fancy dress ready for the evening's celebrations, and Ellie and Izzy laugh when they see a couple of blokes wearing Ant and Dec masks and tap on the window and wave at them.

Soon enough, we've turned onto the beach road and are driving towards the houses on Marine Drive, close to Adelaide Terrace. I'm shocked when, a short while later, we park the car up outside the pastel-coloured houses.

'I thought we were going to the Georgian quarter?' says Ellie.

'So did I.' I turn to Luke with a puzzled frown and he smiles.

'Well, I might have been fibbing a little bit. Although, I did stay there for a few days, before things got sorted with the house.' He holds his hands up. 'I was telling the truth about that.'

We climb out of the car, and I wonder what he's up to, as my eyes fall on the nearby house he once lived in, noticing the

For Sale sign has been changed to Sold. I'm totally surprised when Luke leads us up the garden path to the house.

'The party is here? I don't understand.'

'Having a house-warming party was always on the cards, and what better time than on New Year's Eve?' He's smiling as I glance at the shiny, navy door and the pale-blue walls and the realisation dawns.

'This is your house?' My mouth falls open.

'When you mentioned it was up for sale, I almost let the cat out of the bag but I thought it would be nicer if it was a surprise. I know how much you loved the house.'

'Luke, I can't believe you bought this house!' I'm in absolute shock. But it's more than just about the house. Does this mean Luke is staying?

Izzy and Ellie are admiring a mermaid water feature in the front garden, surrounded with bamboo fencing and several figurines dotted about, including a Buddha statue.

Luke opens the door with his key, and the music from a room somewhere filters through the hall. As I step onto the same parquet flooring that I did all those years ago, a million memories come rushing back.

Luke pushes the kitchen door open and there's at least twenty people in the large kitchen, standing around chatting. There's a fantastic buffet on a table and, along with all the usual party fare of sandwiches and nibbles are mini fish and chips, burgers and all manner of tasty treats alongside a sensational dessert table that has made Ellie and Izzy's eyes widen.

Luke introduces me to several people, and I say hi to his friend Andy, who I've already met. He has his son with him, who looks around the same age as the girls and colours a little when I introduce them. There are two more teenagers at the party, who live next door, and a couple of younger boys. Luke was obviously keen to start off on the right foot with his new neighbours by inviting them all. I think this gathering has suddenly become quite exciting to Ellie and Izzy, with the presence of other young people, including boys.

'Right, I think it's time you met some other people I've invited,' says Luke, leading me to the drawing room as the girls mingle with the other young people.

'Other guests?'

He leads me across the hall, before pushing open the door of the vast lounge and a woman stands up from a chair.

'Hi, Sarah, how are you?' There's a pretty, dark-haired woman smiling at me, and in an instant, I know that it's my old friend.

'Kay! Is it really you?' My hand flies to my mouth.

'It is.'

We practically race across the room to each other, and we're hugging and I don't care that there are tears streaming down my face, as the best friend I have ever had is here with me in this room. There are a million questions I want to ask, but just then an elderly lady appears and I realise it's Luke's mum. She's silver-haired now, but still beautiful.

'Hello, Sarah, it's good to see you,' says Ruth. 'I'm so happy Luke ran into you again,' she tells me warmly.

'Me too. I can't believe he's bought the house. Are you going to live here too?' I ask, still struggling to process everything.

'No, my life is in America now.' She smiles. 'I live next door to Kay. I prefer the weather in Florida and the boys are settled in school there,' she explains.

'Where are they? I'd love to meet them.'

'You probably already have; they are in the kitchen,' says Kay.

'I think you did,' confirms Luke. 'I just didn't introduce them as my nephews.'

'You're getting quite good at being secretive.' I poke him gently in the chest. 'I'm not sure that's such a great quality in a man,' I say, and Kay and Ruth laugh.

'No, maybe not,' he agrees. 'But it was all part of the surprise.'

We have the most wonderful evening, chatting and eating, and everyone seems to be having a great time, on their feet dancing to some wonderful music played through speakers. I spend a good part of the evening catching up with Kay and her life, after she's introduced me to her husband, Pete, who's really lovely, as are her two boys.

'How long are you staying?' I ask as we sip Prosecco in the kitchen, that has only a group of adults now, the youngsters having decamped to another room to play their own music and watch YouTube. And with half of the dessert table by the look of things.

'A week. Luke painted such a great picture of Liverpool these days, we decided to have an extended break for New Year. I'm looking forward to spending some time with my old friend.' She threads her arm through mine, and I feel so happy.

'Well, I'm thrilled you're here.'

As we head towards midnight, Luke pushes open the French doors from the kitchen and switches on the lights that are strung across the fence and immediately the lawn is bathed in a soft light. He lights a large chiminea, and soon several people are standing outside chatting, beneath a black sky. Just before midnight, Luke excuses himself from a couple of people he is talking to, and leads me off somewhere. To my surprise, we head upstairs and are soon standing on a small balcony that leads off a bedroom and overlooks the front garden.

'Quite a view, isn't it?'

I glance out across the Irish Sea, the dark water sparkling beneath the light of the large, white moon.

'It's magical.'

I turn to face him and he kisses me so deeply, it leaves me breathless.

'Oh, and here,' he says, when we finally pull apart. 'Happy birthday.'

He opens a box and reveals a ring that looks like white gold, studded with small diamonds and slides it onto my right hand.

'Luke!' I gasp. 'You shouldn't have; you've already given me the brooch,' I protest.

'That was a Christmas gift. This is for your birthday. It's an eternity ring. I know eternity sounds like a long time, but I'm definitely planning on sticking around.'

'It's perfect. Thank you, Luke,' I tell him as he slides the ring onto the third finger of my right hand.

I want to stand here forever with my first love, who I thought I'd lost forever, but as I glance at my watch, I realise it's just a few minutes until midnight.

'I think we ought to be heading downstairs,' I tell him, so we walk down the glorious staircase holding hands and join the others who are assembled in the rear garden. A minute or so later, someone starts a countdown.

'Mum.' Ellie and Izzy come running over with their new friends and stand beside us.

'Ten. Nine. Eight...'

'Happy New Year!' Suddenly, there are party hooters and cheers and a rocket shoots up into the night sky. People embrace each other and when Luke kisses me on the lips, I see Ellie and Izzy nudge each other.

'What a wonderful evening.' We're standing outside watching the sky light up with colours of pink, silver and green. Just then, Kay appears and hands me a small gift.

'Happy birthday, Sarah. I hadn't forgotten.'

I open the gift, wrapped in tissue paper, to reveal a photo of me and Kay when we were teenagers, inside a gorgeous silver frame.

'I made the frame myself,' she tells me proudly.

'Kay, it's gorgeous, thank you! I don't remember this picture being taken.'

The two of us look so young, smiling and carefree at a time when the future held so many possibilities.

'I think my mum had a new camera she was trying out. It was one of many she took in the garden, I think.'

'I'll treasure it, thank you, Kay.'

I pass my phone to Ellie and ask her to take a photo of me and my friend.

'One for the album. Hopefully we can get another one when we're old and grey.'

'And lots in between,' she says, smiling, and I get the feeling we will.

It's been such a fantastic evening, full of surprises and the best news is that Luke is here to stay. At least for the immediate future, I hope. Plus, I get to spend some time with my long-lost friend this next week. She couldn't have come over at a better time, with the cinema being closed. This really has been the best Christmas ever.

'It's been such a magical evening,' I tell Luke as we stand, arms wrapped around each other, glancing up at the sky still glowing with fireworks. 'I can barely take it all in. I love my life.' I sigh.

'I'm glad to hear it. And hopefully, there are many more moments like this to enjoy together.' Luke gives my hand a little squeeze. 'After all, they do say life begins at forty, don't they?' he says, before he moves in for another kiss.

EPILOGUE

I spent a wonderful week with Kay and her family, visiting tourist attractions and having dinner at both of our houses. We even had a games night at my place, which was a lot of fun. Ellie bombarded Luke's nephews with questions about America, and even though they are several years younger, they bonded over their love of music and films. It was hard saying goodbye at the end of the week, but Ellie and I are going to visit Kay and her family in Florida around Easter, and Ellie is already counting down the days. So am I, as Luke will be coming with us.

The transformation of the cinema took my breath away and I was thrilled to see that Greg had stayed true to his word, and left the last row of the cinema with the velour seats. As it turned out, though, the older patrons were thrilled with the new recliner seats, and said it was about time we changed them. Oh and we've seen a real surge in customer numbers. Mainly due to the refurb of the cinema, but also thanks to a full-page ad in the local newspaper, showing the latest releases. It seems some people, especially young couples who had moved into an estate of new-build houses several miles away, hadn't known the cinema even existed until they saw the advertisement in the newspaper.

The birthday parties are still popular too; we're doing at least one a week. In fact, we have one later today.

'What did you think of Barcelona, then?' I ask Shelley at the cinema one afternoon.

'Amazing. I'd definitely go again. The Gaudí buildings were so cool,' she says. 'We never saw the illuminated fountains, though, so it's a reason to go back.'

'Together?'

'Hmm, yeah. Ed was great company,' she says, with a smile on her face. 'Do you think we'll be offered some birthday cake later?' she suddenly asks. 'I'm debating buying a packet of Haribos if not.'

'*Buying* a packet? We have turned over a new leaf,' I tease.

'I love this job. I don't want my sweet tooth to contribute in any way to the closure of the cinema,' she says, sounding really sincere. I don't bother telling her a couple of packets of sweets a week are unlikely to do that.

Luke has settled into his new home and I've been a regular visitor. We all visited the theatre on Saturday night, four of us including Ellie and Izzy, finally going to see a show as Luke had suggested when we first got together. We stayed over at Adelaide Terrace after and Ellie said it was brilliant having a house in the town, and another in the country, and Luke smiled.

'I like that idea,' he said. 'Splitting our time between a town house and a country residence. I might even dress like a country squire and take up shooting on the weekends I stay at your place.'

Ellie has knuckled down to her studying and is getting to know Luke, who happily she really seems to get along with. Especially as they have a joint love of crime series on Netflix, which they spend time in the evening watching, whilst I read or get on with my sudoku. Crime series aren't really my thing.

Luke's heading off to Ireland tomorrow for a couple of days on business, and tells me I can join him on trips in the future, which I'm sure I'll enjoy. Especially when he mentions he has customers all over Europe.

I'll never forget bumping into Luke that day in the library, and I think Cassie was right. It was definitely meant to be. Of all the buildings in the city, he happened to walk into the library that day. And for that, I will be forever grateful.

A LETTER FROM SUE

Dear reader,

I want to say a huge thank you for choosing to read *Christmas at Red Robin Cottage*. If you did enjoy it, and want to keep up to date with all my latest releases, just sign up at the following link. Your email address will never be shared and you can unsubscribe at any time.

www.bookouture.com/sue-roberts

I really hope you loved *Christmas at Red Robin Cottage*. Christmas is such a special time of year and for me, a time that still feels a little bit magical! They say you should never lose the child inside you, and the festive season can certainly bring that out!

If you did enjoy reading this book, I would be very grateful if you could write a review. I'd love to hear what you think, and it makes such a difference helping new readers to discover one of my books for the first time. It may even inspire some of you to discover the wonderful city that is Liverpool, worth a visit any time of the year in my opinion!

I love hearing from my readers – you can get in touch on my Facebook page, through Twitter, Goodreads or my website. Thank you all so much.

Thanks,

Sue Roberts

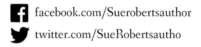

facebook.com/Suerobertsauthor
twitter.com/SueRobertsautho

ACKNOWLEDGEMENTS

I would like to thank my editor, Natalie Edwards, for her input on this, my latest book, *Christmas at Red Robin Cottage*. Writing a Christmas story was a real departure from the usual beach reads I have penned recently and Natalie was full of enthusiasm for the idea, applauding the new venture. I am truly grateful for her input. As always, I would like to thank the fabulous team that make up Bookouture. Big shout-out to the publicity team that are Kim, Noelle, Sarah and Jess along with the whole team behind the scenes who bring our books to life! I am lucky to write for such wonderful publishers.

I must also mention the wonderful people of Liverpool, who are happy to answer any questions you may ask about the city, always with a certain pride. And thanks to my friend Shelagh Walsh for snapping photos of me for my social media pages, stood in front of some of the Liverpool landmarks that feature in the book. We've been friends since high school. It seems some friendships really do last a lifetime.

And finally, to all of the book bloggers, reviewers and you the reader, for choosing to purchase this book. My appreciation is infinite.